Special Delivery

A Mountain Meadow Homecomings Novel

Laura Browning

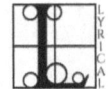

LYRICAL PRESS
Kensington Publishing Corp.
www.kensingtonbooks.com

Lyrical Press books are published by
Kensington Publishing Corp. 119 West 40th Street New York, NY 10018

Copyright © 2014 by Laura Browning

All Kensington titles, imprints, and distributed lines are available at special quantity discounts for bulk purchases for sales promotion, premiums, fundraising, and educational or institutional use.

Special book excerpts or customized printings can also be created to fit specific needs. For details, write or phone the office of the Kensington Special Sales Manager:
Kensington Publishing Corp.
119 West 40th Street
New York, NY 10018
Attn. Special Sales Department. Phone: 1-800-221-2647.

Kensington and the K logo Reg. U.S. Pat. & TM Off.
Lyrical Press and the L logo are trademarks of Kensington Publishing Corp.

First Electronic Edition: May 2015
eISBN-13: 978-1-61650-753-4
eISBN-10: 1-61650-753-5

First Print Edition: May 2015
ISBN-13: 978-1-61650-754-1
ISBN-10: 1-61650-754-3

Printed in the United States of America

Welcome home to Mountain Meadow, Virginia—a small town with a big heart, where love is just around the corner…

All Holly Morgan wants is a safe place to have her baby. Nestled deep within the Blue Ridge Mountains, miles away from her abusive ex-fiancé, Spence, Mountain Meadow seems perfect. Holly can manage a few meddling church matrons if it means Spence can't find her. Harder to handle is Jake Allred. He may be a dark-haired hunk, but he's also someone Holly can't trust: a cop.

Since his time in the military, Lieutenant Jake Allred has lived to protect and serve. And if anyone needs protection, it's Holly. Having been let down by the law before, she's wary of letting Jake into her life. But when an unexpected snow storm strands them together, their attraction is hot enough to melt the mounting ice. Just when Jake thinks he's finally warmed Holly's heart, Spence strikes. Now it's up to Jake to save Holly's baby and bring their fledgling family back together.

Visit us at www.kensingtonbooks.com

Books by Laura Browning

Winning Heart

Mountain Meadow Homecomings
Special Delivery, Book One

The Barlow-Barretts: An American Dynasty
Bittersweet, Book One
Balancing Act, Book Two
Remember Me, Book Three
Broken Heart, Book Four

Published by Kensington Publishing Corporation

To my husband and son who have put up with my long hours at the computer, you have my love and thanks, not to mention the gratitude for the meals and clean-up you guys have pitched in to complete. I'd also like to dedicate this to my friend and teaching colleague, Karen Grayton. Not only have you been my number one fan, you've been a great sounding board for ideas. I love you guys.

Chapter 1

"Tyler, wake up," Holly whispered. Her calm tone masked a heart pounding so loudly she feared her little brother would hear it as well.

Dark hair spiking above his rumpled blankets, Tyler rubbed his eyes and mumbled, "It's still night."

"We're leaving. Now." Some of her urgency finally broke though.

He sat, eyes wide in the dim glow of the streetlight filtering through his curtains. Holly hated doing this to him, but after taking yet another midnight call from Spence, her ex-fiancé, she didn't dare wait any longer.

"I thought we weren't leaving till Saturday," Tyler grumbled as he rose and located the clothes he'd left folded at the foot of his bed. "What's happened?"

Even at eleven, he was no dummy. Tyler had already come out on the wrong end of Spence's temper and knew how vicious it could be. Holly ruffled his hair. God, she loved him. "Nothing we can't handle, but I want to make sure we're the ones staying a step ahead."

No way would she share with him the latest threats Spence had made. Holly had tried going through the legal system. She'd obtained a restraining order right after Spence had gotten physical. Now it wasn't enough. Something was off with Spence, something scary, and Holly wasn't sticking around to see what. If the restraining order wasn't going to stop him, then she and Tyler would just disappear.

"Meet me in the garage in five minutes. I'm going to check to make sure everything's locked. We'll drop the key by the real estate agent on the way out of town."

She'd put the house on the market, but with the economy so slow, they'd had few nibbles, despite cutting the price. Now Holly hoped the real estate agent might be able to find a renter. It could provide some income, but she wasn't holding her breath. Grinding her teeth was more like it.

Laura Browning

She'd already put most of the furniture she wanted to keep in storage, figuring she could pick up odds and ends wherever they ended up. Once she was sure Spence hadn't followed, she would send for the stored items. Still, her small car was packed as they backed out of the garage and eased down the street. Holly couldn't help glancing at the rearview mirror several times. The house was the last tie to their parents. Now they would have to carry those memories in their hearts instead.

On the highway leading out of town, Holly at last dared a glance at her brother, giving him a small, reassuring smile as she squeezed his hand. So what if reassuring him also made her feel better too? Leaving the only home you'd ever known was scary.

His eyes reflected his uncertainty. "Are we doing the right thing?"

She shifted her hand to the swell of her pregnancy. "I hope so, Tyler."

* * * *

When no one answered his call in the morning, Spence Dilby drove to Holly's one-story ranch, snarling at every traffic light that slowed him down. Located in an upper-end area of Lynchburg, it still screamed middle class to him. He pulled to the back of the house where his car wouldn't be seen. No use taking chances. He'd had enough of having the cops on his ass. Only fast-talking had gotten him out of hot water the last time. He didn't need another incident because his father was nearing the end of his patience. At least he'd made his parents happy when he'd agreed to marry Seely.

He knocked on the back door. No one answered. He pounded, wanting nothing more than to feel his fist smash through the wood. Still no answer. Spence peered through the windows. "Open up, Holly! I know you're in there."

Silence was his only response. He walked to the French doors looking into the family room and noted with a burst of fury much of the furniture was gone. He smacked his palms against the wooden panels, the sting making him snarl. The bitch had left! He hadn't believed her when she said she would. Why would she want to keep the baby when he would pay her to disappear out of its life?

Well, she wasn't getting away that easily. No. Fucking. Way.

* * * *

Five-thirty in the morning and the sky had just begun to lighten above the ancient peaks east of Mountain Meadow. Jake Allred sucked in a deep breath, feeling yet again a profound sense of homecoming. More importantly, he could enjoy the imminent sunrise without feeling like he had to check over his shoulder or keep a hand on his sidearm. He knocked on his next-door neighbor's door. The heavy wooden panel swung open to reveal the tall, lean figure of his best friend.

"We have to stop meeting like this, bro. People will begin to think we're dating."

Jake rolled his eyes. "Get off it, Evan. Even the church gossips know I can't stand dating guys taller than me."

Evan snickered. "Ready to run?"

"Ready to beat your ass."

Running had become a morning ritual ever since Jake purchased the stately, blue Victorian home right next to Evan Richardson, the Castle County commonwealth's attorney and Jake's best friend. As their feet pounded the pavement along the deserted streets, Jake thought about the days getting shorter. He and Evan might be running in the dark soon, but Jake didn't want to give up this morning ritual. Hearing their feet strike and lift in unison grounded him. He wasn't on his own anymore. Evan was right there with him, just as he'd been for most of their lives.

The bite of the morning air was more intense. The vibrant colors of fall had already faded. It wouldn't be long before winter blew in with its attendant headaches.

As they finished a route that brought them back to their houses, Evan asked, "Hey, we still on for poker tonight? Sam's bringing someone with him."

"Who?"

Evan laughed. "The new preacher from the Baptist church. Don't tell his parishioners."

"Are we pathetic or what? A Friday night and all we have to do is play poker...the sheriff, the police lieutenant, the lawyer, and now the preacher." Jake grinned and slapped Evan on the back. "Maybe we should just wear signs that say 'Losers.'"

"I don't consider it pathetic," Evan drawled, a glint in his eye. "I consider it once burned, twice shy."

"Ancient history."

"At least I have a history."

"Screw you."

"Later, baby." Evan batted his lashes. "What would the neighbors say?"

* * * *

Holly's stomach rolled. Whether it was from the baby or the sheer drop-off just a few feet away, she wasn't sure. She had pulled off the shoulder of the Blue Ridge Parkway at a place where there was a scenic overlook. With one hip leaning against the car, she chewed on her lower lip, and stared, lost in thought, along the asphalt snaking around yet another curve. She rolled her shoulders and stretched away the tension in her neck.

Tyler stood near the edge of the mountain looking out over the valley spread below him. "This is awesome, Holly, like that miniature-town stuff Mom always set up at Christmas. Come look."

Just a twinge of grief slipped through her consciousness at her brother's mention of their mother. Far greater was the relief that Tyler could talk about her so easily. Holly grimaced in response to his suggestion, though.

"No, thanks. I'll just admire it from here."

She wasn't keen on heights to begin with, but pregnancy had made her even more cautious. Her whole sense of balance had changed. While Tyler put his hand up to shade his eyes and squinted off into the distance, she counted the money she'd managed to come away with and blew out a frustrated breath. They couldn't go much farther. She needed to save her cash reserves for a place to live.

Glancing along the parkway, she noticed the sign indicating travel distances. They'd been on the road for what felt like hours. Surely they had put enough distance between themselves and Spence. Besides, Holly was nearing exhaustion after being up most of the night. She did a quick eenie-meenie-minie-mo and discovered her finger pointing toward a place called Mountain Meadow. Sounded pleasant enough. Probably not much happening there with such an idyllic-sounding name. At this point, its name could be Hell's Harbor as long as she could find a place to put her feet up. More than anything, though, she liked the spontaneity. Maybe it would keep Spence off their trail longer.

"Come on, Tyler."

"Where are we going?"

She pointed to the sign. "Mountain Meadow. Sound good to you?"

He shrugged. "I like mountains, so that would be cool." As they drove toward the town, Tyler laughed. "Hey! We should go check out the road back there."

"Why?" Holly's fingers clenched on the steering wheel. Unrelieved driving along the twisty roads had tightened her nerves.

"It's called Mistletoe Lane. You know…Holly and Mistletoe."

She had to laugh. It felt good to be able to for a change, and on a whim, she found a turnaround and headed back. Spontaneous, that was what they were being. As they bumped down the road, she glanced at Tyler. "This road is the pits, but maybe it will keep Spence away."

Tyler giggled. "Sports cars and potholes aren't a good mix. There's a house up ahead."

"And a truck parked out front."

As they stopped in front of the small, wood-frame house, the door opened and a stoop-shouldered man stepped out onto the porch. He eyed them suspiciously.

"Can I help ya?" he called as Holly got out of the car.

Crossing her fingers behind her back for luck, she said, "I'm new around here. My little brother and I are looking for someplace to live. Do you know where I might be able to find a rental or real estate agent?"

The old man's eyes narrowed. "Might be I could help you. I been thinking about renting this place out. Ain't nothin' fancy, but the roof don't leak and it's cheap."

And right now, cheap suited Holly to a T. Making an instant decision, she smiled. "Sounds perfect. I'll take it."

"Ain't offered it yet."

She smiled. "But you're going to, aren't you?"

The old man laughed. "I like you. You got nerve."

They hammered out a rental agreement, signed it with a handshake, and it was Holly's car that stayed while the old man and his truck bumped back to the main road.

* * * *

If the church ladies could just see him now, they'd have a cow. Cards and poker chips were on the table. Jake grinned as he glanced around the living room. He'd pushed the big table that stood in front of the double window to the middle of the room with the kitchen chairs pressed into service around it. Knowing Sam and Evan would want cigars, Jake had set an ashtray to one side. Beer was in the fridge, along with soft drinks for the preacher. Potato chips and peanuts—check. He'd brought home pizza from Mercer's. He even had some spray cheese and crackers. Yep. He was ready. How freaking domestic.

With just himself for company, he'd admit it would be nice to have some noise around the big old house. He hadn't thought about how empty it would seem when he bought it.

Maybe because he'd pictured it full of kids, like his house had been growing up with his three brothers and Becca, the baby. They had all gone their own ways as adults, but damn it would be nice to have family around. He rubbed the ache in his chest.

Right.

Single and not a woman in sight, and he was thinking kids.

Laura Browning

When the door opened without a knock, he grinned. "In here, Evan."

His friend sucked his teeth. "Aren't you the domestic goddess. Are we having those little canapés on triangulated white bread?"

Jake grunted. "Pizza and beer. You want cucumber sandwiches, you need to hook up with one of those blue-blooded sorority girls your mama and daddy keep tossin' your way."

"Not hooking up with anyone, bro. Not happening."

Jake laughed. "Right. You bought the big house just for you to ramble around in?"

Evan's eyes narrowed. "Pot and kettle, man, and I bought mine before you. You have all the signs, Allred."

"What signs?"

"Of a guy just looking to get hooked up."

Jake snorted.

The door knocker thumped. Jake left his friend and the conversation behind, somewhat relieved Sam and his preacher buddy had interrupted.

"Jake…this is Joe Taylor," Sam rumbled in his deep voice. "You met yet?"

"In passing." Jake stuck out his hand. "Welcome, preacher."

"Joe," the younger man grinned, returning Jake's greeting with a firm handshake. "This is definitely not a parochial visit. I'm hoping to fleece some of my potential flock…all proceeds to go to the church general fund, of course."

Evan laughed. "I like you. Nice addition, Sam."

The sheriff nodded. Sam was a big man, as tall as Evan and as broad as Jake. A little older than the rest of them, he was still a fixture—born and raised in Castle County.

As they sat and the dealing began, Jake thought his earlier conversation with Evan was over and done with, but after so many years, he should have known better. As Jake passed out pizza and paper towels, Evan said, "So, Sam, don't you think Jake has the look of a man just looking to settle down and get busy on the two-kids-and-a-dog routine? I mean, look how domestic he is already all handing out paper towels so we can wipe our fingers."

"Bite me." Jake laughed. "I just don't want greasy fingerprints all over my cards. As to settling down? Unlike you, Ev, I don't have any exes hanging around."

This time the smile left Evan's eyes and Jake knew he'd gone too far. Before he could think up some awkward apology, Sam spoke up.

"You're both thirty. I wouldn't be surprised to see the two of you with rings through your noses or on your fingers before the New Year."

Jake and Evan's eyes met and the two men howled.

* * * *

Almost a month after arriving in Mountain Meadow, Holly began to let down her guard. Tyler was enrolled in the local elementary school. The bus picked him up at the end of the lane. She'd discovered few people braved Mistletoe Lane once they got a good look at the potholes. She lurched her way to the part-time job she'd found keeping books for Crawford Pallets. The job suited her and the pay was okay. Mr. Crawford, her boss, had been desperate to find someone to untangle the company finances, which were in terrible shape with invoices and receipts shoved willy-nilly into file folders and nothing entered on computer.

She'd straightened that out, and he was making noise about bringing her on full-time. Holly grinned. Extra hours would help. Mr. Crawford had been so relieved to have her handling the books, he'd even mentioned allowing her to bring the baby to work. At lunchtime, she knocked on his office door.

"Mr. Crawford, I just wanted to remind you about my doctor's appointment this afternoon."

He smiled over the half-moons of his reading glasses. "Right. Thanks, Holly. We'll see you tomorrow then."

She'd told Tyler to wait for her at the general store after school. With it being right off the town square, she figured it would be safe enough, especially since the courthouse and the police station were both within sight of it.

From Spence, she'd heard nothing at all. Of course, with their tightening finances, she'd had to let the cell phone go, so now he had no way to harass her. And he'd been cautious about calling her cell since the restraining order. No, he was very careful not to provide any solid proof of his badgering.

Her fingers tightened on the wheel as she drove to her appointment. Spence was a chameleon. That had been part of the problem. The face he presented to everyone else certainly wasn't what she saw, at least now. He'd been smooth enough to begin with. That's how she'd gotten sucked in. Only later did she discover he was an adult and much more dangerous version of the kid who was always pinching or punching people behind the teacher's back.

She wasn't fooled anymore. He was a snake, and she needed to stay on her guard to make sure he didn't slither back into their lives unnoticed.

Laura Browning

The clinic was located in a building right next to the hospital. Holly's choice of where to stop had been pretty fortunate. Mountain Meadow was the Castle County seat and laid claim to the sole hospital in a three-county area—something she would need. Holly sat in the waiting area with people of all ages. A family practice wouldn't have been her first choice, but it was close, and she'd had a lot of her prenatal care already done by her obstetrician before she left.

"Miss Morgan?"

As the nurse called her name, the curious stares of two older women zeroed in on her stomach. Holly had experienced censure before. Her gaze skimmed around the room, and she noticed only one other expectant mother, an uncomfortable looking father-to-be at her side.

Holly put her chin up. Well, she couldn't boast any proud papa, nor did she want to if the choice was Spencer Dilby. He had been little more than a sperm donor, and she shuddered to think of that experience.

The nurse showed her into the doctor's office. "Dr. Owens will be right with you."

Holly nodded and sat. Knowing she would be leaving Lynchburg, she'd obtained copies of her medical history and dropped them off a couple of days ago. Medical books lined the shelves along one peach-painted wall, but there were no pictures of a husband or children. Her examination halted when the door opened and a petite blonde entered the room. Her hair was cut chin-length, as sleek and businesslike as the doctor seemed to be.

She held out her hand. "I'm Dr. Owens. Most patients call me Doc or Doc Jenny."

Instead of going behind the desk, she sat next to Holly, softening the businesslike exterior. "I read through your file and wanted to ask you a couple of questions before we do an exam. There was a notice you are a no-information patient. I'll make sure that stays in place."

"Thanks. I appreciate it."

"Has the baby's father been attending any birthing classes with you?"

Holly shifted. Just the thought of Spence having anything to do with her baby's birth was enough to make her queasy. "The father is the reason I'm a no information patient. H-he denied paternity to begin with, then after our split changed his mind. He's been pressuring me to give him the baby."

"Pressuring?"

Holly tucked a strand of hair behind her ear, her hand just a bit shaky. "He's the heir to the Dilby Department store fortune," she explained watching the doctor's eyebrows lift. "It seems his new fiancée can't have kids, so he's decided he 'needs' mine. His words."

"And this pressure was enough you left?"

"I have a protective order in place against him, which did nothing. He didn't leave me a lot of choice. See, in addition to myself and the baby, I'm also guardian to my little brother. I had to think about what was best for all of us."

Doc Owens nodded. "I've seen your ultrasound, so I see you're having a little girl. Are you aware your doctor had written in his notes he had some concern about your cervix?"

"No." A ripple of unease trickled down Holly's spine.

"I'd like to take a look. You're just six weeks from your due date, so chances are there's not a problem, but let's be sure, particularly since it's your first. At twenty-two, your age works in your favor."

A half hour later, they were back in Doc Owens's office once more. This time, the doctor's expression was more serious. "Holly, have you been experiencing any cramps or feelings of heaviness?"

"Some. I figured it was just stress from moving and everything."

Doc tapped her finger against the ultrasound image she'd been studying. "Well, you're already effaced and starting to dilate, like someone a whole lot closer to term. How accurate is this due date?"

Holly sucked in a shaky breath. "Very. There was just one night…"

Jenny nodded, her finger still tapping. "I'd like you on bed rest. You could go into labor any time. If we can get your little girl to hold off, I'd prefer it not be for at least three more weeks. The nearest obstetrician's more than an hour's drive away. It might be simpler to have you in the hospital…"

"No. I can't do that. I have my little brother to take care of. I have a job…and I don't have health insurance." A vision of what might happen if there were complications began to form, but Holly pushed it away. Panic was the last thing she could afford right now.

When she left the clinic, Holly was still trying to take everything in. She'd always tried to take things in stride, but this overwhelmed her. Bed rest. What on earth was she going to do?

* * * *

"I'm sure we can find her, Mr. Dilby."

Spence sat across from the private detective who was looking at the information Spence had given him about Holly. The paunchy guy tapped Tyler's picture. "This might be our best place to start. She'll have to enroll him in school. I've also got a contact who can help me out with tax info. If she's working someplace, she'll show up on his records."

Spence allowed himself a slight smile. "Excellent. Needless to say, this needs to be kept quiet. I'm now engaged to another woman, but I'm concerned about the welfare of my unborn child. Holly has shown signs during the pregnancy of depression, and I just can't help thinking about all those cases involving new mothers..." He let his voice trail off and, as he hoped, the detective's expression grew even more concerned.

"We'll find her. Don't you worry."

Spence stood, shook his hand and exited the office building with a small smile of self-satisfaction.

* * * *

Jake noticed the dark-haired boy sitting on the bench outside of Mountain Meadow General Store when he drove around the square to pull up in front of the small, brick building that housed the police department and his cramped office. An hour later, as he walked over to Tarpley's, what most folks called the store, to grab some chips and a drink, the kid was still there.

"Hey, buddy," he greeted him. "How's it going?"

"Okay." The kid gave him a sidelong glance from eyes that held more suspicion than he was used to from a boy so young.

"Kind of cold to be sitting out here so long. You waiting on your mom?"

"My sister. She's at the doctor." He scuffed his sneakers on the pavement.

"Well come on in. I'll get you a candy bar and you can warm up. Mr. and Mrs. Tarpley won't mind if you sit inside."

The kid glanced at Jake's badge, then at the store. "If you think it'd be okay. My butt is getting kinda cold."

"What's your name?"

"Tyler Morgan."

"I'm Lieutenant Allred." Jake grinned at him and they walked inside together. After introducing him to the older couple who'd run the store ever since Jake could remember, he let Tyler pick out a candy bar. While the kid sat near the window, munching on the chocolate and caramel, Jake spoke to the Tarpleys. "Haven't seen him around here. He new?"

Susie Tarpley nodded. "He and his sister Holly rent the old Crawley place."

Jake raised his brows in surprise. The house had been run-down when he was a teenager, and knowing old man Crawley, he doubted anything had changed. The bell above the door jingled and a burst of cold air entered. Jake glanced over and caught his breath, feeling as if someone had sucker punched him right in the gut. The woman who walked in was gorgeous, with hair the color of aged whisky, pale skin, and cheeks just touched with pink from the cold air.

"Holly!" Tyler jumped off his chair. "I thought you forgot me."

This must be the sister. As she shifted to give the boy a hug, Jake noticed her pregnancy, and disappointment stabbed him. Someone had already claimed her. Her gaze lifted to his, green eyes wide and wary as she took in his uniform.

"We need to go, Tyler," she murmured with an urgency that seemed out of place.

"How'd your doctor's visit go?"

She started to say something, glanced over her shoulder at Jake and the Tarpleys, and said, "We'll talk when we get home."

Jake leaned against the counter, watching the door shut behind them. "Did you say it's just her and the boy in the Crawley place?"

"Yup," Jim confirmed. "They've been in several times for groceries. She's pleasant and polite, but a little shy. The boy's a good kid. He's helped a couple of older folks out to their cars with groceries. They keep to themselves."

And she had something to hide. The thought had popped into Jake's head and wouldn't go away. He'd also gotten the distinct feeling his uniform made her even warier. He must be imagining things. *Or trying to come up with a reason to see her again?*

Jake nearly snorted out loud. She was pregnant, no doubt had a boyfriend or a husband somewhere already. He'd just mind his own business. Out where she lived, she was Sam's concern anyway.

Chapter 2

Where was Tyler? Holly shifted on the sagging flowered couch in her living room, fighting panic. Doc Owens wouldn't let her do anything other than sit, so her comfortable sofa had morphed into a jail-cell bunk. Not that she had any idea what one felt like. She glanced at her watch. Five o'clock and almost dark. Tyler should be here. She braced one hand under her belly, struggling to sit up. He'd walked into town to buy groceries to help tide them over, but even considering the distance, he should have returned by now. What had she been thinking anyway? He was just eleven. Sometimes Holly lost sight of that.

He had always been mature for his age, but in the year since the accident that had killed their parents, Tyler had become even more so. While she had juggled the paperwork involved in their parents' estate and her new role in looking out for her brother as stipulated in her parents' will, Tyler had quietly gone about finding his new normal. Right now, she wished she had more of his stoicism.

She stared at the laptop she'd set aside. While she still brought in some money from Crawford's, working part-time from home had put a real crimp in their budget. She bit her lip. Things weren't turning out quite as she'd hoped the day she'd so optimistically chosen Mountain Meadow as the place to land. Maybe trying to see the bright side of things was part of the problem. Because she'd been so desperate to get away from Spence, she hadn't spent enough time considering what could go wrong before they'd left Lynchburg. Bed rest the last few weeks of her pregnancy had not been in her plan. She took a deep, shaky breath, but it failed to calm her.

Now Tyler was MIA. Holly didn't want to panic, but her options were limited. She should go find him, not sit here doing nothing. She didn't want to call the sheriff. Her last few experiences with the law hadn't left her with much confidence in their abilities. An image of the cop in the

Tarpley's store popped into her head. If the sheriff resembled him, at least the law in this part of Virginia was a lot better-looking. Still, she had her doubts about how effective any of them could be in keeping Spence at bay. Her best bet was to lie low, and having to call in help to find her brother shot that to pieces.

The sudden crunch of gravel and the swift glare of headlights reflecting on the window made Holly jump. She twitched the curtains aside to peer out and her stomach dropped. This time fear, not her baby, caused the lurch. A uniformed police officer waited on Tyler to climb from the big pickup idling out front. Holly swallowed, but her mouth remained bone dry. The cop from the store.

Tyler appeared fine, so her mind conjured other potential problems. Had Spence found them already? Would her restraining order even apply here? Her hand went to her stomach. This was her baby, and she would not give her up. Not to Spence. He could threaten her with as many lawyers as he wanted.

Of course when she'd stood up to him and told him she'd just deny he was the father, things had turned even uglier. He might have money and enough influence to get his way in Richmond, but not here, not if he couldn't find her.

And if he did find her? Her chin lifted. He'd have a fight on his hands. It wasn't Holly's fault his new fiancée couldn't have children. Spence had no right to stalk her, to threaten her.

She pushed to her feet and struggled to the door. No way did she want this police officer to think she couldn't take care of Tyler. With a jerk of the warped wood, she yanked it open. Her eyes darted from her little brother to the tall, broad-shouldered cop at his side. Though she felt the cop's eyes on her, she ignored him to focus on her brother.

"Tyler! Where have you been? Are you all right?" Her hand rubbed the dull, persistent ache in her lower back. "Ar-are you in trouble?" she choked out as her gaze flicked again to the tall police officer.

"No, it's not like that, Holly," Tyler told her. "This is the guy I told you about the other day...the one who bought me the candy bar."

The officer stuck out his hand. His smile eased her tension somewhat, but she still hesitated before she allowed her slender fingers to disappear in his firm grasp. "I'm Lieutenant Jake Allred, Mountain Meadow's assistant police chief. I saw your brother walking with your groceries as I was headed home, so I gave him a lift."

His easy grin and dark hazel eyes, with just a hint of shyness, sent an unfamiliar tingle through her, but he was still a cop, and Holly had good

Laura Browning

reason to be wary. Spence had gotten around her restraining order again and again. It seemed to her the police had been unable or unwilling to stop him. She doubted this place would be much different.

Holly forced a smile to her lips—less than genuine but the best she could do—and pulled her hand away.

"Thank you. I know it was out of your way. I'm Holly, and you've met Ty."

The lieutenant smiled, turning his easygoing grin on Tyler. "Yeah. We're old friends by now. Why don't you grab those groceries since your sister knows you're okay?"

"Yes, sir." Tyler jogged out toward the pickup truck.

"Nice kid. You should be proud of him."

Holly relaxed a little. Tyler was a great kid, doubly amazing considering it had been little more than a year since their parents' deaths. She started to thank the cop and noticed his eyes had dropped to her belly. She splayed one hand across her stomach, her tension increasing. She'd received more than a few odd glances around town and had to assume she was already grist for the gossips.

"The Tarpleys mentioned you'd rented this place. You're a little isolated out here," he commented, looking around at the surrounding hills. "Kind of a long haul for your brother to cart groceries. Is there a problem with your car?"

Why was he being so nosy? As his eyes drifted to her beat-up compact, Holly leaned a shoulder against the doorjamb and rubbed her back. When she didn't answer right away, the tall officer regarded her with curiosity. Holly swallowed. "I—my doctor, that is—put me on bed rest."

Now his eyes did focus on her belly, and Holly rubbed her stomach. When the lieutenant frowned, his glance going from her stomach to Tyler returning with several bags of groceries, Holly's concern increased.

She didn't want to draw attention. She'd figured such a rural area and such an isolated rental were just the thing. But now, here was this dark-haired, hazel-eyed hunk of a police officer standing on her front porch quizzing her. It made her nervous. He made her nervous…and way too aware.

She needed to send him on his way. As soon as Tyler scooted into the kitchen, she gave the lieutenant as much of a smile as she could muster. "Look, thanks for giving Tyler a ride. I don't want to keep you. I'm sure you must be anxious to get home."

Holly started to turn away, but when he spoke again, she paused.

"Your brother said you hadn't been here long." He pulled a card out of his pocket and handed it to her. "Look, you're in Sam's—Sheriff Barnes's—jurisdiction, but I'm out this way a lot. If you need anything, give me a call. I'm happy to help." He shifted, sneaking a glance at her. "You know, not in any official capacity."

She took the card, her brow furrowed. As much as she wanted to get back to the safety of her little house, she had to know. "Why? I mean. We're not your concern." She made a face. "I'm sorry. That was rude. We're fine. It was kind of you to give Tyler a ride."

His eyes narrowed on her for another heartbeat as if he wanted to say something, but then he just slapped his cap against the side of his powerful thigh a couple of times and swallowed. Was that a flush on his cheeks? "No problem. Just remember. Call if you need anything."

Holly watched him go. When only the retreating glow of his taillights remained, she shut the door and leaned against it, willing her heart to calm. She wasn't sure if Jake Allred was the cause of that flutter or if it was just relief it wasn't Spence who'd arrived. They were still safe. Her poor judgment hadn't caught up with them yet. When she opened her eyes, Holly met her brother's innocent expression.

"Don't give me that look. You have some serious explaining to do, Tyler. I sent you out for just a few things." She eyed the bags on the table before staring at her brother. "Then you're gone for hours longer than you should have been, and you come back with way more than I gave you money to buy. I think that calls for some explanation."

"Come on, Holly," he protested. "Don't go all big sister on me. I just wanted to help. You should be lying down. What are you doing?"

She stared at him in exasperation. "Don't distract me. What did you expect would happen when you disappear all day, then show up at the door with a police officer? You weren't buying groceries all this time. How do I take that lying down?"

He pulled on her hand, guiding her to the couch. "I had to do something. Did you think I didn't notice how your back's been botherin' you? Be honest. Thanksgiving sucked. Now Christmas is comin' and…" He flung his thin arms out. "I just wanted to help. The Tarpleys asked about you, and we started talking, so I asked them for a job." He finished in a rush, maybe hoping she wouldn't hear what he'd said.

Holly sat. "Tyler! You're too young to work." She knew from doing the payroll for the pallet company teenagers were forbidden to work in any hazardous jobs. There were a few exceptions to the law that would allow someone as young as Tyler to work—but working at a grocery store wasn't one of them.

He bit his lip as he stared at his sister and began the whole story. "It's not anything full-time…."

"It's not anything *legal*, honey," Holly protested. "Mr. and Mrs. Tarpley could get in trouble."

"Well, I'm not like an employee, you know?"

Holly shook her head. "No. I don't know. I think you're going to have to explain. Does that mean they're not paying you?"

Tyler's gaze flicked to the groceries and understanding dawned. When he took the money she'd given him out of his pocket and put it in her hand, she swallowed.

"I talked to them yesterday after school," he admitted. "Mr. Tarpley said he couldn't pay me money, but if I wanted to stop in, he would find odd jobs for me to do and we could trade. You know. I'd do some stuff for them; they'd give me groceries in return. I didn't want to lie to you, Holly, but I was afraid you'd say no."

She sighed, staring at the groceries. "And I would have. You're eleven, Tyler! I'm supposed to care for you, not the other way around."

He sat next to her and knotted his hands together. "I wanna help. If I can do some odd jobs, you know for Mr. and Mrs. Tarpley, maybe for some other folks, too, after school and on weekends, maybe it will help make up for you having to cut your hours."

Holly wasn't sure whether to laugh, yell, or just cry. "But Tyler…a job?"

He blinked at her, batting his thick lashes over his big chocolaty eyes. "Come on, Holly! You know we can use the help. It's only for a couple of hours a day."

Holly thought about the mounting bills and the meager amount of money still in her account. The truth was it would be a help. Doc Owens mentioned she might be able to get public assistance, but Holly feared it would provide a paper trail leading Spence to them. She needed to keep as much of their finances as she could on a cash-only basis.

She blinked back tears. After a gulp or two, she whispered in a choked voice, "Okay. You're the best brother I could ever have, Tyler. I just worry about you trying to walk home from town so much."

He shrugged. "I'll find a ride with somebody headed this way, like I did today. Will that make you feel better?"

Yes and no. Although she knew he should be safe with most of the people around here, they were still new to the area. "Just promise you'll get rides from people you know, okay?" At his nod she smiled. "Beans are on the stove."

They were having pintos for supper…again. Tyler didn't say anything, and Holly appreciated that. She knew he was tired of them, but until her next paycheck they had few options. Now, thanks to Tyler, they had milk and cereal they could eat for breakfast. There also would be some variety to lunch and dinner.

His dark head was bent over the bowl of beans. He was a nice kid, just like Lieutenant Allred said. Plenty of cornbread and sweet tea rounded out the meal, and Tyler ate like a horse. He must be hitting another growth spurt. Halfway through his bowl, he stopped in midscoop.

"You not hungry?" he asked around a mouthful of beans.

She grimaced. "My appetite's been off. There just isn't much room inside anymore for anything but the baby."

"Holly?"

She glanced up, exhaustion dragging at her. He looked so grown with his serious dark eyes, so like their mother's. He'd tucked his longish brown hair, darker than her own, behind his ears.

"What are you going to do if the baby comes while I'm not here?"

"I'll call 911, or your cop friend," she joked.

"I'm serious, Holly," Tyler said, his brows drawing together.

She smiled to reassure him. He'd gotten so protective of her. It had been that way ever since the accident that had killed Mom and Dad. Holly understood. They had only each other now.

"That's a long way off, Ty, so don't worry. We've got the phone. It's not like we're cut off."

* * * *

The scarred wooden doors of the cramped brick building housing Mountain Meadow's police force banged shut behind Jake. He frowned as he snatched off his baseball-style cap and raked his fingers through his thick hair to get rid of the hat-head look. He glanced at his aging boss. Chief Ernie Jones was just turning away from the ancient Bunn coffeemaker, stirring a spoon in a mug stating World's Best Grandpa in big childish lettering.

"What's got you riled, Jake?" Ernie grinned as if he already had a damn good idea.

"Someone toilet papered the nativity scene at the Baptist church. In her official capacity as head of the ladies worship committee, Betty Gatewood assures me it's some of those folks from the Presbyterian church. She wants a full-scale investigation and seemed pissed I didn't dust for prints. 'Course, Joe hasn't said a word."

The chief stirred his coffee and failed at smothering a grin. Jake narrowed his eyes. The feud between the Baptist ladies and the Presbyterian ladies was legendary. It heated up every holiday season, most often with some help from the town's teenagers. Jake had just never expected to land smack-dab in the middle of it. But thanks to covering for one of their vacationing officers, he'd been the one to answer the call. Now embroiled in the middle of the ongoing feud, he found it hard to appreciate Ernie's good humor.

"Come on, Jake, you grew up around here. You know they're always feuding over something...or it's kids burning off a little pre-Christmas excitement."

"That's what I tried to tell her," Jake said.

"Well how'd you leave it?"

"Joe and I removed all the toilet paper before I assured her I'd make some inquiries."

"Sounds good to me." Jones sipped his coffee, sighed with pleasure and ambled toward the door to his office. "Jenny stopped by a little while ago looking for you. She mumbled something about a patient she was worried about. Wanted to see if you'd go check on her."

"One of her elderly shut-ins?" Jake asked as he shrugged off his leather bomber jacket. Jenny was always going the extra mile for patients, but he supposed they all did in their own way—just part of life in Castle County. People had always watched out for neighbors, like that kid and his sister the other night.

Ernie's thick brows furrowed as he drawled, "Nope. Didn't get that impression from her. Sounded like a younger person."

He thought of Holly Morgan. He wouldn't mind checking on her, but he doubted she was who Jenny had in mind. Too bad.

"Well, I'll try to give her a call before I leave. If not, I can ask while I'm at her place."

Ernie raised his brows. "Something going on there?"

"No. Just friends. Jenny and I know too much about each other to be a couple. Besides, despite what Evan wants people to believe about he and Jenny being past history, no way would I tread on that territory. It's the guy code. No, tonight's a holiday party, not a date."

Ernie laughed. "Too bad. 'Bout time you found someone to settle down with, isn't it?"

"Don't hold your breath." Jake grinned and moved to the short hallway leading to his office, but as he went through the door he thought about Ernie's comment. Jake did want a wife and family. And he guessed Sam and Evan weren't far from the mark when they accused him of showing the signs. Problem was there didn't seem to be a lot of candidates, and he wasn't into the whole dating and small-talk scene. He never seemed to think of anything to talk about, and those long silences sure got awkward. Then it would turn into twenty questions with him answering yes or no. Women always wanted to talk things to death. ESPN and a beer to go with it were a whole lot less awkward.

He tilted his ancient wooden desk chair back, listening to its familiar squeak of protest. He'd put a couple of noses out of joint when he'd applied for, and gotten, the job as lieutenant after his return from Afghanistan. A chill chased down his spine. He still experienced nightmares about those last two years. That's what had driven him back to Virginia. He needed home, roots. His parents and his brothers and sister might have left Mountain Meadow, but he knew the people here, and it gave him a place to belong. Knowledge of the area, combined with his military experience had helped him land the job. He didn't regret it. Most of the time. Hadn't helped the dreams much, though.

There were a few negatives. Most of his high school friends had homes and families. Except for Jenny…and Evan. He didn't like to think about their past. Then there was him, rattling around in the huge house he'd bought. What the hell had he been thinking? The perfect woman would just drop into his lap? Even if she did, how long would she stick around with his nightmares?

Jake straightened his chair, pulling the unfinished reports toward him. He was busy, that was what mattered. Family would come. He just had to be patient. A vision of a pale face with vivid green eyes popped into his mind.

Holly. She was just as thorny as her namesake. She was an attractive woman, even if it did look like pregnancy was draining her. What was she doing on her own? Where was the baby's father? He'd like to ask her, but how the hell did you do that? *Hey, Holly, I don't see a ring on your finger. Are you divorced, or did you just walk out on the father-to-be?* Worse still. What if she was a widow? Jake shuddered. Way too awkward. Besides, a ready-made family was hardly what he'd had in mind when he pictured kids running around his house, filling the bedrooms on the second and third floors.

Laura Browning

No use even going there. She'd made it plain she wanted nothing to do with him. Even as polite as she'd forced herself to be, he knew when he was being hustled out a door. It might be the uniform, but he doubted her wariness was all due to it. A world of hurt had lurked in those eyes.

* * * *

How could you end up on hold just trying to check your bank balance? Holly sighed as she switched the phone receiver to her other ear. She hadn't even talked to a real person yet. Was the computer that busy? When the automated voice spit out her balance, she saw it matched the pittance recorded in her checkbook and disconnected.

Where was the Holly who normally cheered people? She blamed it on the pregnancy hormones, but more factored into it. The insurance money her parents left behind was never intended to cover the costs of her pregnancy. After she'd paid funeral expenses, Tyler's medical bills, and settled her parents' debts, there wasn't much left anyway. What remained disappeared between leaving Lynchburg and getting set in Mountain Meadow. Without selling the house or finding a renter, she was in a bind.

Renting this place had drained her money even more. She had always lived at home until she and Tyler left Lynchburg, so she never had to deal with deposits for utilities and a house. All of those extras had eaten into her meager reserves.

She stared out the window next to the kitchen table. *Damn you, Spence.* He had burst her fairy-tale bubble of what a romance should be. Then his drinking and rambling threats had forced her to pick up and run. Nothing was more important than making sure Tyler and her baby were safe.

Could Spence have done anything? Probably not. But she couldn't take the chance with her baby or her brother. She'd already proven her judgment was way off base when it came to men. She wouldn't make that mistake again.

Now she was confined to the house, working part-time—thanks only to Mr. Crawford's generosity. He'd set her up with a satellite Internet link and a laptop so she could keep doing his books and get paid. But with so little left, remaining upbeat was harder and harder.

A disconnection notice from the power company stared her in the face. If she paid their minimum, she wasn't sure they would have enough for food, but if she didn't pay, the power would be cut off and then not only could she not afford to reconnect it, she would also not be able to get her bookkeeping done. She could ask Mr. Crawford, but she hated to do so if there was some other way to work it. He was already being kind enough. If a solution was out there, she sure would like to know. She glanced up, hoping for a little divine intervention, or at the very least inspiration, but of late even faith—in God or man—was in short supply.

Holly pressed a hand to her back and stood, hoping it would relieve the ache. She just couldn't seem to find any comfortable position. And the bed-rest part? Forget it. Every time she lay down she felt like she couldn't breathe. Between working on the computer and a lack of sleep, Holly's eyes were gritty. She was sure they must be bloodshot. Doc Owens had warned her the last month would be uncomfortable, but it seemed to her the bed rest made it worse, not better. She was so inactive, the last thing her body wanted to do at night was sleep.

The baby rolled and shifted. Holly rubbed her belly. The muscles across the top of her stomach tightened, then relaxed. Doc told her these practice contractions weren't anything to worry about, but they happened more and more often. She smiled as she stroked her abdomen again. *Wish me luck, baby, because Ty and I are going to need it.*

She called the power company. She tried to time her bill-negotiating calls for when Tyler was out of the house. He didn't need to hear her working deals for partial payments on their phone and electricity. She would pay the minimum and just hope the money she had left combined with what she could still earn would get them through. At least if Ty brought groceries one worry was off her mind.

* * * *

Jake locked his office and grabbed his cap and coat from the peg next to the door, realizing he didn't have time to run home before he was supposed to be at Jenny's house. He grimaced at the idea of going to her party in his uniform, but hell they all knew who and what he was anyway. Wasn't like jeans and a shirt would make them any more comfortable.

"Get in the car, Jake."

"Evan?" Jake started. "What are you doing here?"

Evan straightened from where he'd been leaning against the side of his car and grabbed Jake's elbow. "You forget. I know you too well. You were getting ready to go to Jenny's in your uniform, weren't you?"

"Well…" Jake slid in the passenger side.

"Fuck well," Evan said as he buckled his seat belt. "I'm running you back to your house so you can change. Then we'll go."

Jake glanced at Evan's profile as his friend drove the few short blocks to where their homes stood side by side. "I still don't get why you want to go."

"I'm a masochist." Evan pulled into the drive. "Hurry up. I can't wait for Dr. Owens to give me an eat-my-assectomy."

Jake sighed. Evan was right. They did know each other too well, and he knew Evan was up to something. He'd dropped hints all week until Jake invited him along. Jenny had said he could bring a friend, but Jake knew Evan was not who she'd had in mind. So why was he going along with it? Because he was a sucker. That was why. They might not remember, but Jake did. Evan and Jenny were supposed to be together.

In just minutes, Jake climbed back into Evan's car, uniform gone and jeans and a sweater in their place. Christmas music blared from the radio as Evan flicked his wrist to turn on the ignition.

"I figure we can both use a little mood music."

Jake laughed. "Doesn't feel like the holiday spirit's infected anybody this year."

As they passed the road leading to the old Crawley place where he'd dropped off Tyler and met Holly, he frowned. He'd given Sam a heads-up about the Morgans so maybe he and his deputies could keep an eye on her. What would she do if she went into labor and couldn't drive? Mistletoe Lane was little more than interconnected potholes. He doubted either of the county's two ambulances could even negotiate the road.

One thing was for sure, Mountain Meadow was small enough chances were good he'd see Holly and Tyler again. He grinned as he realized he wouldn't mind at all. He'd liked the kid a lot, and if he could get past some of Holly's wariness… Jake wasn't quite sure how to finish that thought. Anyone could see she loved her brother and the baby she carried. He had to respect that kind of commitment.

"What are you grinning about Allred? My imminent demise?"

Jake snorted. "You were the one who invited yourself along. Don't whine if you're welcome's less than you expect."

"So why the grin?"

"Thinking of the woman and her brother who've rented the Crawley place."

Evan laughed. "You're thinking about a woman? Careful, next thing you know, Sam's prediction will come true…hooked and landed before the new year."

"Asshole."

Evan turned into Jenny's drive. Her home, tucked into the trees on the side of one of the mountains, was ablaze with light when they arrived. Some of the doctors and nurses from the hospital as well as friends they'd gone to school with were already milling about. When Jake showed up late, Jenny smiled—until she saw who followed him in.

"Hi, Jake." She ignored Evan and pulled Jake to one side. "When I said bring a friend, Evan wasn't who I meant."

"Come on, Jenny. He's my best friend and my next-door neighbor. Besides, I was running just a bit late and he was waiting for me." He needed to change the subject. "I was up this way last night. Dropped a kid home on Mistletoe Lane. Tyler Morgan. Lives with his sister, Holly. I guess y'all are neighbors of sorts."

"Oh. Then you've met her," Jenny said with a smile. "I hoped Ernie would remember to give you my message."

"What message?" Jake asked in confusion. "When I saw him today, he just said you wanted to talk to me about a patient."

Jenny tucked her short blond hair behind one ear. "Yes. Holly Morgan. Didn't you stop at her house?"

"Well, yeah, but only because I gave the kid a ride home yesterday. Why'd you want me to check on her? It's not my jurisdiction. I can give Sam a call, though."

Jenny sighed. "I know it's not your jurisdiction. I wasn't talking about official business. Ernie didn't listen. Sam had already left the courthouse, so I left a box of food at the station for you to take by. There's no way my car will make it down her road, and I knew you were headed out here anyway."

Jake quirked a brow. "You're feeding your patients now?"

Jenny punched him in the arm. "I had to put her on bed rest. She's only worked at Crawford's pallet warehouse for a couple of months or less. I think he's arranged some work-at-home stuff for her, but still. She's got no family and few resources. I mentioned Medicaid and food stamps to her, but she shut me down cold."

Jake's brows drew together. "Where's the dad-to-be?"

"She has a protective order against him. I know his name and a medical history, but I can't talk about it. Her file is no information."

He had his own sources for information, and he'd get some too. She and Tyler needed help. Jake didn't even want to examine why he felt compelled to be the one to give it.

"She did seem a little spooked when she saw me in uniform," Jake offered to fill the silence. "Wouldn't even let me get past her front door."

"She was lying down wasn't she?" Jenny's golden gaze sharpened.

He thought about the way Holly had flung the door open when they'd stepped on the porch. "Not exactly."

"I was afraid of that. At this rate, she'll go into premature labor. I'll give her a call Monday. I'd like to get her out of that house and closer into town. I have some real doubts about the safety of Crawley's house. There's no telling how old the well is, not to mention the paint, probably loaded with lead."

"Well, there are those apartments not far from your clinic…"

"I checked. They have a waiting list." She eyed him. "You've got extra room in your place."

"So do you, Doc, and I'm not in the market for either boarders or roomies. What about some of the church ladies?"

"She already said no when I mentioned moving closer in." Jenny shook her head. "You know our town. I'm guessing she's already come in for the evil eye. I mean, get real. Can't you just see her boarding with Betty Gatewood? Your place would be a perfect solution. What better way to make sure her PO is enforced than to board with the police lieutenant."

He saw the glint in her eye. *No, sir.* As sexy as Holly Morgan was, even pregnant, that was too much. He'd just keep an eye out, make sure Sam knew about the protective order so he could send guys by more often.

Just the thought of a woman invading his house made him shudder. She'd want to watch sappy chick flicks or get pissed off when he wanted to watch football. *She'd find out I cry like a baby every night from nightmares.* There must be something closer in, and he could pull a few strings, maybe get her a break in rent. He doubted Crawley had done anything as formal as a lease. Hell, he was surprised she got the old man to rent the place at all.

The doorbell pealed and Jake saw Evan open the door to one of the young nurses. The perfect diversion to save him from Jenny's well-meant meddling. As soon as the thought occurred, Jake was sorry about it. Fireworks were a forgone conclusion whenever she and Evan crossed paths. Playing host in her house was bound to get the sparks flying.

He supposed he should try to head Evan off. He knew his best friend far too well. Evan was never one to back down from a confrontation, and Jake should have realized what Evan had been angling for when he'd kept nagging Jake to let him come with him.

Jake started to move in for the interception, but he was already too late. Jenny was ahead of him. She smiled at the nurse, but the look she gave Evan would have made most men turn tail and run. Her golden eyes narrowed.

"I didn't get a chance to greet you earlier, Counselor. Did you stop by to see if I'd taken over running Daddy's still?"

Evan's gray eyes were as cold as chips of ice. "Moonshine wasn't the only thing your daddy ran, Dr. Owens. Last time I was by this place, it resembled a turnstile for the basketball team. But then you always were popular with the boys, weren't you?"

Jake winced. Well, now. That was taking things just a little too far a little too fast. Evan wasn't even attempting an end run, he was plowing straight through the defensive line. Jake stepped in to block. "Hey, Evan! I'm working on a case I need your advice on. I forgot to ask you about it on the way over. Got a second?"

He noted Jenny's tense expression and dragged Evan away from her. No one would ever believe they had lived in each other's pockets all through high school. Since his return to Mountain Meadow, he'd juggled his relationship with them. Both were good friends of his and he didn't want to lose either one. He pulled Evan over to the refreshments.

"What the hell were you thinkin', Evan? Do you go out of your way to make her mad?"

Evan arched one thick brow and let his shuttered gray eyes survey the room. "I didn't go out of my way at all. You invited me."

"Don't be an asshole! You know what I mean. And you invited yourself."

Evan stared Jake dead in the eye. "I don't make it a point to have anything to do with her at all, Jake, but neither am I going to avoid her. Meeting in a social situation was inevitable. I won't be driven out of my town just because she's decided to return. So, I chose the turf. Hers." His lip curled as he took in the comfortable surroundings. "Looks to me like the good doctor's done pretty well for herself. I'm sure she can handle a little heat."

"It's the holidays, Evan. For God's sake, leave it alone for one night."

Evan's mouth thinned and he said nothing, but nodded acquiescence. Jake sighed. It would take a miracle to bring those two together. He kept an eye on Evan, noting just how often his eyes tracked Jenny's movements. Say what he wanted, Evan wasn't over her, and Jake was sure she was the same.

He was not much surprised, when Evan found him later, wanting to leave. That was fine with Jake. He had plenty on his mind but hoped he'd get a decent night's sleep for a change.

* * * *

Jake picked up the box of food for Holly and her brother the following morning when he stopped by the station. He shook his head. Ernie was starting to get forgetful. It seemed to him the chief had a lot on his mind these days, and played most of it pretty close to his chest. Jake hefted the box, which contained some nonperishable snacks—healthy of course.

Doc wouldn't load her patient with nabs and Moon Pies. Though if you asked him, they'd taste a whole lot better than squirrel food. Maybe he'd stop by Tarpley's on the way and grab a couple of bags of chips and some candy bars for Tyler. A boy needed decent guy snacks, not the granola crap Jenny stuck in there.

It would be easy enough to drop it by before he drove the additional hour along the interstate to ski on his day off. Fresh snow on the higher peaks would be a change from the icy texture of the man-made snow at Thanksgiving, and Jake looked forward to it. He could enjoy the day and still do his good deed by looking in on Holly like Jenny wanted. Doc didn't ask much, and she was a good friend. He knew she asked now because her fancy car couldn't negotiate that pisshole of a road Holly and Tyler lived on. Besides, it was an excuse to see Holly again. And how pathetic was that? He'd hardly been able to carry on a conversation with her between her wariness and his klutziness with women.

As he drove down the rutted lane, one thought nagged. How did Holly plan to get out if she went into labor? He hadn't considered it before, but now he had a better idea just how bad their circumstances were.

Tyler opened the front door as soon as the truck stopped. When he saw who it was, he grinned.

"Hi, Lieutenant!"

Jake grimaced. Holly sure didn't need reminders he was a cop. It seemed obvious to him if she'd run, her protective order hadn't done much. "Just call me Jake, Tyler."

"What're you doin' here?"

"Doc Owens asked me to bring this box of food. Don't you have school today?"

Tyler grinned from ear to ear. "Teacher workday. Come on in."

When he stepped inside, he noticed the chill and glanced over to the cold woodstove. His eyes went to Holly. She sat on a stool at the kitchen sink, up to her elbows in suds. When she saw him, she stopped and dried her hands nervously on the towel she'd slung over her shoulder. Her belly might be poking out, but her arms and hands were still delicate.

Her mouth twitched into something he guessed was a smile, but he knew it fell short of the mark. Not a warm welcome. He had to fight the urge to fidget as he cast around for something to say that wouldn't sound like he was a complete idiot.

Her wary gaze went to the box in his arms. "What's that?" Her chin tilted.

"A box of food."

Her face suffused with color and then went very pale. "We don't need charity, Lieutenant Allred. As I told you the other night, we're fine."

Jake's eyes narrowed as he set the box on the small kitchen table with a definite *thud*. It was one thing to be proud when you had just yourself to worry about. That wasn't the case here. "It's not charity, Miss Morgan. Call it being neighborly. It's what we do around here. Doc Owens sent the food over. For some reason, she seems concerned because she believes she's put you on *bed rest*." He stared at where she sat.

Now the color flooded her cheeks in a guilty blush. Tyler came into the room. "Holly," he interjected into the tense silence. "There's no more wood to bring in for the stove. It's gone."

For just a moment, Jake thought he saw her chin tremble. Then she bit her lower lip. Neither Holly nor her brother was in any shape to chop wood. Tyler wasn't big enough to wield an ax, and she was supposed to be in bed. How the hell had they gotten along until now?

Jake sighed and admitted he'd been looking for an excuse to hang around. Now he had it. Forget skiing. He stripped off his coat and pushed up the sleeves of his sweater.

"What are you doing?" Holly's eyes widened.

"What needs doin'." He pointed at her. "You go lie down like Doc says." He pointed at Tyler. "You show me where the axe is. I'll chop wood while you finish the dishes for your sister."

"Look, you can't just walk in here and…" Holly's protest trickled off after one look at him. She swallowed. "All right. Thanks."

He'd expected more of a fight, but then she looked tired.

Tyler handed him the axe a few moments later out on the dilapidated front porch. "Uh, Jake?"

"Yeah, kid."

"I have to go into town. I'm doing some odd jobs for the Tarpleys. They give us food and a little bit of money."

Jake paused. "Is that where you were coming from when I gave you a lift Saturday?"

"Yeah. I'd just started. Holly…well, Doc said she can't work. She does some stuff from the house, but it's not full-time or anything. I thought I could help out. She's awful worried about money. She thinks I don't know, but I see her at night trying to figure how to make it work. Sometimes… sometimes she cries."

The boy was so serious for someone so young. "What time you supposed to be at Tarpley's?"

"Noon, but it takes a while to walk."

"No walking. I'll run you into town when I go. In the meantime, I'll chop wood, and you do those dishes. Your sister's supposed to be lying down 'cause Doc's afraid the baby's trying to come too soon."

"It's a girl," Tyler confided. "Holly wants to name her Noelle, 'cause she's supposed to be here right around Christmas."

Jake's mouth quirked into a lopsided smile. Holly and Noelle. "That's cool."

"Yeah. That's Holly. Or it was. She used to be so happy all the time. I kinda miss the way things used to be."

Jake struggled to imagine the serious young woman he'd met as someone who was happy all the time, but then circumstances could change folks. Look at Jenny and Evan...and him. Jake ruffled Tyler's hair, trying to reassure the kid. "Well, I guess she has a lot on her mind getting ready for a baby and all. Maybe we can make her smile again. What do you say?"

Tyler grinned. "That'd be great. I'll go finish the dishes, then help bring the wood in."

"Can you get a fire started?"

"Yeah. Holly showed me how. Mine aren't as good as hers, though. She says I'm too impatient."

Jake laughed. From what he had seen of Holly, she didn't strike him as the patient sort, but then he was sure he wasn't seeing her at her best. As he split the oak logs and stacked them, he pictured her. Along with her almost Madonna-like face was a stubborn, pointed little chin. Other than the baby bump—hell, mountain—she was thin, with long arms and legs and narrow shoulders that gave her a fragile air. Her breasts...he stopped there and swallowed. *Whoa, boy.* Pregnant. About to be a mother any minute. *Better not to think on those lines.*

Tyler joined him in a few minutes. Together the two of them stacked plenty of wood on the covered porch. Jake watched Tyler build the fire, giving him a few tips. He glanced away and found Holly observing, her brows drawn together.

He spoke to Tyler. "Do you need to clean up before I run you into town?"

The boy glanced at the dirt on his shirt. "Yeah. I'll be back in a minute."

An awkward silence fell. Jake stood near the stove, feeling like the Jolly Green Giant in the small house.

"Why are you doing this?" Holly asked at last, wary and just a little defensive.

Somehow he doubted she wanted to know he was attracted. He wasn't sure he wanted to know. He spread his hands. "You need the help, and I like your brother."

For just an instant, he saw the first trace of humor flash across her face. "Just not me," she commented.

Heat flooded his cheeks. "That wasn't...what I meant," he sputtered.

"It's okay, Mr....I mean Lieutenant Allred. I haven't been at my best."

"Jake," he corrected. "Call me Jake."

"Would you like a glass of tea before you go? You must be thirsty after all that work. There's some in the fridge."

A peace offering. "Yeah. I'll get it."

Jake opened the refrigerator. Christ. There wasn't enough food in there to feed a gnat, but he didn't say a word. It would humiliate her, and heaven knew she was a prickly thing. He took the tea pitcher, grabbed one of the clean glasses from the dish drainer, and poured before putting the pitcher inside. The tea was good. Strong and sweet like he preferred. As he set the glass in the sink, he said, "I'll bring him home—Tyler, that is—after he gets done at Tarpley's."

She stiffened. He wondered just who had done such a number on her she would let herself and her brother almost starve before she asked anyone for help.

"You don't have to."

"Yeah. I do. It's who I am, Holly." He'd provided a friendly shoulder for as long as he could remember, and he couldn't stop now, even if there were times when he just wanted to be alone.

"You must have other things to do, things with your family."

"My family's moved away. My sister and brothers couldn't wait to shake the dust off their shoes and get out of here. Then my parents decided this wasn't where they wanted to retire, so they moved to Florida."

"Why'd you stay?"

Jake shrugged, not ready to admit just how much he'd needed the comfort of someplace familiar where he didn't have to wonder if a sniper would pop out from behind the next house. Realizing he needed to say something, he swallowed.

"Didn't, really. Stay, that is. I spent the last ten years mostly in the Persian Gulf and Afghanistan. Why are you here?"

Her hand covered her belly, and that gesture was as close to the truth as he'd get. He saw it in the way her steady gaze shifted away from him. "Just a desire for a new start, although so far it's not going quite as I expected."

Her evasiveness disappointed him, but what had he expected—that she would pour her heart out and let him comfort her? Hoped. Maybe. Before he could say anything, Tyler returned to the room. His long hair was combed and his shirttail tucked in.

"Ready, kid?" Jake asked.

"Yeah. I don't wanna be late."

Jake glanced at Holly. "You have my number if you need anything."

She nodded, but he already knew she wouldn't call. She didn't want to owe anybody anything. Someone had shown her all too well there was always a price to nice.

Chapter 3

Thoughts of Holly nagged Jake all night. First thing the next morning, Jake was in the station and on the phone. Mountain Meadow might be a small police force, but they still had resources they could call for help. And friends. And right now he was calling in a favor.

"Trev, it's Jake."

"Hey, dude! How are things hangin' out there in the Blue Ridge? Longing for the big city yet? You know there'd always be a place for a man like you here at the bureau."

"Not a chance," Jake shot back. "I'll leave the big city and the politicking to you, buddy. Give me my mountains any day. Look, I need a favor."

"Anything. I still owe you for that night in Kandahar."

Jake shook the memory off. Not something he wanted to think about, let alone talk about. "I need some information about two people: a Holly Morgan and her brother Tyler...same last name. Tyler's just a kid."

Trev laughed. "You got anything other than names? You know, maybe ages, descriptions, some basic ID I can use?"

Jake passed on what he'd gotten out of Tyler on the way into town. He'd been hesitant to try to pump too much information from the kid. "Until about two months ago, they lived in Lynchburg, She graduated from a college or university there."

"Well now. That's more to go on. I'll get back to you as soon as I can."

Jake hung up, then called Jenny.

"Hey, Jen, it's Jake. Busy?"

"I'm a family practitioner in a small town with the only hospital in a three county area. What do you think, Jake?"

"No need to be testy. I won't take much of your time. I just want to know what Holly Morgan's due date is."

"Jake, I'm overjoyed you're showing such personal interest, but you know I'm not supposed to tell you anything. Besides, I still haven't forgiven you for your choice of friend to bring to my party."

"Come on, Jen. I just want to help."

"Okay, I will give you one interesting tidbit. You're the second person today to ask the very same question. Someone else called first thing, claimed they were planning a shower for her. Sure didn't sound like anyone from Crawford's, so I think it might have been somebody just fishing."

Jake's senses went on alert. He hadn't gotten the impression from Jen or Holly she'd been around long enough to have friends wanting to give her a shower.

"Did you tell them anything?"

A snort sounded from the other end of the line. "No. We didn't even let them know she was a patient. And I'm not telling you anything either."

"Look you already told me she's all but lost her job. What else is stressing her? I mean, she looks at me like I'm Jack the Ripper—not Dudley Do-Right as you keep calling me."

Jenny's exasperated sigh floated over the line. "I am so violating confidentiality here. Her ex-fiancé hassled her to give him the kid after they split. He wants her to play incubator and then hand the baby over to his new fiancée. That's why she's got the PO."

Jake grimaced. "Damn! That's cold." He jabbed the pencil he'd been tapping on his desk blotter back into the cup holding a half dozen other pens and pencils. If a woman like Holly were having his child, there wouldn't be anyone but her.

"Okay. So now I've told you way more than I should've because you're one of my very best friends, and I think Holly could use a friend like you. I hope the information is for a good cause."

"I thought I'd take more food over later this week. The weather forecast calls for snow, so I don't want her and the kid stuck with nothing to eat. Jeez, Jen. I opened her fridge to get a glass of tea yesterday, and it was almost empty."

The pause stretched. "Like I said, Jake. She could use a friend, even if she doesn't think so."

He ended the call so he could take his turn doing patrol duty. As he drove, he kept turning over the mystery call to Jenny's office. If someone was sniffing that close, chances were they had a lead on Holly already. Jake blew air out in frustration. If it turned into knowing her address, she and Tyler would be in deep trouble. Crawley's place was way too isolated.

He had just cleared a domestic argument, sparked by a husband who spent too much of the family paycheck on holiday cheer, when his phone rang. He pulled his unmarked cruiser into the parking lot of the Presbyterian church.

"Jake here."

"Hey, dude. Got you the info you were looking for."

Jake pulled out a notebook and a pencil. "Okay, Trev. Shoot."

"Holly Marie Morgan. Twenty-two years old. Bachelors degree in Accounting from Lynchburg College in May of this year. Legal guardian of Tyler Matthew Morgan. Eleven years old. Parents were Matthew and Marie Morgan, both killed in a car crash Thanksgiving of last year. Tyler was injured, but survived. Until five months ago, Holly was engaged to Spencer Dilby, of Richmond."

Jake raised his brows. "Would that be like Dilby Department Stores?"

"You got it."

And the guy wanted her kid? That was some serious pressure with the money and pedigree to back the name.

"Who ended it?"

"He did, and is now engaged to a Celia Segal whose family is from Fairfax. Pretty straightforward stuff. Hope it helps."

"More than you know, Trev. Thanks."

"Anytime, bro."

Jake sat in the car and drummed his fingers on the steering wheel. That would explain why the ex-fiancé might be after the kid-to-be. The child had a claim on the Dilby fortune. It would also explain some of her wariness around him. She no doubt figured the Dilbys could pressure anyone with all the money they had backing them, protective order or not. If so, they hadn't ever been to Mountain Meadow. Folks in this part of Virginia didn't take to people who flashed their cash.

* * * *

Just as Holly suspected, the phone company cut service Wednesday. They'd told her the last time she'd called a partial payment wouldn't be enough. She rubbed her back as she returned to the couch from her latest trip to the bathroom. She had the radio tuned to one of the local stations for some background noise because, with no satellite and no cable, they got almost no television reception in the hollow where they were, even with the box to convert the digital signal.

Her forced inactivity drove her bananas. Used to working, she made a list of baby items she still needed, but all she did was frustrate herself when she realized she had neither the time nor the money to be ready for her daughter's arrival.

Jake stopped by Thursday with another box of food in hand. Without Tyler as a buffer, he swallowed, and after he handed the box to her, he took his cap off and slapped it against his leg a couple of times. She was relieved when he mumbled something again about chopping wood and hurried outside.

The window gave her a great view while he worked. He made it look so effortless, and for him it no doubt was. There wasn't an ounce of flab anywhere on him. Holly bit her lip and let the curtain fall into place. He was handsome, but she had no business looking at him. She had no business looking at anyone. Still, she twitched the corner of the curtain again, drawing some comfort from the smooth swing of the ax. She was disappointed when he just stuck his head in the door and mumbled a good-bye.

What did she expect? She'd been pretty bitchy to him. Holly bit her lower lip. This wasn't who she was or what she was like, but after the mistake she'd made about Spence, trusting anyone else was nearly impossible, even someone like Jake.

Jim Tarpley brought Tyler home most of the week. On Saturday, he stepped into the house for a minute to say hello.

"Susie had me bring this box of baby clothes and whatnot. We kept items around when our grandchildren were tiny, but most of them are in their teens now, and she thought you might could use it."

Holly smiled in genuine pleasure. "Thank you, and please thank Mrs. Tarpley, too. You've been such a help."

His eyes twinkled when he smiled. "Anything we can do, you just let us know. Tyler's a hard worker, and we're real fortunate to have him with the holidays coming. You let us know if you need anything, you hear?"

Holly smiled. Tarpley waved his good-bye and shut the door behind him.

While Tyler did his homework, Holly went through the clothing, blankets and small toys. In addition, several items appeared brand new. Baby wipes and powder, diapers, a bulb syringe, and a couple of bibs. She blinked back tears.

They had met some nice people since they came to Mountain Meadow. Folks like the Tarpleys, Doc, even Jake. Maybe things here were different. Jake called it being neighborly. Until Spence, Holly had trusted in the basic goodness of people. Then he opened her eyes to reality, but maybe that was Spence's version of reality. Her eyes drifted to the full wood box.

Somehow, she bet Jake's reality was a lot different. And given a choice, she wanted Jake's version.

After Tyler went off to bed, Holly doused the living room lamp and settled on the couch. She now slept half-propped just to find some comfort and still be able to breathe. Even so, she was getting far less sleep than she needed. By Tuesday morning when Tyler set off for school, she was achy and lethargic.

"Pay attention to the weather, Tyler," she told him as he started out the door. "They keep calling for snow."

He waved at her. "I will."

Just after noon, Holly realized the weather wasn't her biggest problem. Her labor had started. The first hard pains hit about the same time the snow began to cascade in thick, fluffy flakes. As the contraction rippled through her, Holly clutched the edge of the kitchen counter and tried to regulate her breathing. She stared at the phone in frustration. She had no way to call anyone. Stupid.

Well, it would be hours before she needed to worry. Weren't first labors generally long? And someone would bring Tyler home. She could get a ride into the hospital then. In the meantime, she would pack a bag for her and the baby.

* * * *

Spence tapped his finger on the manila envelope in front of him and smirked. The detective hadn't brought much, but it might be enough. Tyler was enrolled in the Castle County Schools, a fifth grader at Mountain Meadow Elementary. He'd made some other phone calls, but had so far come up empty. His information didn't include a physical address, just a PO box.

Maybe it was time for a ski trip. He and Seely could go through there, giving him the perfect excuse to stop and nose around just a little. Holly's baby should be born any time. A Dilby. That was all his parents cared about. So if he could deliver, they'd quit pestering him.

Yep. Time to head to the mountains.

* * * *

Snow blanketed the town square, and Jake thought of the additional box of food he had for Tyler and Holly. He had to let Jenny know not to say anything. He told Holly the boxes were gifts from Doc, but aside from the first one, Jake had packed them. He hated to think the grief she would give him if she found out. Hell, Evan was already calling him Father Teresa. Yeah, he hated the way he smirked when he did it, too, like he thought Jake was going all moony over Holly. He was just being neighborly, like his parents had taught him.

He called the general store and talked to Susie Tarpley, letting her know he'd run Tyler home in a couple of hours. In the meantime, he finished the paperwork on his desk. It included a proposal to the town council for an expansion to the building and the force. Right now they had just six sworn offices. Jake hoped to add two more. Ernie had shuffled more and more of the administrative work on him. About four-thirty he grabbed his coat and cap and checked in with the chief.

"I'm gonna get out of here early. I told Jim and Susie I'd run the Morgan kid home, so I'll be in my truck. I'll have my cell phone with me, though."

"Careful. Scanners are starting to light up with a lot of traffic problems north of here along the interstate. Looks like this is switching over to freezing rain."

Jake frowned. All they needed was an ice storm. Snow was one thing, but when things iced up, nobody moved no matter what they drove. He stopped by his house and grabbed the food he'd forgotten, tossing the box onto the backseat of the four-door truck. A half hour later he halted in front of Tarpley's.

The snow indeed switched over to thick drops of freezing rain. They plopped like syrup on the windshield before the wipers whisked them away. Why was he doing this? Holly didn't even live in Mountain Meadow, and she hadn't given him any come-hither looks. Hell, maybe that was it. She was so determined to do everything on her own... Tyler slipped and slid his way to the passenger door and climbed in. Jake waved to Jim and Susie across the seat.

"Buckle up. This could be an interesting ride home."

"Yes, sir."

"Have you talked to your sister to let her know you're on the way?" Jake put the truck in gear. When Tyler didn't respond, he glanced over and saw the boy shift. "Tyler? Did you call her?"

"Our phone's shut off."

Jake started to swear, remembered the boy sitting next to him, and bit his tongue, smacking his palm against the steering wheel instead. "You mean to tell me your stubborn sister is all alone out there on bed rest with no way to call anyone?"

"Yes." Tyler's voice shook. "We couldn't pay it, so they cut it off last week."

Last *week*? Why hadn't she said anything? He'd been by several times. Did she mistrust him so much? Jake pressed his lips together. "Okay, okay. We'll get you home, then come hell or high water, I'm taking you and your sister out of there tonight. Even with a phone, I'm not sure any help could get to y'all in an emergency." Thinking of the protective order, he added, "You can stay with me until you find someplace closer in where Holly can get help if she needs it." And by God, if she bowed up on him, he'd carry her out over his shoulder, pregnant or not.

As they set off, Jake realized he was doing what Jenny had angled for at her party. He realized something else. It didn't matter. He couldn't let Holly and her brother stay in that piece-of-shit house any longer. The place should have fallen in years ago.

* * * *

How long had it been since the last contraction? Holly huddled in the bathroom. She'd been sick a couple of times as the contractions rolled through her. The pains came harder and faster, and now she wasn't sure just how much time she had. She put clean towels on her bed and boiled water. What the water was for she had no idea, but it seemed like people always wanted boiling water when they screamed about birthing babies in the movies.

She checked her watch. Five o'clock. She'd been in labor about four hours. Not very long. She remembered other women at Doc Owens's talking about being in labor for twelve hours and more. She checked her watch as the next contraction hit. Less than five minutes. The freezing rain hit the windowpanes with an ominous ticking noise.

For the first time, unease stirred and with it the realization she was in very real trouble.

When she heard a vehicle outside, she braced one arm on the edge of the tub and tried to stand, but she was tired. As she shifted one more time, something popped and was followed by a gush of warm liquid that drenched her clothing and left her gaping in horror. The front door opened and Tyler called to her.

"Holly? Where are you?"

Another contraction hit, and she moaned.

* * * *

Jake pushed into the house right behind Tyler and stomped the snow off his boots. He heard Holly's moan as soon as the door shut. He took in the scissors and string on the table, the pot of water on the stove, the towels and a book on pregnancy and birth. Dropping the box he carried into the chair next to the door, Jake shot past Tyler.

"Holly!" Fear drove him down the hall.

She knelt on the floor of the bathroom in a puddle. His throat ached. Her eyes swallowed her pale face. He had seen the look before: pure, unadulterated fear. For soldiers, it could be deadly, and Jake had no doubt this could be just as dangerous. *Calm down.* He had to be the strong one because she must be scared spitless.

"Holly, honey, it's Jake," he murmured, not sure how aware she was. "You need me to help you?"

She nodded. "My water just broke, but I've been in labor for a while." She sucked in a shaky breath. "Oh, Jake. Thank God you're here."

He picked her up, mindless of her wet clothing, and carried her down the hall to the room he assumed belonged to her. He was relieved to see the bedcovers turned back and towels already covering the sheets. He glanced at her with new respect. She'd prepared to get through this on her own. As he settled her on top of the towels, he asked, "How long have you been having pains?"

"They started around one."

He glanced at his watch. About five hours. "How far apart are they?"

She swallowed and whispered, "The last ones were three minutes."

Jake pulled out his phone, checked to see he had a signal, and punched a button. It rang just two times. "Doc? It's Jake."

"Hmm, you're calling me Doc, so this must be business."

"It is. I'm at Holly's house. I brought Tyler home. She's in labor. About five hours. Pains three minutes apart."

"Shit." There was a pause and then she said, "Why didn't she call someone? No. Never mind that now. Think you can deliver a baby?"

"Uhh, Jen…we covered the basics in training, but I've never done it."

"Jake, I'm at home and stuck. If you move her on this ice and get stranded, the situation could go from bad to worse—life-threatening worse for her and the baby."

Jake closed his eyes then opened them to stare at the ice hitting the windowpane with its rhythmic *tick, tick.*

"Give me a refresher. Her water's already broken."

"How's she holding up?"

"Other than being scared, breathing and color seem okay. I haven't checked her pulse."

"It'll be elevated. I'm not so worried about that. Has she said anything about feeling the need to push?"

"No."

"Chances are she's not fully dilated yet. Clean her, get her changed, and make her comfortable. Check to see if you can see the baby's head, then give me a call."

Jake punched End and stared at the blank phone screen. What the fuck? He was barely on a first-name basis with Holly and Jenny wanted him to… He looked at Holly's pale face and wide eyes. Jake blew out a deep breath. Time to put his personal interests aside. This was professional. Right. And he was no doctor.

"Holly?" Tyler's voice came from the doorway. His face was pinched and pale as he took in her soiled clothing. "What's wrong? It's too soon for the baby, isn't it?"

Jake heard the edge of hysteria in the boy's voice and realized he must be thinking about losing his parents the year before. Now the only family member left was bloody and in pain.

"It's okay." Holly's smile vanished as another contraction slammed into her. "Just a little early. No big deal." She panted and closed her eyes as if to hide her fear from her brother.

So Jake smiled. "Your niece, Uncle Tyler, has decided it's time to be born, and she and Holly will need our help. Can you be a big man and do that?"

Tyler straightened his thin shoulders. "Y-yes. Yes. I can."

"Good. I just got off the phone with Doc Owens. She says we need to get Holly cleaned up and make her comfortable. Can you find me a nightgown?"

"Yeah." Tyler went to the chest of drawers and pulled out an oversize T-shirt. "Here you go. It's what she usually sleeps in."

Holly lay against the pillows, sweat beading her brow. She must be so tired, and he felt nearly helpless to change that.

"Great, buddy. Now get me a warm washcloth and a clean towel so Holly can wash." As soon as Tyler left the room, Jake stripped off his jacket. "Can you clean up, or do you need help?"

Her gaze slid away from his. "I—I'm going to need some help."

Jake skimmed her cheek with his fingertips. "Now's not the time to be embarrassed. You and I are gonna get to know each other a whole lot better in the next few hours. Doc says not to move you."

Holly's eyes widened. "Have you done this before?"

"No," he admitted. And he wasn't sure he wanted to do it now, but he couldn't tell her.

She smiled, weariness plain on her face. "Couldn't you lie to make me feel better?"

He stroked the hair off her face. "No. We need to be straight with each other about what's going on. It's the only way to get you, the baby, and Tyler through it too." And me, his internal voice shouted.

Holly nodded. Her expression relaxed somewhat. If she still didn't quite trust him, she at least didn't look petrified anymore.

Tyler returned and handed them the cloths.

"Thanks, man. Say, if you've got any coffee around here. I could use a pot."

"There's some in the freezer," Holly said. "You remember how to make it, Tyler?"

"Yeah."

Jake grinned. "Then get to it while I help Holly."

As soon as Tyler left the room, Jake hefted her to her feet, supporting her with one arm while he helped her remove the damp nightgown with his other. He wiped her, patted her dry, and then slipped the clean shirt over her head.

As much as he tried to be objective and impersonal about the whole process, his insides were in a knot. He'd never seen a pregnant woman's body before and he marveled at all the changes. When he looked into her face, she blushed and looked away.

"Don't, Holly," he blurted. "You're beautiful." Jake felt heat in his cheeks, but he refused to look away. She was pretty. She needed to know that.

Her laugh was half sob. While she sat in the chair near the bed, Jake put additional towels over the mattress. He'd never seen a human baby born, but he had helped with cattle births on the farm when he was a kid and knew clean and easy weren't necessarily part of the process. When he was done, he helped her onto the bed just as another contraction began. He sat next to her and held her hand. How the hell was he going to do this?

"Doc said I should make you comfortable. Would you rather sit on the bed or move around a bit?"

Holly's eyes were so bright they almost glowed. "Sit for now. Have Tyler get the extra pillows out of his closet. I'm so tired. I guess the pains I've had since yesterday weren't false labor like I thought."

"If you'll be all right for a few minutes, I'm just gonna check on Tyler, and then I need to call Doc and the chief. I'll bring those pillows, too."

Holly laid a hand on his arm, and he stopped to look at her.

"Thanks, Jake. I know you didn't expect this, but I can't tell you how glad I am you're here. I thought…"

He squeezed her hand. "You thought you were going to have to do it by yourself."

She let out a relieved breath. "Yeah."

He grinned. "You'da done it, too."

* * * *

The weather deteriorated as the night wore on. The *tick, tick, tick* of freezing rain continued to beat against the windows and onto the rusted tin roof. In a strange way, Holly found it soothing, like being cocooned inside the small house.

Jake's presence was more reassuring than she might have imagined. He sent Tyler out to his truck to bring in the emergency kit he kept in the backseat and then had her brother fill two of the collapsible five-gallon water containers he pulled from the kit. Tyler gave him a questioning look.

"Why ya having me get all this water?"

"In case the power goes out, buddy. If you lose power, you'll lose the well pump—so no water. After you've filled the containers, fill the tub, too. I'm gonna call Chief Jones to let him know where I am and talk to Doc Owens."

He sat in the chair next to her bed to make his calls. Holly shifted position, rolling to her feet awkwardly. When Jake started to rise, she waved him back.

"I'm okay. I just need to move around some."

While she walked around the room, she listened to Jake's end of the conversation with Chief Jones. The weather situation was worsening. Jake pinched the bridge of his nose while he listened.

"Look, I'm sorry to leave you in the lurch like this. I know it's not our jurisdiction…"

When he hung up a few minutes later, Holly said, "If being here is getting you in trouble…"

He glared. "Don't even finish that sentence. Ernie told me to stay right here. Sam and his deputies can cover until I get back." He studied her belly. "You doing okay?"

Holly nodded. "A little tired." Another contraction started, so she held onto the bedpost and rode it out. She knew Jake was worried. She tried to smile. Then he surprised her by coming around to rub her shoulders and her back.

"That help?"

"Yes." Another stronger contraction doubled her over. "I think I need to sit, and Jake?"

"What?"

"I think you should call Doc again. I feel like I need to push."

Jake helped her to bed, propped her with the pillows, and left the covers over her. This wasn't how Holly had pictured the birth of her baby. This man was little more than a stranger, but as he moved around her with easy grace, his hair falling over his brow and his gaze flicking her way with concern, she realized if Doc Owens couldn't be here, she was glad Jake was.

He was on the phone with Doc. He listened for a few moments, huffed out a breath, and ran his fingers through his hair before he said, "Yeah, I'd already kind of figured that, Jen." He paused an instant and then handed the phone to her. "Doc wants to talk to you. I've got to go scrub."

"Hi, Doc."

"You okay with this, Holly?"

She smiled as Jake left the room. "I don't have a lot of choice, but yes. Jake's doing a great job."

"Good. I know you're a little uncomfortable with people you don't know, but he's a good guy. You're going to be pretty busy here in the next little bit. Just keep in mind everything Jake does is to help you and the baby. Okay?"

"Yes. I feel like I need to push."

"Sounds like you're close. Let me talk to Jake again."

He had just returned from the bathroom and used a towel to grab the phone from her. After a minute or two he held it out to her. "Hit the End button, please."

That's when the lights went out. Jake swore, and Holly's heart skipped a beat. As if he sensed that flutter of panic, Jake squeezed her knee. The gentle pressure reassured her.

"Tyler?" he called calmly.

"Yeah?"

"Get in my emergency kit. You'll find two flashlights, some candles and matches. Bring them here, please."

"Yes, sir."

Tyler walked in with a flashlight beam already bobbing in front of him. In another minute, several candles cast a soft glow around the room. Jake's lips quirked. "Someday you'll have some great stories to tell your little girl."

Holly's laugh cut off as another strong contraction started.

"I need to take a look to see how close we are to the real work." He glanced at her. "Still feel like you need to push?"

"Yes." She panted.

"Easy, honey. Big breaths. Just relax. We'll get your baby here right and tight. Tyler, I'm sorry, buddy, but you're going to have to be an active participant. I need you to hold the flashlight so I can see."

"Okay."

This had to be tough on Tyler and was no doubt more than he wanted to know about how his niece was getting into the world. "Ty, if you're not okay with this, we'll figure something out."

He swallowed. "I'm okay. Really. I watched Jimmy Pruitt's beagle have her puppies, so I have some idea."

If Holly hadn't been in so much pain, she would have laughed. In fact, she could have sworn she heard Jake do just that.

"I remember delivering a few puppies," he said, "but I think we'll bypass the part where you swing the little guys to get them breathing, and I don't think Holly will need to bite through the umbilical cord."

"Ooh." Tyler made a face. "That's just gross."

Jake's eyes twinkled. "What do you think?"

"I'm all for snipping," Holly assured him.

Jake put a hand on her knee. "I'm just gonna take a look, okay?"

The heat of his palm offered some comfort, but everything took a backseat to the simple need to push the baby. "Hurry."

"Oh, wow!" Tyler whispered at the same time Jake spoke.

"I see the top of her head, Holly." A note of excitement crept into his deep voice. He glanced at her and grinned. Her contraction eased. When Holly half laughed and half sobbed, he patted her leg. The touch was enough to reassure her. "You're doing fine. Doc says you should push with your contractions, but easy. As soon as the head's out I'll need to suction and check to make sure the cord's good."

She nodded, feeling a mixture of awe and fright. The life inside her had taken control, and she had no say at all in what was going on. As another contraction began, Holly sobbed and began to push. It hurt, more than anything she could have imagined, but even the pain paled next to the anticipation.

Jake told Tyler, "Prop that flashlight right there. Take the other one into the kitchen and bring me the bulb syringe I saw on the table. More towels, too.

"You mean the thing with the squishy rubber end on it?"

"Yeah. Then come sit next to your sister and tell her what a great job she's doing."

Laura Browning

Jake's gaze reassured her that everything was okay. Her nerves settled. When the next contraction came, she concentrated on bearing down, the effort almost enough to overcome the pain. She was nearly done. Just a little more and her daughter would be here.

Jake laughed. "That's it. The head's out, honey. Relax a minute." He reached for the bulb syringe. She supposed he must be suctioning the baby's nose and mouth, but she couldn't see. Holly tried to catch her breath.

"Jake…" Her body took over and the next contraction sent the baby out into Jake's waiting hands. He cradled the infant for just a moment, and even with her blurring vision, she saw his eyes well over as well. As if he realized, his expression went blank and he blinked several times before he laid the infant on her stomach and began drying the baby. There was just the faintest tremor in his big hands as he touched the newborn, but he made no attempt to hide it. Jake was as overwhelmed as she was. The baby cried, angry mewling sounds, and her tiny face screwed up as she voiced her displeasure at this unwelcome change in her surroundings. The warm weight of her daughter now rested on her instead of inside her. Her miracle.

Holly reached trembling fingers to stroke her child. Her baby. She swallowed against the thickness in her throat. "Is she okay? Is she perfect?"

"The most perfect baby I've ever seen."

Holly smiled and let her head fall against the pillows. She was okay. "Thank you, Jake," she managed to choke out.

Tyler's eyes were huge.

"How you doing, Uncle Tyler?" Jake murmured.

"I'm good. Wow!"

* * * *

Jake stared at the umbilical cord. "We're not done yet. Call Doc, Tyler. Just hit Redial while I wash."

Tyler held the phone for him as he came out. Jenny ran down the directions to deal with the cord, then explained Holly should try to nurse the baby to help stimulate contractions to deliver the afterbirth. "Don't worry, it's nothing compared to the baby, just a little messy."

The afterbirth was a snap compared to delivery, but fatigue had worn them down. By the time Jake settled Holly on clean sheets so she could nurse, cleaned everything, and put it away, he was exhausted. He returned to her bedroom to find Tyler curled on one side of the bed watching as the baby slept. Jake sat in the chair next to Holly's bed. When she smiled, the wariness she'd treated him with had disappeared. For right now, trust had replaced it. The change floored and scared him. He swallowed past the thickness in his throat.

"You were amazing, Holly. I don't know many women who would have been so calm in this situation."

"I didn't feel very calm. I don't know what we would have done without you. I was so scared, and then you got here…thank you." Tears welled again, spilling down her cheeks.

He touched the wetness, brushing it away. "I'm just glad I was here. I'll bring you some Tylenol, then you need to rest." He tapped his fingers against his thigh. "You…uh…you didn't tear or anything." Shit, he so didn't want to go into this. "I just thought you should know. Doc will check you out and all."

Holly smiled. "I had a great delivery guy."

At Jake's signal, Tyler scooted off the bed and blew out the candles. Jake waited for the boy to precede him out of the room, then said to Holly, "I'll leave the door open. If you need anything, I'll be in the living room. Just call me."

He checked in on her a couple of times and found both her and the baby sleeping. She looked exhausted, not even stirring when he brushed a stray lock of hair off her face. His gaze moved to the tiny bundle of the baby, as delicate as a porcelain doll. A fierce surge of protectiveness moved through him, and not just for the baby, he realized. His emotions had been riding a roller coaster since he walked in the door. Now looking at them both, he realized a connection was there. He'd been interested the first time he saw Holly, and that had only grown as she tried to juggle her pride with what she knew was best for her brother and her baby—and how what was best always won. He would get them both to the hospital just as soon as he could, and then? Then he would move them in with him—her, the baby, and Tyler.

Now, all he had to do was convince her. He hadn't told her his suspicions about someone looking for her. Eventually, he would have to. For a moment, Jake wondered if moving her in was for them or him. He'd wanted a family, and fate had put one right in front of him.

Holly and Noelle. Tyler'd said Holly wanted to name the baby Noelle because her birthday was supposed to be around Christmas. Well, it was December. An early Christmas gift. He touched the infant's head with his big palm and shifted his gaze to Holly's pale face. He had helped her bring this baby into the world. He hadn't counted on how that changed things. Emotional ties bound them together, and he wondered where it would lead.

Chapter 4

Jake stamped his feet and blew on his gloved hands. Ice glittered on tree branches like a million prisms the next morning, but he had a lot more to do than admire its beauty. His focus was on getting his precious cargo out of here. That meant clearing the trees and branches littering the rutted road.

By chance, his chainsaw and a can of gas sat in the bed of his truck. He'd loaned them to one of the patrol officers who had taken his kids to cut a Christmas tree. Now Jake could put the saw to better use clearing a path for a holiday package to get to town.

As he and Tyler dragged the last of the branches off the still slick road, the boy asked, "Are we taking Holly and Noelle to the hospital today?"

Jake slapped bark and snow from his uniform with his gloved hands and grinned. "I hope so. I'll call Chief Jones and Sheriff Barnes in a minute to see how the roads are. If they say four-wheel drives are moving okay, we'll take Holly and the baby to see Doc."

"They're okay aren't they?" Tyler asked.

Uncertainty clouded the boy's face, so Jake put an arm around his shoulders. "'Course they are, Tyler. We did a great job helping Holly. It's just a precaution. Kind of like having the teacher look over your work at school."

"Oh. Okay." Tyler tossed branches on the pile near him with renewed energy, a grin back on his narrow face.

After Ernie and Sam reassured him about the roads, Jake bundled the sleeping Noelle nice and tight. He strapped the infant carrier into the backseat. Jake hummed Christmas carols as he turned on the truck to warm it. He didn't want Holly or Noelle getting chilled. He laughed to himself. *Careful, man.* He sounded like a new father.

"Ready to go?" he asked Holly as he entered her room. She sat on the bed's edge, frustration evident. "What's the matter?"

She sighed. "I feel useless, like I can't do anything."

Jake leaned against the doorjamb. "You just gave birth. If you're exhausted, you should be. Relax. Let someone take care of you for a change. It looks to me like you spend all your time trying to care for everyone else."

Her mouth quirked. "It would be a switch."

"Good. Because I'm giving you a ride out to the truck." While he carried her out and belted her in, Tyler followed with Noelle cradled in his arms. Jake smiled as he secured the baby in her carrier. Noelle couldn't ask for a more protective uncle.

Jake climbed in. "Everybody ready?"

Holly leaned forward to touch his shoulder. "Thanks, Jake."

Their eyes met in the rearview mirror, and he answered her with a small smile before putting the truck in gear.

* * * *

Holly stroked the baby's cheek. Noelle had woken once during the night wanting to be fed, then again just after dawn. Feeling her nestled against her, tiny mouth pulling at her breast, had filled Holly with awe. This tiny, perfect human being trusted and depended on her totally and completely. Holly had vowed then and there to try to be the best mother she could every single day.

As far as Holly could tell, things were going fine. Somehow the smell of sweet, sweet baby was already erasing the pain of labor and birth. She smiled as she thought of changing her first diaper. Even that was something new and wonderful, another way to bond with her baby.

Icy patches still dotted the roads where trees shadowed the curvy highway. Holly was glad to see Jake was so careful. From the rear seat, she studied the back of his head and the part of his profile visible in the rearview mirror. She would have been in real trouble if not for him. The whole experience drove home just how isolated they were.

Maybe now was the time to ask for help. Filing for assistance was bound to leave a paper trail and make it easier for Spence to find her, but maybe it was time he did. She knew people here now. They could help her stand against him and all the influence the Dilby money could buy. More than anything, she had to remember Tyler and Noelle were what mattered. Maybe she could work from home and keep books for more than just Mr. Crawford. If she could get her own computer, she could work on taxes, too. That would support them if they could find someplace inexpensive to live in town, maybe rent a couple of rooms instead of trying to take on a house.

She'd ask Doc. Maybe Jake, too. They'd both grown up here, so they could help. Her gaze settled on Jake again. Those broad shoulders of his made her want to run her hands across them. Mr. Hot Cop was good inside and out. Sharing the experience of Noelle's birth proved it. She would never forget the wonder on his face when he laid the baby on her belly. Why couldn't Spence have been like Jake? Spence's care and consideration had evaporated the moment he'd taken her to bed.

Jake watched her in the mirror, and she blushed, fidgeting with the baby's snugly wrapped blankets. Holly had slept with Spence one miserable time. She couldn't be sorry. Noelle was the result, and she wouldn't trade anything for her little girl.

The storm had forced her to put her trust in Jake. She wasn't quite ready to test these feelings, but she'd already seen how well he related to Tyler. She'd thought then he was just a cop with a big heart, but between delivering Noelle, and helping her the past day, she realized something basic had changed between them. She could depend on him, but more than that, he made her breathless.

When their gazes met again, they held for just a moment, and Jake looked away first to watch the road. He was as unsure as she was. Good. She'd had cocky and seen how empty that was.

Holly smiled at her tiny daughter, resisting the urge to once again unwrap her to examine the delicate fingers and tiny toes. For the first time since she'd told Spence about her pregnancy, Holly hoped things might return to normal. She wasn't going to run scared anymore. Mountain Meadow was the place she was going to stay, and let Spence bring on his worst.

They arrived at the emergency entrance of the small regional hospital. Holly protested when an orderly brought a wheelchair out for her.

"It's standard procedure," Jake reassured her. After helping her out, he placed Noelle in her arms. He and Tyler followed as they wheeled her in. Jake spoke to the receptionist, then crouched next to Holly.

"Doc will be here in a couple minutes. Then they'll get you settled in a room."

Holly clutched his arm. "Jake, I don't have enough money. The baby and I are fine. Won't they be able to just check us out and let us go home?"

"I don't know. You'll have to ask Doc. Don't worry about Tyler, though. If Doc says you need to stay, he can bunk with me. I just live right down the road. And don't worry about the bill either. Sometimes these things have a way of working themselves out. It's not like they'll keep the baby till you're paid in full."

"That's not funny." Holly glared and Jake just chuckled.

"Good afternoon, Holly." Jenny Owens approached, cutting her off before she could tell Jake she'd find a way to pay her own bills. She smiled at all of them. "Let's see what we have here."

Holly placed the swaddled infant in the doctor's outstretched arms. For just a second, something flashed in Jenny's eyes. Pain, nostalgia, Holly wasn't sure, so she blurted into the brief silence, "She's doing well. She's nursing just like she should be."

"And how are you handling that?"

"It was strange at first, but Jake helped, and we got the hang of it."

Jenny arched one perfect brow at Jake. To Holly's surprise, he blushed and looked away.

"Yeah. Jake's been great, Doc," Tyler chimed in. "He didn't even panic when the lights went out while Holly was havin' the baby!"

"Really? You didn't tell me that, Jake."

Jake coughed. "Yes, well it turned out okay. I had my emergency kit with a couple of flashlights and some candles."

"A candlelight delivery," Jenny drawled. "How...old-fashioned."

Jake glared and flushed again, his gaze darting from Holly and Tyler to the doctor. "Enough, Jen," he snapped. "We all did what we had to do."

One of the nurses paused to look at the baby in Doc Owens's arms. "Did you just say Jake delivered this cutie by candlelight?"

Jake groaned. Holly studied his face. He was embarrassed. Was it because they were linking her to him? The idea hurt, but it didn't fit with what she knew of him. So why was he worried?

Jenny glanced at Holly. "Come on, Mama. Let's get you and the baby settled in a room. There are a few tests I'd like to run on both of you, and we need to record all of Noelle's vital information. We'll keep you tonight, just like we would any new mom who gave birth here, but I see no reason you can't go home tomorrow. We'll see about Noelle."

"What do you mean?" Holly gasped. "Won't she be able to go with me?"

Jake moved closer, resting his hand on her shoulder, and a sense of comfort moved through her. Jenny handed her the baby.

"We just want to be careful. Even though you were pretty much full term, since she was just a little earlier than expected and born at home, we'll check her over. I'm sure everything's fine, Holly," Jenny soothed. "I didn't mean to alarm you."

* * * *

As the nurse wheeled Holly and the baby away with Tyler following, Jake spun on his longtime friend. "Nice bedside manner, Doc."

Her golden eyes narrowed as she countered, "You helped her and the baby get the hang of nursing?"

"Don't divert." Jake blushed again. "I read the manual to her while she," he gestured with his hands, "you know, handled everything else."

"Well, I knew you'd made a thorough study of breasts during high school, Jake, but I didn't realize it extended to their practical uses." Jenny laughed, enjoying his discomfort.

"Come on, Jen! Cut me some slack. It was me or the eleven-year-old. I did what I had to, what anyone would have done."

Her tawny eyes examined him again. "From the blush on your face and the soft look in your eyes, I suspect you did a lot more than what just anyone would have done."

"I was there."

Jenny arched a brow. He hated when she did that. "You know what I think, Jacob Allred? I think you're already crushing on Holly Morgan."

Jake was speechless, which was just as well since Jen wasn't done with him. "I haven't liked how closed in you've been. I noticed it as soon as I got back, and I suspect you've been that way since you returned to Mountain Meadow. I look at you and see someone so withdrawn, so alone, even when you're surrounded by the people you've known all your life. That's not like the Jake who was always there for everyone else with a shoulder to cry on."

He shifted his feet and slapped his cap against his thigh. "Jen…don't pry. You have no idea. I can't…I can't talk about it. Okay?"

"Let me ask you something. All kidding aside now. You've got a ton of room in your big old house. I didn't understand why you bought such a huge place, but it's a godsend now. Would you take them in? I don't want them at the old Crawley place. Between the well water and the paint, I'm not sure how safe it is."

Jake wadded his cap in his big hand and returned to slapping it against his leg. He could picture Holly, Tyler, and the baby filling the emptiness in his big house. What he couldn't picture was actually talking to Holly about it. He slapped the cap harder. He'd stared into the eyes of enemies, risked gun and mortar fire to help his fellow soldiers, but asking Holly to move in? He needed help. "I thought of suggesting that, but I wasn't sure she would go for the idea. Think you could sell her on it for me?"

Jenny smiled. "I'll try. In the meantime, I asked one of my nurses to get her and the baby some of the basic things they need to get started—on me of course."

Jake shuffled his feet. "I could help. She doesn't have much."

Jenny smiled. He narrowed his eyes. She looked way too smug. "Great, Jake. You know, you've got a great argument on your side."

"You mean the PO, and your phone call?" He glanced at the exit doors. "I better go. I need a shower and a shave, and I need to check in with the chief. I'll be by later to see Holly, if you'll let her know. I'll take Tyler home with me then. I told her he could bunk with me."

Jenny touched his sleeve. "I'd be happy to. And Jacob?"

He rolled his eyes. "Only my mom calls me Jacob, and you've done it twice so far in this conversation. So before I kill you—what now?"

"Thanks. You did great."

He grinned, embarrassed at just how fantastic that made him feel. "Well, thanks, but Holly did the hard work."

Jenny arched a brow. "Come on, Allred. We both know better."

He laughed and waved as he left the building, his step lighter just knowing Jenny was in his corner.

* * * *

Holly bit her lower lip as a pediatric nurse took Noelle from her and left the room. Maybe it was stupid, but she wanted to cry. Noelle hadn't been out of her sight since her birth. Until now.

The remaining nurse smiled. "Don't worry, honey. We're just going to weigh and measure her, then record the information we would already have if you'd given birth here. When was the last time you nursed?"

"About an hour ago," Holly murmured.

"We'll have her back for her next feeding, okay? You just get some rest. You'll find out just how much you need it over the next few months."

Holly tried to smile, but it didn't quite make it. She was uneasy about having Noelle out of her sight and knew she would get little rest. Leaving Lynchburg had stopped Spence pestering her about the baby, but Holly feared he hadn't quit trying to get his hands on her. Noelle was a means to an end, a way to turn everything into the ideal picture of marriage and family life.

Sure, he could shower Noelle with money. But what about love? Her mouth thinned as she looked out the window at the sunlight sparkling off ice still coating the tree branches. She would never let him have her. Spence wouldn't love Noelle. She would be a possession. And he'd already shown he tired of his toys in no time.

"Holly? Are you okay? You look mad or scared or something."

She started, recalling Tyler still sat in the room. "I'm okay. I was just thinking."

"About him—about Spence. Right?"

Holly stared at her brother. "Yeah. How did you know?"

"You always get the same look when you think about him. Don't worry, Holly. Jake and I will protect you." Tyler jutted his chin.

She laughed. "Jake and you, huh? You've gotten pretty tight." Tyler's reaction to Jake just ramped Holly's attraction that much higher.

Tyler flushed. "He's great. Did you know he fought in Afghanistan and Iraq? He was in one of those units no one knows about."

"Where did you hear that?"

"Jake told me he'd been in the Middle East, so I asked Mr. Tarpley. He told me."

His military background would explain why he always seemed prepared to handle any situation without getting rattled—except for the odd blush or two. Holly smiled. She'd never met a man who blushed. Jake always looked so capable, so it made him less intimidating.

"You're right, Tyler, Jake is a great guy." And Holly had gotten used to having him around. Would it feel lonely without him?

"Is this Jake's fan club?" Doc asked as she stepped across the threshold. "Because if it is, I want a membership."

Tyler and Holly laughed.

"We owe him a lot." She continued. "You and the baby are in great shape, Holly. You've come through labor and delivery with no problems we can find. I would say Jake did as good a job as I could have done, but that might put me out of a job."

"I'm sure he'd like to hear that from you," Holly said. "Being thrown into it wasn't easy. The power going out just made it more difficult. We would have been lost without him."

Jenny sat in the chair next to Holly's bed, leaned back, and crossed her slender legs. "I'd like to talk to you about where you're living. The Crawley place was fine for you and even Tyler, as big as he's getting to be, but I'm not sure it's healthy for a baby."

"It's all I can afford," Holly mumbled, uncertainty about where they would go once she left the hospital tightening her chest. "But I'd already realized the same thing. Having to deliver Noelle there...well, if Jake hadn't come along it would have been bad. I thought maybe you might know where I could rent something closer. A couple of rooms even. I don't have money to put a deposit down, but I can still do books for Mr.

Crawford, and I thought I might be able to work a deal to do bookkeeping and taxes for other people."

Jenny smiled, the gentleness in her expression like a lifeline. "I see you've already given it some thought. I think I can help you out with a place. It might just be temporary. I know someone who has one of those big old Victorian homes. Lots of bedrooms. Bright. Airy. Just the place for a baby and," she added looking at Tyler, "for a boy running errands and doing odd jobs not too far away."

"Is it Jake?" Holly asked and saw the doctor's guilty expression. "He's already done so much, I don't want to impose."

"I think it's safe to say Jake doesn't see it as an imposition, but talk to him about it."

"I-I don't know." He had already done so much. She should stand on her own two feet. Look what had happened with Spence. "This is such a tightly knit area. I was thinking more along the lines of an older woman hoping to supplement her retirement."

"We have those, too. But I want you to think about Jake's place. He said he would stop by tonight and visit before he takes Tyler home with him. Talk to him and see what you can work out. God knows he's got plenty of room."

The nurse returned with Noelle. The tension that had vibrated along her nerves since Noelle had left the room, eased. As long as she could see her, she was safe. After peeking at the baby, Jenny left.

Tyler stared out the window while Holly cradled the baby to nurse. Noelle rooted and latched on. For several minutes, only the sound of the baby nursing interrupted the silence in the room. Holly's eyes drooped as she relaxed. She could be safe here, and she had people willing to help her. All she had to do was reach for it.

* * * *

For just a moment, when Jake returned, the sight of mother and baby took his breath away. Holly was beautiful. His heart filled. The whole picture was perfect. A lot of her previous tension was gone, as if she'd made some decisions and gotten herself in balance. Her hair fell in loose curls around her shoulders, framing a delicate, porcelain-skinned face tilted toward her child. Together they looked like a painter's ideal of mother and child. He wanted to take a picture, find some way of burning the image and the feeling on his brain and in his heart so he would never forget it.

"Jake!" Tyler noticed him, and the mood was broken. Holly's wide green gaze met Jake's. He held it while he spoke to Tyler.

"Hi, kid. How's it goin'?"

"Great! Both docs—Holly's and Noelle's—say they can go home tomorrow. Doc Owens says we can stay with you."

"Tyler!" Holly blushed. "Jake and I still have to talk about that."

Tyler frowned. "Okay, but if I get a vote, I vote for Jake's. I'd be closer to school and the store. And, Holly, any place is better than where we are now."

Jake handed Tyler a couple of bucks. "Thanks for the vote of confidence, buddy. Why don't you go to the snack machines and buy something to eat and drink while Holly and I talk about this?"

"Adults never let you hear anything good," Tyler groused.

Jake stared out the window, waiting until Tyler left. "Jenny said she mentioned the idea to you," he murmured. "You can't keep on at the Crawley place. You've got no heat other than a woodstove, and this time of year it's too risky."

When he glanced at her, Holly's lips were pressed together, her gaze on the baby rather than him. Crap. She was going to refuse. Time to fight dirty.

"There's another reason, too, Holly. Doc's practice got a call not long before you went into labor. We think somebody's fishing for information about you."

Her eyes widened. He had her attention now. "What did Doc tell you?"

"Only that you had a protective order in place." Jake took a deep breath. "The rest I found out on my own." It might piss her off, but he had to be honest. "I guess it's the cop in me. I got the basic info on you and Tyler. So I know you were engaged and your fiancé broke it off when he found out you were pregnant."

Her eyes snapped. "You *checked* us out?"

He grabbed his cap and popped it against his thighs. "It's my job, Holly. You were running from something, and I just wanted to know if it was something you'd done, or something someone was trying to do to you."

"And what did you find out?" She eyed him warily. Trust was such a fragile thing, and her doubts hurt.

"I discovered what I already knew. You were trying to do the right thing for your brother and your baby. Damn it, Holly. Let me help. Not every guy's out to hurt you." Especially not him.

"I've been burned once," she whispered. Yeah. He hated that, but he sure as hell wasn't going to be the one to burn her again. "I just wish you would've asked me before you did a background check."

"I should have. Can we agree we'll both keep that in mind?"

"Yes. Things will get better now. I can take care of Tyler and Noelle. I can still work on the pallet company's books from home. I couldn't pay you much."

Jake sat in the chair next to the bed. "I won't take your money."

Holly stared at him. "And I won't stay for free. People will talk enough as it is."

"Let them."

"You don't mean that."

"I sure as hell do."

"Don't swear."

"Shit, Holly..."

"Jake. I've got my little brother to look out for. I don't need him to have the potty mouth of the fifth grade. Look. This just feels weird, you know? Spence...my ex-fiancé...things didn't go well. He made threats, called me at all hours, and showed up at the house. It's why I left. So I want us to understand each other. I'm not looking for a relationship, not looking for a baby daddy. I'll cook and clean. Then when I get paid again, I'll pay rent."

And he wasn't looking for a quick lay. He needed to say something. Reassure her. He met her eyes again, his voice reserved. "Call me old-fashioned, but I believe relationships between men and women must be built on trust and equality, not on one person taking advantage of a position of power. I don't take advantage of anyone. I won't deny I find you attractive, and I refuse to close my mind to the idea we could have a relationship. But I happen to believe intimacy should be reserved for a committed relationship. Besides, as I understand it, that's out of the question right now anyway."

Holly stared at him. "Are you for real? Do any men think about things like honesty and honor anymore?" Tears sprang to her eyes, but she blinked them away.

Jake once again slapped his cap against his thigh. Her tears were like bullets to him. "I won't abuse your trust," he muttered. "I would never ask you to do anything you didn't want to."

"I'm sorry. I didn't mean to make you mad. It's just. M-my ex-fiancé... he was my first, and..."

"And he burned you," Jake finished for her, feeling a knot in his chest.

"Yeah, so I'm gun-shy...or guy-shy I guess I should say. Can we just be friends?"

He wanted her in his house. And the more he learned of her, the more he wanted to know. "Friends, yeah. I can do that." *Please let that be true.* "So, will you move in?"

She nodded. "On two conditions. First, you let me take care of the house and the cooking."

He stopped slapping the cap against his leg. "Count me in, as long as you take it slow. What's the second condition?"

"You'll figure a fair price for rent, and I'll pay as soon as I can."

"Fair enough. You owe Crawley anything?"

"Next month's rent. I agreed to thirty days' notice."

"Did you give him a month as deposit?"

"Yes."

"I'll talk to him. He can keep it for next month if he insists."

Holly looked at Noelle's sleeping face. Gently she detached her nipple from the baby's little rosebud mouth. She put her to her shoulder and patted her until she got a burp.

"Here," Jake murmured. "I'll hold her while you fix your gown."

He rocked the newborn, feeling as if he'd done it all his life, and said, "My house has five bedrooms and three baths. I rattle around in it like I'm lost sometimes. I could use the company."

Jake handed the sleeping baby to her, then retreated to the window again.

Tyler walked in with a bag of chips and a Coke. "So are we gonna live with you, Jake?"

Jake smiled, a little nervous. He could just picture their reaction the first time he woke up screaming. "Looks like it."

"Yes!" Tyler exclaimed, punching the air with his fist. "Can I pick the room I want?"

Jake laughed. "Within limits."

* * * *

At nine the next morning, the phone in Holly's room rang. Thinking it was Jake, she picked it up.

"Ms. Morgan? This is Amanda Brown, the staff writer for the *Messenger*. I'm working on a series of stories about hometown heroes, you know, people who've gone above and beyond the call of duty."

"So how does that involve me?" Holly asked, already steeling herself to say no. Publicity carried too much risk that Spence could find her.

"Well, I heard Lieutenant Allred delivered your baby during the ice storm. Would you be willing to do an interview about it?"

Holly hesitated. Jake deserved recognition, but for her the attention was like putting out a welcome mat for Spence...or worse, like waving a red flag. Right on the point of giving the reporter a straight-up no, Holly remembered the look on Jake's face as he held Noelle in his hands.

"Miss...Brown, right?"

"Yes."

"This is just the county paper it would run in, right?" Spence couldn't know for sure where she was. The call at the clinic could have been anything.

"Yes."

"Well, okay then. Noelle and I get out of the hospital around noon, though."

"I can be there in a half hour if that's okay?"

"Sure." Holly hung up the phone, not entirely comfortable with the idea, but thinking it would be a nice surprise for Jake. She did the interview with the reporter and let her take a picture of her holding Noelle. The blonde, just a year or two older than her, had been gone about fifteen minutes when Jake arrived. His brow was furrowed as he walked into the room.

"I had a call from Amanda Brown with the *Messenger* wanting to talk to me about delivering Noelle. Did you talk to her?"

"Yes," she replied. "She said it was just a story for the local paper. That's not a problem is it? I thought it would be nice if people knew how you'd helped us. How—how did the paper find out?"

Jake laughed without humor. "Welcome to small towns. The hospital gossip line leaped into overdrive as soon as we walked in the door. According to the county dispatcher, Nancy, the nurse in ER told the story of Noelle's birth to Josh, a county EMT. He passed it along to his wife whose sister is married to a highway-patrol dispatcher. He passed the story to the staff writer for the county paper when she made beat calls late in the day. So there you have it."

Holly blinked. "That's a little frightening."

"Tell me about it." Jake crossed the room and twitched the curtains at the window. After just a moment, he asked, "Tell me the truth, Holly. What is Spence Dilby up to?"

"What do you know about it already?"

"Whatever you choose to tell me is what I know, and it will never go any further than this room."

They stared at each other for what seemed like an eternity. She could decide to trust him or not. It would shape where they went from here on.

Holly's fingers plucked at the blanket. There were no answers there. She would simply have to go with her gut.

"My ex-fiancé was pressuring me to let him have the baby," she began, "but I knew he didn't want her. When I first told him I was pregnant, he got angry and walked out. He claimed I was trying to trap him. He wanted me to abort." Holly halted. She had to. Spence's request was even more incomprehensible now than it had been when he initially made it. She met Jake's steady gaze as she whispered, "How could I *trap* a man who'd already asked me to *marry* him...?"

Jake didn't say a word. He didn't need to; the tightness around his mouth said it all.

"Then all of the sudden he was engaged to someone else, and he wanted my baby. I said no and he started putting on the pressure. When he started threatening Tyler," she continued, "I decided to leave."

Jake eased a hand around the back of his neck. "The phone call to the clinic worries me. I think we should be careful. Someone's nosing around. They might be doing it blind, but I don't want to take that risk with you." Jake flushed. "With you and Tyler and Noelle."

"Do you think the newspaper article could be a problem?" Holly persisted.

Jake shrugged. "Maybe I'm just being overly sensitive. Just to be safe, I'll call Amanda, see if she'll scrub using a picture of you and Noelle."

Holly's exhale was ragged. "Thanks. I should have thought, but she said it would be a local story. I mean, what are the chances Spence would stop in Mountain Meadow?"

Jake touched her hand, his work-roughened fingers as reassuring as a warm blanket, and for just a fleeting second, their eyes locked and her nerves tingled. Did he feel it? Lord, she hoped so.

"Cut yourself some slack, Holly. Just helping you exhausted me. I can't imagine being the one going through giving birth. You're tired. We all are, and maybe we're not thinking as clearly as we could be. So, let's get out of here, get you to my place, and you can rest."

* * * *

Jake let the conversation go amid the details of checking out of the hospital and taking Noelle home, but he would have to get on Amanda fast. The chances he could talk her out of the story altogether were nil, but the picture? Maybe.

Jake found his mouth dry as he turned off onto the quiet side street where his house was. Would she like it? The wood trim wasn't to everyone's taste. Would she be mad when she discovered he'd furnished a nursery? He and Tyler had set it up last night and had a blast doing it. He pulled into the drive and switched off the engine. He stole a glance at her, worried because she hadn't said anything. She hated it.

"Oh, Jake. What a beautiful house. It's like something out of a Currier & Ives print. This is yours?"

He grinned, heart lifting. "Yeah. I wanted something to feel like home. My parents sold our farm, and I figured it would be better to live in town anyway, so I used some of my savings to buy it."

When he glanced at her, a tear shimmered on the tip of her eyelash. "Holly? What's wrong?"

She wiped her eye and sniffed. "You're so nice," she choked out. "I wish…"

Okay, nice was a little vanilla. He'd hoped for more. "What do you wish?"

Her eyes softened. "I wish I'd met you a year ago."

Better. A lot better. He touched her cheek. "You know me now. A year ago I wasn't even here. So what do you say we just start where we are?"

Holly laughed. "Okay. Can we go in? I'd like to see the house before I have to nurse again."

"Right." Jake swallowed.

After carting in Noelle and all her paraphernalia, he began the tour of his pride and joy. Since Tyler was still at school, Jake showed her the room the boy had picked on the third floor with its dormer windows and a ceiling in line with the pitch of the roof. He saved her room and the nursery adjoining it for last. Jake didn't tell her it was the master suite or that he had moved all his stuff into the room across the hall. He gauged her reaction as she walked into the room.

"This is great…so airy, but are you sure? I love the curved bay window with the bench seat beneath, the king-size bed and the thick carpeting, but we'll have to get a crib or something for Noelle."

Jake tapped his cap against the side of his leg as he crossed the room silently and opened the door to the nursery. "This room's for her." He held his breath while he waited for her reaction.

She stopped dead in the doorway, her bewildered gaze swiveling to find him. "It's a nursery. How…when…why?"

He shifted his weight, not sure how to explain it to her. He spread his hands helplessly, then jammed them in his pockets. "You needed it. Think of it as a gift. Tyler and I set it up."

Holly took in the crib, the changing table, a chest of drawers, and a platform rocker with a stool, then brushed her fingers beneath eyes now welling with tears. "It's beautiful, but Jake…it's too much."

It wasn't even close to what he would do for them, but he couldn't say that. Way too soon. Instead, he swallowed and cupped his wide palm around Noelle's head with its little pink cotton hat. Somehow, he needed to find a way to lighten the mood. There were too many emotions swirling around.

"We could always pull out one of the dresser drawers in your room and bed her there if you're determined, but I didn't want my littlest guest to have any reason to complain. Think of it as Noelle's first Christmas gift. I'm not creeping you out, am I?"

Holly shook her head, seemingly at a loss for words, then stood on tiptoe and kissed him on the cheek. "Thanks, Jake. I feel like I keep saying that."

He blinked, feeling a flush once again stain his cheekbones. What would she do if he turned his head, let their lips meet instead? "No problem. Uh…if you want to get settled in, I need to go to the station for a while. I figured we could go out to the Crawley place this evening and get your stuff. Evan, my friend who lives next door, said he'd help with any heavy lifting, and I've got a garage where we can store whatever doesn't fit in the house."

"Okay."

He set his cap on his head. "Right. I'll just go to the station. You can call there if you need anything."

* * * *

Holly nearly called him back. He was incredibly sweet. She thought again about the blush she'd witnessed. She never would have guessed from their first meeting he was shy. He seemed too much the local football hero type. What would her life be like had she met Jake Allred before Spence Dilby? As she crossed over to the rocker and sank onto its padded seat, she fantasized.

While Noelle nursed, Holly imagined the baby was Jake's. They were a family—her, Tyler, Noelle, and Jake. He'd make a wonderful dad. She'd seen how patient he was with Tyler, yet he never talked down to him or treated him like he couldn't do things. Then he was so careful with Noelle, but so natural, like the way he'd rocked her in the hospital room yesterday.

Holly sighed. His offer tempted her, and not just for security. Just thinking about Jake made her heart beat faster in ways it never had for

Spence. Where Spence had always scared her just a little, as soon as she'd gotten past Jake's uniform, his presence had made her feel safe. And now? She had no doubts about her safety, but she there were plenty of unsafe things she'd like to try with him. She needed to be careful not to read too much into Jake's actions. What he was doing for her, he'd do for anyone. He was just that kind of guy. She'd said friends and he'd agreed.

* * * *

No matter how Jake tried to mask it, he knew his voice held an edge of irritation as he spoke to the reporter from the *Messenger*. "Look, Amanda, there are facts you don't know, things I can't tell you. Isn't there any way you could just forget the story and replace it with something else?"

"Jake, we go to press tonight. This is a major feature this week. My editor would fire me if I told him the story needed to be pulled."

Jake drummed his fingertips on his desk. That was a no, so he tried a different tack. "Would you at least consider using a picture of me instead of Holly and Noelle? After all, the premise is supposed to be hometown heroes," he pointed out.

"May I ask why?" she asked and Jake went on the alert. He had to remind himself the woman was first and foremost a reporter.

"No. It's not my story to tell." Jake waited her out. He'd been around enough to know she would be reluctant to burn a possible source for future stories.

"I'll swing by and take your picture, but I can't promise anything. Rick has the final say."

"Fair enough."

There was a pause on the other end. "You know, I appreciate the fact you didn't threaten to go to him over my head."

Jake drummed his fingers. "That doesn't do either one of us any good. You burn me, you lose. I burn you, I could lose."

Chapter 5

Almost home. Just a couple of minutes and he'd see Holly again. It scared him to realize how much he looked forward to that. Jake pulled his truck into the driveway just as Tyler bounded up the walk. No doubt the kid had stopped off at Tarpley's store. Evan was standing on the porch, leaning against one of the pillars. Jake exited the truck, keeping one eye on Tyler. Evan intimidated a lot of people, let alone a kid. The boy's steps slowed as he noticed Evan. Jake hung back next to his truck to watch.

"Who're you?"

"Evan. Who're you?"

"Tyler. Whatcha doin' here?"

"Helping Jake. What are you doing here?"

"I live here."

Evan stuck his hand out. "Nice to meet you. 'Bout time Jake got some company."

Jake moved forward as Tyler's gaze traveled over Evan from head to toe before he grasped the outstretched hand. "Nice to meet you, too. You're real tall, but I s'pose you know that."

Jake halted next to them. "Hi, guys. Why don't you go on in? I called Holly from the station and let her know I was on the way so she could get Noelle ready."

"God, Allred," Evan's voice dripped disgust, "you sound like you enjoy all this domesticity. Got the ring through your nose already?"

Jake cocked a brow at his friend as they stepped inside. "You might try it yourself sometime."

Evan shuddered, his gray eyes wary as Holly descended the wide staircase with Noelle in her arms and a diaper bag on her shoulder. He examined the wrapped bundle she held. "Is there something alive inside?"

"Evan," Jake snapped. He took the baby from Holly and peeked under the blanket before he rocked her back and forth.

Evan arched one brow, smiled at Holly, and stuck his hand out. "Hi. I'm Evan Richardson. I live next door. Jake and I have been friends since kindergarten, and I try very hard to have nothing to do with babies."

Holly laughed. "Wow. After that introduction, what's left to say? I'm Holly Morgan. I'm guessing you've met my brother Tyler…"

"Indeed." Evan glanced over his shoulder before turning back to Holly. "And after a very thorough inspection, I received tentative approval to be allowed into your presence without making a blood sacrifice, although I believe it was touch and go there for a while."

Holly smiled. "He's a little protective. The wad of blankets is Noelle. You're in luck right now because she sleeps almost all the time, but I understand that will change."

Evan eyed the baby again. "Hmm. Just don't expect me to do anything for it."

Jake shook his head. Since it looked like Sam had accurately predicted their future, he just hoped Evan ended in the same boat. His glance strayed to Holly. Correct that. He hoped Evan ended just as lucky. Jake took a deep, steadying breath. "Let's go."

* * * *

They bounced their way down Mistletoe Lane while Evan muttered about how a road could have such an idyllic-sounding name yet be suited only for mountain goats.

Holly enjoyed Evan's sarcastic sense of humor and wondered why such an attractive man was just as single as Jake. Were the women in this part of Virginia blind? At least Jake had been overseas for years and had just come home. However, the way Jake talked, Evan had left only for college and law school. So why hadn't someone snapped him up? He was good-looking, just a little intimidating. She knew from reading the paper he served as commonwealth's attorney for the county. So he must be one of the area's most eligible bachelors.

When they parked in front of the house, light glowed from the small windows and smoke curled from the chimney. Holly smiled. "Great. Doc made it. She said she was a half mile as the crow flies and she would try to get the woodstove going."

"Jenny can build a fire?" Evan remarked. "How unexpectedly domestic."

Holly's eyes narrowed at his tense expression in the glow of the dashboard lights. Something in his tone warned her that Evan and the doc together might not be the best idea, but it was too late now.

Jenny hurried off the porch, but her step faltered and her smile faded as she saw Evan unfold from the passenger side. Ignoring him, she spoke to Holly. "It's warming…at least enough you can bring Noelle in. I packed your dishes while I waited. I hope you don't mind."

Holly laughed. "How could I? Thanks, Doc."

Jenny's gaze skittered to Evan. "Just call me Jenny, okay?"

Holly glanced over her shoulder at his glowering expression. "Okay, Jenny. Here. Would you take Noelle while I unhook the baby carrier?"

"Sure." Jenny cradled the baby in her arms, cooing to her as she rocked her back and forth. "Aren't you just the most beautiful baby?" She glanced at Evan again, her expression almost stricken before she hurried into the dilapidated house. Evan had definitely put a chink in her polished, professional exterior.

Evan's jaw twitched, his expression bordering on furious. "Let's get this done. I've got some briefs to go over tonight."

He stomped to the back of the truck and dropped the tailgate. His actions were rough and choppy, not the smooth, graceful man she'd seen up until this point. Holly looked at Jake. "I—I guess I shouldn't have asked Jenny to help."

Jake squeezed her shoulder. She'd really needed that silent reassurance. "It's not your fault. It's a long story. I don't even know all of it, and I've known them both my whole life." He wrapped his arm around her shoulders. "Come on. Let's get to it. Let me know if you get too tired."

Holly smiled. "I will. Thanks again for all of this."

His hazel eyes softened and his lips curved into a smile. Friends, she reminded herself. They were just friends. Too many other things were on both their plates right now.

True to her word, Jenny had already packed most of the kitchen. While she continued to keep an eye on Noelle, Holly sent Evan in to help Tyler get his belongings packed while she and Jake went to work on her bedroom. Once all the personal items were out, Evan and Jake loaded furniture in the back of the truck. With some clever maneuvering, they fit everything into the truck's long bed. As Jake locked the house and pocketed the keys, Holly spoke to Jenny. She couldn't bear to see two such close friends of Jake's at war—even if it was only a verbal one.

"Why don't you ride back with us? We'll unload this stuff, get some dinner, and then Jake can run you home."

Jenny's eyes swiveled to Evan and back to Holly. "I should get home. It's not far, and the moon's out."

"Running away?" Evan taunted.

Jenny glared. "No. There's nothing around here worth running from."

The hostility was out in the open, the air nearly crackling with animosity.

Holly put her hand on Jenny's arm. "Please join us."

Jenny's eyes strayed to Evan as he slammed the tailgate. "Okay. Just for a little while."

In the end, Tyler rode in front with Evan and Jake while Holly, Jenny, and the baby sat in the backseat. When they reached Jake's house, he let Holly and Jenny off near the front door, waiting while they released Noelle from her car seat before he pulled around back.

Holly led the way inside. "If you could help me, I would appreciate it. I have homemade spaghetti sauce that just needs to be heated, and there's a salad in the fridge. I need to nurse Noelle, but I can come back to the kitchen and tell you where everything is while I do."

Jenny grinned at Holly. "You're a fast worker. You've only been here since noon and you already know your way around Jake's kitchen?"

Holly laughed. "Jake doesn't know it yet, but I rearranged his kitchen to suit me since I'll be the one cooking in it."

Now Jenny truly laughed, her tawny eyes alight. The shadows Holly saw earlier were gone. "That's priceless, but take it easy. You just gave birth."

"I took plenty of breaks. I mean, it's not like Jake has a ton of stuff anyway."

While Holly nursed the baby, Jenny bustled around the kitchen. In no time at all, the spaghetti sauce bubbled, the pasta boiled, garlic bread heated in the oven, and the salad sat on the table, which she had set, ready for them to eat. By the time the men came in, Jenny had drained the pasta and put it in a large bowl. Bread and sauce sat to either side.

Jake's eyes rounded as he stepped inside. His gaze took in the nearly completed meal. "How did you...?"

Jenny laughed. "I just followed orders. Holly already had most of this done."

"Of course," Evan sniped from just behind her, "you wouldn't want to be caught doing anything domestic. It might not fit with the image of the mighty doctor."

Jenny stiffened, and the light in her eyes dimmed. Her voice was cool and clipped. "Well, sit. Let's eat. The sooner we finish, the sooner Evan can spend the evening examining his briefs."

Evan's eyes narrowed to icy shards, but before he could say anything in return, Jake tapped his fork on his tea glass. "Time out! It's my dinner table, and I'd like to eat without verbal sniper fire ricocheting off the walls."

Holly took a deep breath, only now realizing she'd been holding it as Jenny and Evan threw their verbal knives.

When they were all seated, Jake said, "Tyler, would you say grace?"

To Holly's surprise, the boy nodded and bowed his head. He paused just a moment and murmured, "Thank you Lord for this wonderful meal. Thank you for the wonderful friends you sent to help Holly and me. And thank you most of all for Noelle, the best Christmas gift ever. Amen."

Out of her little brother's mouth, the truth. All of the adults echoed Tyler's amen, and when Evan and Jenny lifted their heads, Holly saw shame on their faces. She smiled encouragement. "I don't know about you all, but I'm starving. Dig in."

She did her best to keep the conversation light. She asked Tyler how his odd jobs with the Tarpleys were going, and he launched into stories of some of the tourists who stopped in to take a break from driving along the Blue Ridge Parkway.

"Do you enjoy helping out in the store?" Evan asked.

"Yeah." Tyler grinned. "All sorts of interesting people come in there. Besides, you know Mr. Tarpley has a bad back and he was havin' a real tough time stocking shelves, so I help with that. Mrs. Tarpley says when I get old enough to really work for them, she'll show me how to run the cash register and wait on customers."

"That's great, Tyler," Jenny said. "Holly must be very proud to have a brother like you."

Holly ruffled Tyler's hair. So many times recently, she would have been in big trouble without his help. "I am. How many people have little brothers who pitch in to help make ends meet and then turn right around and coach you through labor?"

"And if I hadn't decided to walk along the road to get home that first night, you might not have met Jake either."

Holly smiled. "You're right. I couldn't forget meeting Lieutenant Allred." She finished in a deep-throated imitation. Everyone laughed, including Jenny and Evan. But then the two of them halted, staring at their plates. Holly sipped her tea and wondered what kept them apart. Something still burned there. It had just become twisted into an awful parody.

When everyone finished, Holly asked, "Anyone up for homemade chocolate chip cookies?"

"You made cookies, too?" Jake grinned.

Evan went one step further. "Will you marry me and move in with me tonight?"

Holly arched her brows. "I come with the squirming thing in the blankets, remember?"

Evan leveled a look of mock horror on her. "Never mind. Jake can handle the baby thing."

Jenny's chair scraped back. "I'll get the dishes."

Holly started stacking plates. Every time the subject of the baby came up in some way, you could almost see the frost coming from Evan and Jenny the coldness between them was so great.

Jake cleared his throat. "Evan, Tyler. Why don't you give me a hand and we'll move Holly and Tyler's personal belongings in? That way maybe there'll be some coffee to go with those cookies."

Holly smiled. "We can do that."

All three men disappeared from the kitchen. Holly studied Jenny. She stood at the sink with her back to the room, her hands clutching the counter in a death grip.

"I should have just walked on home," Jenny whispered. "Coming here was a mistake."

Holly laid a hand on her arm. "I take it you and Evan share some history."

Jenny's laugh was bitter. "We dated all through high school. We were the couple voted most likely to marry first, but as you can see, that didn't happen."

"Was there a reason?"

Jenny dashed away a tear on her cheek and raised her chin. "We wanted different things."

"Not so different," Holly whispered. "You're both still here in Mountain Meadow."

Jenny stopped, her lips parted, and raised her eyes to meet Holly's. "I never thought of it that way." For just a moment, a wild kind of hope flitted across her face, then disappeared. "No. There are too many other issues. Too many misunderstandings. I've learned from experience, Holly. The only thing that really kills a relationship is lies." She grimaced. "So many separate Evan and me it's as if we stand on opposite sides of a river with no bridge across."

The cool, calm doctor was back, and Holly knew Jenny was through baring her emotions.

By the time Jake, Evan, and Tyler trooped into the kitchen again, the cookies were on the table and the dishwasher hummed in the background.

Jake and Evan looked like they had died and gone to heaven as they helped Tyler munch his way through most of the plate. Jenny ate a couple, but Holly just sipped a glass of milk.

"No cookies?" Evan teased between bites.

Holly shook her head. "I just make them. I don't eat them."

"She doesn't like sweet stuff," Tyler clarified. "But put some popcorn or some fries within reach and you could lose a finger if you get in the way."

Holly pulled a face at him. "Thanks, Tyler."

He grinned and finished his glass of milk. "What are brothers for?"

"'Bout time for you to hop in the shower, kid," Jake said. Holly's jaw dropped when Tyler told everyone good night and headed out of the room. She stared after her brother and then back at Jake.

"What have you done to my kid brother?" Holly narrowed her eyes.

Jake grinned. "We made a deal. I told him he could have the attic room if he could show me he was man enough to follow the house rules and not whine."

She just shook her head. Jake was just the positive, male role model Tyler needed. Tyler seemed to agree.

"I should get home, Jake," Jenny interjected. "I have rounds to make in the morning."

Evan cleared his throat, eyes focused on the far wall. "I'll take you, so Jake can get Holly settled for her first night."

Jenny's brow furrowed, worry clouding her features. Before she could refuse, Holly jumped in. "Great, Evan. That's so thoughtful."

He grimaced and said self-deprecatingly, "I manage it every once in a while. I'll get my car."

After he'd left, Jake asked Jenny, "Will you be okay?"

She nodded, but her brows were still drawn together. "We've sidestepped each other for almost two years. It was bound to come to a head. I guess tonight's the night." Jenny pulled on her coat and gave them a wan smile as Evan honked out in the driveway.

Jake touched her arm. "You have our number if you need it."

"Thanks." She hurried from the room and a moment later the sound of the door shutting drifted down the hall.

Our number...like they were a family. No. Holly shouldn't think that way. She'd said she wanted to be friends, and that's how it needed to stay. Depending on Jake was too easy.

Noelle chose that moment to cry, and Holly hurried to get her. Practicalities were what she should concentrate on.

* * * *

Evan didn't open the car door, Jenny noticed. Just another sign of how their relationship had deteriorated. Evan had always stood apart. He'd had class. His family counted themselves among the area's original settlers, but they had always been just a bit different, a little more refined than most families. The Richardsons traveled to New York and Washington. His father had served two terms in the United States Senate before he abruptly retired from the political scene.

His parents had been appalled when Evan chose to date Jenny Owens, whose mother had long since taken off for parts unknown and whose father everyone knew made the best moonshine around. Of course nobody said that out loud, but they still lined up to buy it. The funny thing was her daddy was just as upset she was dating "one o' them snooty Richardsons" and she'd never understood why.

Her father had wanted her to get out of the Blue Ridge, to be a doctor in some big city, anywhere besides Mountain Meadow. Jenny wanted to come home. They both got their wish. And so had Evan's parents. They'd wanted whatever would keep Jenny Owens away from their golden boy. For more than a decade, she and Evan had stayed as far away from each other as possible.

Jenny buckled her seat belt and sat in the passenger seat. After a brief glance, Evan put the car in gear and headed out of town. Animosity filled the silence between them.

"You surprise me." Evan's lip curled as he maneuvered over the twisty roads. "I wouldn't have thought you'd allow any competition for Jake."

"Competition? Jake and I are friends," she snapped as Evan turned onto the long road leading to her house.

"Would that be friends like you were with half the basketball team?" Evan's tone changed from just biting to as cutting as a hunter gutting his kill. While she was still reeling from that, he stopped in front of her house and added, "I guess it's a good thing you got rid of your baby, huh. It might have been a little difficult to ask half the senior class to take paternity tests."

Dead silence reigned for just a fraction of a second as she struggled through the pain drowning her. Her hands shook so much she fumbled with the seat belt. Jenny sobbed in frustration before it loosened so she could rip open the door. As the overhead light blazed, Evan sucked in his breath, but Jenny barely spared him a glance before she ran for her house. She had to get away from him, away from the pain.

He leaped from the car, sprinting after her. Just as she stopped to open the door, he caught her arm and spun her to face him. "Did you really think I didn't know?"

Jenny's eyes burned with tears she refused to shed. "You know nothing. Nothing!" she yelled at him.

"Like hell!" he shouted right back. "Your father, your own father, let me in. I saw you lying there with them. Half my teammates! Your dad just thought I'd come to join the party. More fool me."

Jenny shoved at him. "It's a lie. You're lying."

"No," Evan snarled. "You were the one lying. Lying with your legs spread and your clothes scattered all over the room. The night after you promised yourself to me." He stopped and raked a hand through his hair. "There I was with an engagement ring burning a hole in my pocket. The night after you told me about *our* baby. Whose was it, Jenny? Did you even know?"

She felt whatever blood remained drain from her face. Her eyes and nose ached with frustration about a night she couldn't remember. But she'd seen it. Oh yes, she'd seen it. "The baby was yours," she whispered. Her jaw tightened so she could barely continue. "They raped me. My daddy drugged me and let them in. They raped me, and I miscarried our baby because of it."

Her words hung in the air like ice crystals of pain. A split second of silence followed in which neither of them moved or even breathed. The past had reared up, pulling them back in with suffocating hands. She had buried it and simply couldn't relive the awful pain again.

"Jenny!" Evan's voice was choked.

She blinked feeling as if she'd come out of a trance. What did it matter now? "Leave me alone, Evan."

She was drained, her anger gone, leaving only the horrifying emptiness of the past twelve years. Jenny walked through the doorway and shut it in his face. He pounded on the wood.

"Jenny! Open the door, damn it. Open the door!"

She twisted the dead bolt instead. Stay away from Evan. Stay away from the pain. There was a long pause in which all she heard was her own breathing before he spoke again.

"Please, Jenny," he whispered. "Please let me in."

She closed her eyes as she leaned back against the door. Her breath came in short, sobbing gasps. Jenny hadn't meant to tell him. She hadn't told anyone, not in all those years...

Both men she had ever loved betrayed her that night. Her father had drugged her, desperate to keep her from marrying and settling down, and the boy she had loved since she was old enough to even think of boys believed his eyes rather than his heart. But even that wasn't enough. When her father lay dying her final year in medical school, he had confessed. The drugs he'd used came from Stoner Richardson. Even the money for her college education and medical school had also come from Evan's father. Hush money.

It would be so easy to drop that bombshell on Evan, but Jenny still couldn't do it. Too many lives and too many relationships had already been destroyed.

She heard his car start, then the crunch of tires as it pulled away. She slid along the door until she sat with her knees drawn up. Resting her forehead against them, her hands clenched into fists at her sides, Jenny cried.

Chapter 6

They were pinned down. Along with the *rat-a-tat* of the insurgents' machine guns were the deeper punctuations of explosive charges. But that wasn't what drummed in his ears and hammered on his brain. *Help me, Jake!* The same cry of pain repeated again and again. His best friend lay wounded across an open expanse of unprotected ground. *Leave no man behind.*

Their mission had gone south before they'd even known anything was wrong. On paper it had been simple. Drop into the camp, complete their objective—in this case rescuing a businessman taken hostage by extremists—and signal the helo for a pickup.

In his dream version, Will continued to call Jake between groans of pain, the screams and cries getting louder, and Jake unable to do anything to end it. Helpless, frustrated rage filled him until he thought he would explode.

He sat upright with a gasp. For just a moment his groggy mind couldn't assimilate his surroundings. His house in Mountain Meadow. Not Afghanistan, but the nightmare never changed. At least he no longer awoke screaming. As he sat in his bed waiting for his breathing and his heart rate to return to normal, he heard another noise. This time someone else cried, but it didn't sound like Noelle. He pulled on a pair of sweatpants, snatched the bedroom door open, and the source of the noise became clear.

"I'm sorry, baby," Holly sobbed. "I don't know what's going on."

Noelle was fussy and irritable, but Holly's sniffs tore his insides. Something was wrong with the baby? With Holly? Jake hurried across the master bedroom to the door of the nursery, his nightmare fading in the face of a new worry.

"Holly?"

She raised a tear-streaked face to him. "I can't nurse. She can't latch on, Jake. Something's wrong."

He swallowed as he realized Holly's nightgown was unbuttoned, exposing her breasts. He forced his gaze away. "Do you want me to call Jenny?"

In his peripheral vision, he saw her shake her head. A beat later, she whispered, "No. Just grab the book. It's next to my bed. See if you can figure out what's going on. If that doesn't work, then I guess we'll have to call."

The book, as thick as a dictionary, had everything about taking care of babies. Relief coursed through him. Reading a book he could handle. "Tell me some of your symptoms," Jake called as he crossed the room to her bed, feeling much more confident now. He turned on the reading lamp.

"My breasts feel hard, and Jake...they're huge. I—I have milk leaking, but Noelle can't get her mouth latched onto me."

Jake's mouth was dry as dirt. Her breasts were huge and hard and leaking milk? He gulped and sent a prayer God would somehow make it so he didn't have to torture himself by seeing Holly's bare breasts again.

"Have you found anything yet?" she asked, her breath hitching yet again while Noelle continued fussing. Jake frantically flipped through the table of contents until he came to the chapter on breast-feeding. He scanned the subtitles until he landed on one labeled "What happens when your milk comes in."

"I've found something. Hang on." He scanned it "...around the second or third day...breasts may double in size...may have difficulty nursing..." Okay, this was sounding like what was going on and the timing was right. Now what were they supposed to do? *Please God, don't make me have to touch them! She'll know then what a fraud I am. How much more than just friends I'd like to be.* "You or your partner should express some of your milk so your baby can latch on." The book slipped out of his nerveless fingers and dropped onto a very sensitive part of his anatomy already throbbing for very different reasons.

Jake groaned, leaning over with his face screwed in pain while he clutched himself.

"Jake? Did you find anything?" Holly called.

He blew a breath out. "Yeah. Hang on. I'll be right there." At least his voice hadn't gone all soprano on him. He hobbled toward the door.

"Why are you walking funny?" Holly inquired.

"I...uh...stubbed my toe."

"Is that all? So what's wrong?"

Jake stared at her then her breasts, and for the life of him, for just a moment, his brain went blank. They were huge. Big beautiful breasts, the most beautiful breasts he'd ever seen. *Mine.* Oh, his body didn't need thoughts like that thrumming through it right at this moment.

"Jake?"

"Um…yeah. It says your milk has come in. You were producing colostrum, but now the real stuff has arrived. It says you might overproduce until your body and the baby get in sync."

"Okay." Holly gestured to her chest. "What do we do about it?"

We? *We?* Jake closed his eyes. He could think of a couple things but doubted if Holly would go for either suggestion. He licked his lips. "The book says you need to express some of the milk. Once the pressure is reduced, Noelle will be able to latch on."

"Well how do I do that?"

"Shit." He angled one hand across his front hoping to hide his arousal. "Didn't you take some class to show you this stuff?"

"Busy avoiding the stalking ex…remember? Look, if you don't want to help, it's okay." Irritation crept into her tone.

"Sorry." Oh man. He was so fucked.

Holly sighed. "Here, take Noelle. Are there pictures in the book?"

Oh there were pictures all right, but nothing like the real thing. Jake nodded as he took the fussing baby. Holly snatched the book off the floor and disappeared into the master bath. An angry cry brought his attention back to the baby in his arms, and he smiled at Noelle as he rocked her. "Mama will help you in a bit, honey. Seems both the women in my life are mad at me right now."

Holly stopped what she was doing, looked into the mirror, and swallowed. She'd left the bathroom door open, and even as quiet as Jake's words were, they carried enough for her to hear him. *Women in his life?* Did she want to be the woman in his life? Other than Noelle, she wanted to be the only woman in his life. The admission left her gaping until the pressure in her breasts reminded her why she was in there.

Holly went back to work, studying the pictures, and trying to release enough milk to ease the painful throbbing. The pictures made it look much easier than the reality, but she was able to express enough to ease the pressure. At least she wouldn't have to wake Jenny in the middle of the night. But Holly was going to face up to one reality right now. Bring Jake Allred's *friend* was no longer possible.

* * * *

Jenny rolled over, checking her bedside clock. Two AM. Someone pounded on the door. From years of rising at all hours, she was awake instantly, but then her sleep had been disturbed anyway. Who could it be at this hour? She jumped out of bed, pulled on the thick satin robe lying across the foot of her bed, and belted it. Then she picked up the baseball bat she kept next to her bed. She wasn't paranoid, just cautious. After all, she was a woman alone out in the middle of nowhere.

When she reached the first floor, she crept forward. The pounding continued, slower and more irregular than before. Jenny peered through the peephole, but all she saw were feet. Large feet, encased in boots like Evan had been wearing.

"Go away, Evan!" she yelled through the door.

"Jenny! Thank God." His voice was muffled. "Please, let me in…"

"Go away," she yelled again. He must have gone off and got drunk. She couldn't take it, couldn't face him again. She had tried so hard to put the past behind her where it could never hurt her again…

"Bleeding. So cold." His voice sounded slurred.

Jenny's fingers trembled against the wood of the door. *Bleeding?* She'd wanted him gone, not hurt. Never hurt. She twisted the dead bolt and yanked the door open.

"Evan! What happened?"

The doctor in her kicked into gear. She squatted next to him where he lay slumped in her doorway. Blood trickled from a laceration along his hairline. He gazed at her with dull and somewhat unfocused eyes.

"Wrecked. When I left. Hit a tree on the curve of your drive."

"When you *left*? But that means you've been out in the cold for hours. The cut might just be a minor part of your injuries. I can't carry you. If I help, can you get up so I can bring you in?"

"Yes."

He was huge compared to her. Evan had always been tall. He'd played forward on the high school basketball team and been talented enough to warm the bench at UVA, but Jenny realized the man had added muscle and mass since his teens. His shoulders were heavier, and his arms and legs more muscular. Jenny grunted as she helped him to his feet, realized her robe had come partway open, and belted it back again. He leaned on her and stumbled as she led him into her den. They staggered before Jenny regained her balance and guided him to the couch near the fireplace.

"Sit. I'll get my bag and we'll take a look at you before I call the EMT."

"No ambulance. Court case in the morning."

All doctor now, she frowned at him with her hands braced on her hips. "Just from what I've already seen, Counselor, I can assure you there will be no court case for you. Now sit still until I get back." Jenny grabbed the blanket off the back of the couch, wrapping it around his shoulders. She snatched another one from a nearby chair and covered his legs.

From habit, she kept a medical bag sitting next to the front door, a little old-fashioned, but necessary in Mountain Meadow because there were times she had to go to her patients. When she returned, his head rested against the back of the couch.

"I'm turning on the lights," Jenny warned before she switched on the recessed lighting overhead and a lamp on the table near where he sat. Evan blinked. Jenny stood behind him as she cleaned the cut near his hairline.

"This needs stitches. What did you hit?"

"Don't know for sure. Car's pretty beat-up."

"Well, you'll need an X-ray at the very least, maybe a CT scan to make sure there's no skull fracture and so we can see the extent of any concussion." She moved in front of him and pulled out her penlight. As she tested his pupils to see if they were reacting the same, she asked, "Any headache or nausea?"

"No."

"Dizziness? Or ringing in your ears?"

"No."

As he warmed, his speech grew stronger, more normal. Jenny sat back on the coffee table. "Follow my finger with your eyes. Don't move your head. Okay. Now tell me what happened."

"I missed the curve in the drive, went off the road into the woods, and hit a tree."

She leaned away from him in surprise. "How did you miss the turn? It's marked for heaven's sake."

His eyes dropped. "I didn't see it," he mumbled.

"How could you not?"

His cheeks flushed with anger or embarrassment, which she wasn't sure. "Just leave it alone. I wrecked, okay?"

Jenny drew a deep breath and pressed her lips together. "Sorry. Were you unconscious?"

"Yes. I don't know how long. I came here as soon as I could."

She sighed. So he had been unconscious for more than just a few seconds. Jenny grabbed her cell phone and punched 911.

"What are you doing?"

"Calling the ambulance to have you transported."

"I don't want to go to the hospital."

Jenny glared. "You don't have a choice. You have a head wound needing stitching, and a concussion. While there've been plenty of times I would have liked to see your sorry ass dead, I'm not letting it happen because I didn't do my job."

"That's what it always comes back to isn't it? The mighty Dr. Owens."

"Shut up, Evan," Jenny snapped as the dispatcher answered.

"911, What's your emergency?"

"Joyce? It's Doc Owens. I have a thirty-year-old white male with a head laceration and concussion from a motor vehicle accident. I need him transported to the ER."

"Sorry, Doc. The guys are working an accident on the parkway. Some kids out joyriding. They're going to be tied up for some time. We've already had to call for mutual aid. Can you bring him in?"

"Hmm. I suppose. But if you have accident victims coming, this one will get shoved down the list by the triage nurse. I'll keep him at my place. Just make sure a deputy gets out here to look at the accident scene tomorrow. If you need me in on the parkway accident, call. He'll have no choice but to come with me then." Jenny put her phone down. Evan appeared as uncomfortable as her, and she didn't like how pale he was. "You're stuck with me for now. I'll go ahead and stitch your head. I've got sutures and local anesthetic in here." She opened her bag.

Evan glared at her. "No. Way. I'm not letting you near me with a needle and thread. You'll make me look like Frankenstein's monster."

That would be a cold day in hell. Jenny arched a brow at him. "When did you become such a narcissist?"

"Since you started talking about practicing your sewing on my skin," he retorted.

Jenny frowned. She studied her hands for a minute, then lifted her eyes to his suspicious gaze. "Evan, no matter how much I detest you, I would never let my personal feelings affect my work. That cut needs to be stitched. The longer you wait, the greater the chances you will be left with a nasty scar. Let me stitch it. I'm good at it."

"Fine. Do it," he conceded.

He complained about the anesthetic. He complained about the stitches. Heavens, he was a whiny patient, Jenny thought as she worked. She tuned him out as she continued making a series of minute sutures to draw the skin together. The laceration was close enough to his hairline it wouldn't be very obvious even if it did leave a scar, but she was doing her best to make sure it didn't. Evan was handsome. No matter how Jenny felt about him, it would be a shame to mar that.

* * * *

Evan closed his eyes because when he opened them, her breasts were at eye level. Her robe gaped as she worked, so if his eyes were open his gaze feasted on one smooth, creamy globe. He remembered how good she'd always tasted. From the very first time he kissed her when they were both freshmen in high school, it had always been Jenny. She was still the most beautiful woman he knew. He shut his eyes to block her image, but he could still smell her unique, spicy scent. He didn't want to tell her he'd missed the turn because tears in his eyes had blurred his vision.

"Jenny?"

"Hmm?" she murmured as she tied off the last suture and set her materials on the table.

"Did your dad really drug you?"

Her hand trembled in her lap before she clenched it into a fist. "Now's not the time for this."

"Then when?"

"Not now." She began packing everything and wouldn't look at him. "Let me help you off with your jacket and your boots. You can stretch out on the couch. I'll give you a ride to the hospital when I go in for rounds."

Her voice was cool, impersonal just like she would talk to a stranger. He would get nowhere with her tonight, but he could be patient. He could wait. And in truth, he felt terrible. Sleep was what he needed. Evan leaned forward as she helped him off with his jacket. Then she knelt at his feet, unlacing his boots and taking them off. He stared at the short, practical style of her golden hair. It suited what she'd become, and he hated it. Was it as soft as it had been? Unable to resist, he touched a strand.

"Don't!" She cringed from him, and he let his hand fall to his lap. This wasn't his Jenny. This was a stranger. This was Dr. Owens. He wondered if Jenny was still there somewhere.

* * * *

Holly reemerged from the bathroom. Jake tried, but he couldn't help it. His eyes gravitated to her chest and he swallowed, looking at Noelle instead. He was still rocking her and she was still fussing.

"I think I've got it," Holly said. The relief on her face was obvious. "Here, let me have her and I'll try again."

He handed the baby to her and then lounged against the doorway. Holly sat in the rocker and opened her gown. Jake studied his bare feet until the silence told him Noelle had latched on. His gaze drifted up again. Holly

Laura Browning

stared at her daughter's small face with such intense love he couldn't look away. He should go. He shouldn't be here, but there was no place else he wanted to be.

"I guess I'll go to bed if you don't need anything more," he mumbled, but he didn't want to leave. He wanted to sit with her, wanted to hold them both and feel that human connection.

Most often when he awoke from a dream, the last thing he wanted was to be around other people. Tonight had been different. When he awoke shaking, Holly's needs had overshadowed his. She'd made him forget the horror with the most basic of pictures: a mother feeding her child.

He came back to where he was and what he was doing when Holly cleared her throat. She moved her legs to one side on the stool. "Would you sit with me? I could use some company."

Jake nodded, trying to be casual, but sure his relief must be obvious. "Me, too."

He perched on the stool, forearms resting on his thighs and hands clasped between his knees, but he kept his face half averted. He didn't want to spook her or make her uncomfortable so she asked him to leave.

"Jake?"

"What?"

"I'll be feeding Noelle a lot while we're living here with you. About every two to three hours right now."

Jake was careful to keep his eyes above her throat. "So?"

"I have to bare my breast. I try not to flaunt it, but let's face it, if we're going to live in the same house, you're going to have to get used to it."

Heat suffused his cheeks. His gaze skittered to where Noelle suckled. "Yeah, but I feel like I'm staring."

She tilted her head. "I don't feel that way. In fact, it makes me more uncomfortable when you don't look. I-I like having you here."

Jake felt himself melt as watched her and the baby. "It's so beautiful, Holly. You can't imagine…a miracle. I thought so as soon as I saw her little head crown."

Her lower lip trembled before she pressed her lips together. He touched her knee and murmured, "I didn't mean to make you cry."

A tear rolled down her cheek she could do nothing to hide. "It's just so different than what I imagined. I-I guess I built this fairy-tale picture when I discovered I was pregnant."

"The handsome prince would marry you and carry you off to his castle where you would all live happily ever after?"

Holly nodded. "But it wasn't like that."

"You don't have to tell me."

"I do," she whispered. "Because...because..."

He touched her cheek, sure of what she was going to say and needing to ease the way. "Because there's already something between us?"

She nodded, obviously relieved he understood. "Yes. Even though we said we'd just be friends. I don't want there to be any lies. I've already been through that."

Jake swallowed. "Okay."

* * * *

Holly stared off into the distance. "I met Spence at the beginning of my final year in college. I was bowled over. Now I suspect he intended that. I guess some of my awe was due to his name and his family. I was naive. We dated off and on when he came to Lynchburg, then after my parents died, Spence started putting the pressure on me to take our relationship to the next level.

"Here I was, now legally responsible for Tyler, trying to help him cope with losing our parents even as I was coming to terms with my own grief, and Spence was right there. He seemed supportive at every turn and I began to depend on that. Spring break rolled around. He found a woman to stay with Tyler and took me to New York. We shopped, went to museums, took in a Broadway show and he was a perfect gentleman until the last night." Holly bit her lip and her brows drew together with the memories of what had occurred.

"I realize now he kept plying me with drinks, and when he took me to my room... He proposed." Holly paused. "I was so overwhelmed I said yes, and then one thing led to another and...sex wasn't like I thought it would be. He was impatient and it hurt."

Why was he so easy to talk to? She hadn't told anyone the things she was telling Jake.

"It was your first time?"

Holly nodded. She swallowed and picked Noelle up to burp her before she switched the baby to her other breast. Jake waited patiently, and this time she noticed he didn't look away. She saw the banked heat in his eyes and felt warmed by it. In just the short time since they'd met, she already trusted him. Jake would never hurt her. She knew it. She touched his thigh, so close to hers, and smiled.

"I told him I didn't want to do it again. I wanted to wait until we were married. I hoped it would give me some time to get used to the idea. He said he was okay with it, but he was angry."

Holly stared around the nursery Jake had fixed for her and the baby. Actions. Spence gave her words. Jake gave her actions.

"He would make remarks, even when we were out with friends. And he started putting pressure on me again, but Jake," she added, "I didn't want to do it with him. I was scared."

He waited. Another thing she liked. He didn't mouth some platitude. "Then I found out I was pregnant. When I told him, he was furious. He broke it off with me, accused me, said I was just trying to trap him into marriage for his money. I was wearing his ring." Her chin wobbled, but she pressed her lips together for a minute so she could regain control. "He had already asked me to marry him, so how could I be trapping him?"

Jake leaned toward her this time and stroked the hair off her face. It would be so easy to lean into that touch, but she didn't yet have the nerve. "Shhh. It's okay. Here, let me take Noelle and put her down, she's drifted off." He reached over to lift her from Holly's arms, then put the drowsy baby to his bare shoulder and burped and rocked her to sleep again. He laid her in her crib as if he'd been handling babies his entire life. Holly closed her gown and her robe.

"I thought you would be awkward with her," she observed, "but you're not."

Jake chuckled. "It's a fluke. It's just because it's her, I guess. I helped her be born, so it just seems natural to handle her. She's out like a light. I could use some hot chocolate. What about you?"

They worked together in the kitchen, then carried their steaming mugs into the den. Jake sat on the couch and patted the spot next to him. "Sit next to me and keep me warm. I think we still have some talking to do, don't you?"

Holly nodded, warmed by more than just the cocoa. "Yeah."

Jake rested his arm along the back of the couch. It felt like a silent offer for her to get closer, so Holly took advantage of it, curling against his side. "You told me at the hospital that Spence threatened you. Did you involve the police?"

Holly leaned forward and set her mug down. "I did. I got a restraining order after Spence stopped by a couple times drunk."

Jake's arm moved from the couch to her shoulders and he squeezed with his hand. "Did he hurt you or Tyler?" he growled.

She hesitated. "He backed off for a little while when I got the restraining order."

Jake's eyes narrowed. "So he did hurt you."

Holly swallowed. "The Dilby name can make a lot of people look the other way. I couldn't risk my baby or Tyler, so I packed our stuff and we left."

"So why did you stop here? Mountain Meadow's not a final destination for most folks."

"I was almost out of money. I had to pick a place. We were parked along the parkway near a mileage sign and…I just picked. I knew I had to save what was left to pay for some place for us to live, and Mountain Meadow sounded so peaceful. You know?"

Jake chuckled. "It drew me."

"From the military?"

His jaw tensed. "I left the army two years before I returned to the States, so I was ex-military. I did special jobs for money. Some of them involved getting people in and out of places. Sometimes I worked for the government, sometimes not."

"A mercenary?"

Jake snorted. "I guess you could call it that."

"What happened?"

He raked a hand through his hair. "I had to pull what was left of one of my best friends from the wreckage of a blown-up Humvee. The next morning I realized I was losing touch with me. No amount of money was worth that. I came back to figure out what I wanted out of life."

"Did you?" Holly held her breath for his answer.

"Yeah," he whispered. "Just recently. You'll be safe here, Holly." Jake set their mugs aside, then tilted her chin up. "I want to kiss you."

She wanted it, too, so much it made her breathless. As his face moved closer to her, Holly trembled. Spence had been rough. Subconsciously she braced for that, so when Jake's touch asked rather than took, she relaxed. He nibbled at her lower lip, so gently it was like the brush of a butterfly. Heat filled her to overflowing. Hands she'd rested against his chest, almost in a position to push him away, instead inched around his strong neck and into his silky hair. His kiss was like nothing she had ever known.

"Holly." His voice was a whisper, a benediction. He rested his chin against her forehead, tucking her against his chest. His heart beat as fast as hers. "This is the wrong time for this. I'm aroused as hell, and you've just given birth. And what are we supposed to do about that?"

Holly stared at him, uncertain how to take his humor. Spence would have been infuriated, but not this man. She stroked his beard-roughened cheek.

Laura Browning

He chuckled. "I'll take a cold shower. Our time will come, but I think we both have to admit there's a lot more than friendship happening here."

Holly closed her eyes. There was. So much more.

* * * *

Jenny woke at four to check on Evan. He slept with one arm behind his head and the other dropped off the couch. He snored lightly, his lips parted and his wide mouth looking softer and more vulnerable. The cover had slipped onto the floor. Jenny picked it up and recovered him. The throw was too short to cover his long, narrow feet, so she grabbed a second throw. He was watching her.

"Don't stop," he drawled. "I was just enjoying this picture of domestic bliss."

Jenny tossed the blanket over him and straightened, her hands fisted on her narrow hips. "I came to see if you were alert. Well you are. So see you."

"Not going to soothe my fevered brow? Charm me with your bedside manner? Kiss me and make it better?" he taunted. Once she might have. Now it just made her sad. "You've become a frozen caricature of a woman. You stand there in front of me with your fists clenched at your sides and look at me like I hurt you? If I took you right now, would you even react like a normal woman? Moan with pleasure like you did after our senior prom?"

"Go to hell, Evan." Jenny stormed out of the room, his cynical laughter following her. She ran back to her room, shut the door, and leaned back against it, her breath coming out in harsh, silent sobs. How could he despoil what they'd had?

How could she get through the rest of this ordeal with him here? How could she check on Holly with him right next door? What had she been thinking to get Holly to move in with Jake…Evan's very best friend?

* * * *

When she woke him again at six, she had showered and changed. "Get up, Evan," she ordered. "There's coffee and toast in the kitchen if you're hungry. I'm leaving in fifteen minutes."

"Not a morning person, Jenny?" he sniped, wanting to strike back at her, needing to see the dislike in her face. Needing to see anything but that pale, wounded look of last night or the way her golden eyes dulled, like someone snapped off the light inside. "I guess that's just one more reason why we would never have worked out."

She stopped in the doorway and looked at him as if he had just crawled out from under a rock. "I'll take you to the hospital. Dr. Razawi will handle any follow up. I've already e-mailed him the details of your case, so he'll be aware of what happened when you see him."

She left the room before he could say anything else. Evan smacked the arm of the couch with his forearm and fist. Fifteen minutes later, he folded himself into the little BMW she drove. She had already warmed the car, and his seat had a heater under the leather covering to make it comfortable.

"Big house, nice car," he observed. "Not strapped by school loans? Your daddy's moonshine business must have been even better than everyone knew."

"Oh, he didn't..." Jenny halted, not finishing whatever she'd been about to utter. She tucked her hair behind her ear and put the car in gear. She had always fidgeted with her hair when she was nervous—or hiding something. Her daddy didn't what? Evan wondered. He didn't pay for her schooling? Then who had? She'd gotten her undergraduate degree from Carolina and gone on to Wake Forest's medical school. Not a cheap education.

The prosecutor in him was like a terrier with a bone, and he wanted to keep tearing at it. But for once in his life, Evan stopped himself. There was something vulnerable in the twist to her mouth and the shadows under her golden eyes. What had put those shadows there?

As if she couldn't stand the silence, she glanced at him. "What? No snotty comeback?"

She slowed the car as they rounded the curve. Over the embankment, the tail end of his Nissan was just visible. Her breath caught, and he glanced her way. If possible, her face had gone even paler.

"Just think, Jenny," he needled her, unable to stop this time, "you nearly had your wish. I did almost go to hell."

She cringed at his tone. "Don't," she choked. "Don't, Evan." She didn't say another word as she sped to the hospital. She halted in front of the emergency entrance. To Evan's mortification, an orderly came out with a wheelchair. Evan glared at Jenny.

"Very funny. I will not get in that."

"Suit yourself. They're expecting you. I've done my job. You're here. Good-bye, Evan. Get out of my car."

Once he was standing on the curb, she slid behind the wheel and drove around to the physicians' parking lot without looking back.

* * * *

Holly curled against Jake, her cheek resting on his furry chest, his arm snuggled around her. He was the one who heard Noelle's cries first. He tried to shift from underneath her, no doubt thinking she was asleep, but she stirred.

"What time is it?" she murmured, a little groggy.

"Five-thirty." As she started to move, he pressed her back. "Stay there. I'll change her and bring her to you, okay?"

"Yeah."

"Are you okay or do you need to…?" He gestured toward her chest.

"No. I'm fine. A little full, but I think it'll be okay."

He nodded and sprinted up the stairs. Holly stared after him just a bit befuddled. He'd kissed her several times. He hadn't scared her, but his searching mouth had left her aching and wanting in a way she'd never experienced with Spence. Holly leaned back into the corner of the couch, turning her cheek against the back of it. It still retained Jake's warmth and the tangy smell of the soap he used. She smiled as she inhaled.

Holly had stepped into the fantasy she'd spun so many months ago, but instead of Spence Dilby, Jake Allred was the handsome prince. She heard his step on the stairs. Jake had thrown on sweats and sneakers and had Noelle tucked in the crook of his arm. He bent and laid the baby in her arms before he kissed Holly on the mouth. The heat, even from his light brush of lips, was almost more than she could handle.

"Good morning," he murmured.

She blinked at him. She had spent her first night with Jake. "Where are you going?"

His mouth quirked. "Morning run. I'll be back by the time you finish nursing. Then I'll take Noelle while you get Tyler going. The bus stops out front at seven-thirty."

Holly laughed as she offered breakfast to the already rooting infant. "You sound like you've been doing this forever."

He grinned. "It's kind of nice."

With a wave he was gone, the door clicking shut behind him. Holly stared at the heavy oak panel. Jake was right. They were so far beyond mere friendship. Sharing Noelle's birth had made their relationship more intimate than it probably should be. They didn't really know each other that well. It scared her, but also made her want to grab hold with both hands. She wanted security for Tyler and the baby, but she didn't want to use Jake to attain it.

After Spence, Holly wasn't sure she could put her complete trust in another man again. She wanted to stand on her own.

Chapter 7

"Good morning, Ernie!" Jake grinned at his boss as he entered the cramped police station and nodded to the other two men already there.

The patrol officer on duty overnight nursed a cup of coffee while he debriefed the officer just coming on. Two other officers rounded out their numbers. Everyone pitched in, and if something big happened they couldn't handle, there was always help from either Sam Barnes and his guys, or they could go to the state. With the proximity of the parkway, even the rangers provided assistance when needed.

"Reports are on your desk, Jake," Ernie called over his shoulder as he stirred a healthy dollop of sugar into his coffee cup. He followed Jake into his office and shut the door. "Got a minute?"

Jake sat on the corner of his desk. "Sure, Ernie. What's doin'?"

The older man scratched his head. "You're mighty cheerful this morning. Don't you have a newborn sharing your house right now?"

"Yeah," Jake said. "She's beautiful."

"Mother or baby?"

Surprise rolled through Jake. He laughed as he said, "Both, I guess. Yeah, both."

Ernie smiled. "Great, Jake. Listen, there's something I've been meaning to talk to you about for a while now, and I can't put if off any longer. I'm retiring at the end of the year."

Jake blinked and dropped into the wooden chair behind his desk. "I guess I knew it was coming, Ernie, but not this soon. That's just three weeks. You don't give a guy much warning."

"I've been puttin' more and more of the workload off on you, and you're handlin' it just fine. I've recommended you for the job, by the way. It should be yours for the taking if you just give the town council the word."

Laura Browning

Jake smiled, touched by the praise. "Thanks. I appreciate that. I've only been here a year. You sure about this?"

"I can't think of a better man for the job. Hey, speaking of good men, have you seen the *Messenger*? The story of you deliverin' the baby is right on the front page, big color picture and everything."

Ernie opened the door and yelled down the hall. "Hey, Brandt! Bring me the *Messenger* sitting on my desk." A couple of seconds later a beefy hand appeared through the door waving the paper. Ernie grabbed it and handed it to Jake.

When he unfolded the paper to look at the story, his smile faded. Holly and Noelle stared back at him.

"Shit." Jake swore. "*Shit.*"

Ernie frowned. "What's wrong?"

Jake tossed the paper on the desk. "Holly ran away from an ex-fiancé who was stalking her and harassing her to give him her child. She has a PO in place. I tried to talk Amanda out of running the story, or at least to hold off on the picture of Holly and the baby. Amanda seems to think it'll just run here, but you know how it is this time of year. Everyone's looking for those peace-on-earth-goodwill-toward-men stories. I'm afraid some news service will pick it up."

Ernie grimaced. "I can understand your concern, but it's pretty much out of your hands at this point, Jake. It's a little late to close the barn doors. The horse's already out."

"Yeah." He pursed his lips. "I'll just keep my fingers crossed it doesn't go any further. What are the odds any of the Dilby family will pass through this area?"

"Dilby? Like the stores?"

Jake made a face. "*Just* like the stores."

"Wow. A lot of women would give them the baby and walk away."

"Not Holly. She's real protective of Noelle and her little brother." He changed the subject. "Court in session this morning?"

"Yeah, I think so. Why?"

"Just wondered. Evan's car was already gone when I went for my run this morning. Seemed a little early for him. In fact, a lot of mornings we run together."

"Can't say as I've heard anything."

Jake shrugged. "Oh well. I stopped trying to be his keeper twelve years ago after his breakup with Jenny."

"Never did understand what happened with those two," Ernie said. "Oh, Brandt caught our Nativity toilet-paper perps red-handed last night."

"Who was it?"

"The city attorney's son and his next-door neighbor."

"Isn't the city attorney a deacon at the Baptist church?"

"Uh-huh." Ernie chuckled.

"Well, guess the Presbyterians are off the hook."

Ernie laughed with him. The long-running feud between the women's groups from the two churches was legendary. Ernie was still chuckling as he left, leaving Jake to go through the reports from the previous day.

Jenny called him a half hour later. "Jake, I need a favor."

"What's up? You know I'd do almost anything for you."

She laughed. "Wow! Holly's already had an impact. Last week you told me you would do anything; now I've been bumped to *almost* anything."

"She's great, Jenny, you know?"

Her laugh was softer. "Oh, Jake. That makes me so happy."

He grinned as he stared out the window of his office. "Thanks. Though you might be a bit premature. So…what can I do for you?"

"I want you to come talk to the pigheaded person you call a friend."

Jake's grin widened as he shifted positions and stared at his ceiling. "Would that pighead's name happen to be Evan Richardson?"

"Yes. He's giving my nurses fits and refuses to let Dr. Razawi treat him."

"Whoa. Whoa," Jake said letting his chair fall forward again with a *thump*. "Back up. Treat? For what?"

She sighed. "I hoped you would have already heard through the police grapevine. It seems to broadcast everything else around here. Evan missed the curve in my drive last night after dropping me off and wrapped his car around a tree. The first I knew of it was when he managed to make it to my door at two this morning. The EMTs were working an accident on the parkway, so I stitched his head, kept an eye on him, and brought him in this morning. Jake, he's being a prick. Razawi hasn't even gotten him into the CT scan yet."

"He's got a concussion?"

"Yes. I stitched a three-inch laceration right at his hairline, and when I talked to him about what happened, he admitted he was unconscious for quite a while. He keeps insisting he's going to court at ten."

"I'll be right there."

"Thanks, Jake."

Ten minutes later, Jake and Jenny walked into the cubicle where Evan was already on his phone, in blatant disregard of the sign asking all cell phones be turned off. He ignored them as he snapped into his phone,

"They're being obstructive. At this point, I don't see an option. Ask for a continuance until January." There was a pause and then Evan snarled. "Tell her honor the commonwealth's attorney is being held hostage at the hospital because of a little car accident."

After punching End, he turned on Jenny, a taunting twist to his wide mouth. "Had to call the cavalry? Couldn't handle it on your own, *Doc*?"

"That's enough, Ev," Jake ordered. "Jenny, close the door and the curtains and leave us alone for a few minutes."

When the door shut behind her, Jake stared at his friend. A neat line of stitches edged Evan's forehead along with bruising there and on his jaw. Otherwise, Evan's face was pale and his gray eyes overbright.

He remembered the Evan he'd grown up with. The friend who'd always had his back, no matter what. The friend who'd spent a lifetime trying to make people think he didn't care about anything because he usually cared too much.

"Ev?" Jake prompted, tilting his head as he walked over to him. "You look like hell, bro."

"I crashed my fucking car. I'm supposed to look like hell."

Jake crossed his arms over his chest and waited. It took less time than he expected before it poured out of Evan in a rush.

"I should have let you take her home. We had a fight. I said some nasty things. Even for me." Evan looked away and swallowed a couple of times. "She told me some stuff. I—I can't even tell you. I kept going at her and at her and when I left I was crying and I couldn't see the fucking road, Jake, so I crashed. And then even when she took me in and stitched me up, I started in on her again."

"Evan." Jake tried to interrupt, but his friend kept on, his expression tormented.

"She dumped me at the door of the ER and said this other guy would be treating me, but I want her."

Jake put his hand on Evan's shoulder and squeezed. "Don't push, Evan. It's a miracle she came back here at all. She has secrets no one knows. Give it time. Right now, you need the CT scan. You've got a concussion. I've lost enough friends over the last ten years, man. I don't know what I'd do if something happened to you. You've been my friend since we beat each other up in kindergarten."

Some of the tension left Evan's face. He smiled, a little watery and his eyes were a little red, but it was still a smile. "Okay."

"So I can tell Jen and Razawi you'll do the scan and what they tell you to?"

"Yes."

Five minutes later, Jenny stood next to Jake as they rolled Evan away. She studied Jake with tired eyes. "How'd you do it, Allred?"

"Let him talk. He was tighter than a tick and just needed to vent."

Her eyes still on the bed disappearing through the swinging doors, Jenny muttered, "Prick."

Jake's eyes narrowed. "I don't know what happened between the two of you all those years ago, and I don't want to. You'll have to work it out, but, Jenny, don't think he doesn't feel. He feels too much. You hear sarcasm and cynicism. I hear a guy who's spent his entire life trying to win approval from a father colder than an iceberg." Jake paused and lifted Jenny's chin with his forefinger. "Don't make me choose between the two of you. I can't. I love you both."

* * * *

Spence Dilby glanced at the woman riding next to him. Seely, the fiancée that made his parents happy, looked studiously out the window, her entire posture screaming boredom. Whatever. Spence had promised to take her skiing, but in reality he was on a mission. They were traveling to the ski slopes via the backroads so he could swing through Castle County and Mountain Meadow. It would surprise the hell out of him if the place was any more than a wide spot in the road. If it was that small, he might luck up and spot Holly or her obnoxious brat of a brother.

The state highway widened out after a curve. As the speed limit dropped, Spence smirked. It might be a bit more than a wide spot in the road, but not much.

"Why are we stopping?" Seely asked with a yawn.

"I need something to drink."

He left Seely in the SUV while he stalked toward the entrance to Mountain Meadow General Store. Probably some freaking tourist trap that would charge him out the ass for a soft drink. The bell above the door jingled as he entered. Behind the counter was a white-haired old woman who looked like her wrinkles had wrinkles. Spence shuddered.

"May I help you?"

He forced a smile. "Just need a soda."

"They're in the case there to the side."

Spence nodded. As he made his way over to the side of the store, he saw movement out of the corner of his eye, but when he glanced toward the back of the canned food aisle, it was empty. Spence shook his head. Weird-ass people lived in these parts. Probably inbred. As he walked back to the counter, the paper on the newsstand caught his eye. Holy shit. It was Holly, holding a baby.

"This is your local paper?" he asked the old broad, trying to keep his satisfaction hidden at how easy his quest had suddenly become. At her nod, he continued, "What a great story idea, featuring hometown heroes. And this new mother's from around here?"

"She sure is," the woman said sucking in a breath as if she was getting ready to tell him the whole town history. Yes. This was just the break he needed.

For just a second, the old woman's gaze darted away, then back to him. Her smile faltered, and whatever she'd been about to say died with it. She smiled again, but not as brightly as before. "Is there anything else for you, young man?"

"I'll take one of the papers. I like good news stories."

The woman took his money and handed him back his change, shoving the paper and the drink toward him now as if she couldn't get him out the door fast enough. Spence glanced over his shoulder, scanning the parts of the store he could see, but no one else was in sight. Taking his purchases, he went back out. As soon as he opened the SUV's door, he shoved the newspaper over the sun visor of the SUV and buckled his seat belt. Seely studied him.

"What's that, Spence?"

"Just the local fish wrap. I figured it would be good for a few laughs when we're not on the slopes the next few days."

As he anticipated, mentioning skiing took Seely's mind right off the newspaper. While he negotiated the narrow highway leading to the interstate, Spence's mind turned over what he'd found out. In two months, the damn detectives he'd hired hadn't been able to discover a damn thing about Holly, just that the kid was going to school in this Podunk town. And look how easy it was. It might not be a bad idea to stop on the way back to see if he could find out anything else.

So Holly had the kid—a little early if his math was right. After all there'd only been one, tedious night. Who'd have thought in this day anyone would be still a virgin at her age. He hated inexperienced women. They took way too much time. He wanted a woman who knew how to get off quick, so he didn't have to worry about her pleasure. Seely fit that bill perfectly.

That one time in New York had been more than enough. Holly had been frigid, not worth the trouble. Seely was a different matter. He glanced at her—blond hair, blue eyes, and big tits. Man, you couldn't get much better. Who cared she didn't have many interests outside snow skiing and keeping her tan intact. She was a good screw and she'd look great as his wife.

Now, if he could just get the kid away from Holly, they could complete the family picture and make all the Dilby clan happy he'd procreated something for posterity. It would be easy enough to hire a nanny, and then private boarding schools would keep the kid out of his hair until he could marry her off. Too bad it hadn't been a boy, but he wouldn't be too picky.

Yeah, he would stop by that hokey store again to see if he could get any other info out of the old broad, and then he was going to find little Holly so they could chat. Maybe he just needed to up the ante. Everyone had a price.

* * * *

Jake had had a frustrating day. Two of their guys had called in sick so he'd helped cover some of the patrols during the morning and shoved the paperwork off until afternoon. Problem was, the pile didn't seem to get smaller. Realizing it wasn't going to get finished today, Jake started organizing everything to work on tomorrow.

He was just getting ready to leave when the outer door rocked back on its hinges. The noise made Jake spin in reaction. Then he saw it was Tyler. He took a deep breath and tamped down the instinct that had nearly made him reach for his sidearm.

"Hey, kid. You come to hitch a ride?"

"I gotta talk to you, Jake. Right now." The kid was breathless and a little shaky looking.

Jake voiced his first thought, a shaft of gut-wrenching fear stabbing through him. "Is everything okay with Holly and the baby?"

"Yes. I mean, I think so. I-I don't know." Tyler looked like he was ready to burst into tears. Jake knew enough about Tyler now to know whatever was troubling him was serious.

Seeing the curious looks the boy was getting from the two other people in the front, Jake hung his jacket back up and held his hand out. "Okay, buddy. Come on back. We'll go talk in my office."

As soon as Jake shut the door, Tyler buried his face against his ribs and hung on for dear life. The boy trembled, so Jake wrapped his arms around the thin shoulders. "Hey. What's wrong, man?"

Tyler shook his head.

"I saw *him*. In the store. He was there."

Jake sat in the nearest chair and let Tyler perch on his knee. "Slow down, Ty. Who'd you see in the store?"

"Spence! Holly's Spence. He was *here*."

Jake went still, coldness spreading through him. "When? Where?"

"He came into the general store to buy some stuff, and I heard him. He saw the paper and bought one. He asked if Holly was from around here. Mrs. Tarpley told him yeah. She didn't know." Tyler's face crumbled.

Jake pulled his cell phone out, hitting speed dial. "Hang on, kid, okay? It'll be all right, I promise."

Evan answered with a gruff, "Yeah."

"You at home?"

"Doctor's orders, so here I am."

"I need a favor fast. Go next door. Stay with Holly and Noelle until I get there. Mooch some more cookies off her or something. Make it seem like just a social visit."

"What's up, bro?"

"The ex-boyfriend appeared at Tarpley's less than a half hour ago."

"I'm on my way out the door."

"Thanks."

After disconnecting, Jake pulled Tyler against his chest in a tight hug. "We'll take care of her. Everything will be all right." He held his fist for Tyler to bump knuckles with him. "You and me, bro."

Tyler grinned weakly. "Yeah."

* * * *

Holly had just put Noelle down when she heard a knock at the front door. She frowned. She didn't know anyone, and folks knew Jake wasn't here. She came downstairs but couldn't see anything through the stained glass bordering each side of the doorway. She hesitated, then shook off the paranoia. No way could Spence have found her. She opened the door and smiled when she saw Evan's rangy frame standing on the porch. He turned as she opened the door wider, revealing the bandage on his head.

"Oh, Evan! What happened?"

His expression was rueful. "I wrecked my car last night when I took Jenny home. They let me out of the hospital, but," he added, "I'm supposed to have someone keeping an eye on me for a couple of days. A concussion, you know."

Her heart went out to him. As sarcastic as he could be, she sensed vulnerability beneath it. "Come on in. You have to stay here. Jake won't mind. Aren't you supposed to have someone check on you every few hours?" Before he could open his mouth to answer, she continued. "That won't be a problem because we're up with Noelle anyway, so you can spend a couple of nights. I was just getting ready to start dinner. Come back to the kitchen."

She pulled him into the house and shut the door. As she led the way back to the kitchen, she heard the *click* of the dead bolt. She spun, narrowing her eyes. "What's wrong?"

"Just locking the door again." Evan's expression was innocent. After a heartbeat or two, Holly nodded.

"Come back and have a seat, Evan," she invited. "Would you like tea or coffee?"

"Coffee if it's not too much trouble." He smiled, oozing charm. "And some of those great chocolate chip cookies if you still have any."

Holly flushed with pleasure. "Sure."

Underneath the glower he normally wore, he was very attractive. Holly saw why Jenny was drawn to him. Too bad they were estranged. She set a plate of cookies and a cup of coffee in front of him.

"Cream or sugar?"

"No."

Holly plopped into the chair across from him and leaned her elbows on the table. "Is Dr. Owens all right?"

Evan paused with a mouthful of cookie, his expression startled. He swallowed. "It happened after I dropped her off. I…uh…missed the curve in her drive."

Holly touched his forearm. "Well, I'm glad you're all right. And you must stay here. I know Jake will say the same thing. There's plenty of room."

Evan quirked an eyebrow. "He likes you, you know."

"I like him, too," she admitted totally unable to stop the huge smile that curled her mouth.

They both heard the key in the lock. Tyler and Jake were coming down the hall. Holly grinned at them, but her smile faded as she saw Tyler's pinched, pale face and Jake's serious expression. When she started to rise, Jake waved her back. Her stomach tightened.

"Tyler? Jake? What's wrong?"

"Tyler saw Spence Dilby at Tarpley's this afternoon," Jake said.

Fear grabbed her by the throat. Her first instinct was to grab Tyler and Noelle and take off. Then she locked gazes with Jake, his hazel eyes steady, reassuring. She took a deep breath and addressed her brother. "Are you okay, Ty? Did he see you? He didn't do anything, did he?"

Jake circled the kitchen table, crouching next to her. "Holly, it's okay. He didn't see Tyler."

She buried her face in Jake's shoulder. For a moment, just the two of them existed. "He saw the newspaper article, honey," he whispered. "He saw your picture and knows you're living here."

Jake stroked her hair off her face. She brushed away her tears, and blew out a breath. "I won't let him threaten me, Jake."

"I know, and I'll be right beside you to help."

Evan leaned forward. "Did you list Dilby as the father on the birth certificate?"

"No. When I told him I was pregnant he denied being the father and broke off our engagement. Only after he discovered his new fiancée couldn't have children did he come back claiming he wanted the baby."

"You've already met the criteria required by the commonwealth to establish you as natural parent. After all, you've got two witnesses right here with you who can verify you gave birth to Noelle. Dilby will have to go through the courts and present genetic tests, but I take it from your reactions legalities aren't your primary concern."

Jake pulled his handkerchief from his back pocket and handed it to Holly. "You're right, Ev, that's not the main worry. The last time Spence Dilby was around Tyler and Holly, he shoved Tyler and slapped her around. I don't think his approach will be through the courts."

"He's a mean man," Tyler whispered. "Spence scares me."

"Oh, honey." She put her arm around him. This was exactly why she had left Lynchburg.

"Don't worry, Tyler," Jake said at the same time. "We're going to make sure you're okay and Spence can't get to any of you."

Evan grinned at them. "Holly invited me to stay here the next couple days since I'm supposed to be taking it easy with my concussion—if it's okay with you, bro."

Jake laughed. "Okay? It's great, a perfect solution, Evan. She won't be here by herself while I'm at work and Tyler's at school. Then we hit the weekend, and I happen to have both days off. After…well, we'll figure it out."

Holly leaned against Jake's muscular arm and glanced at Evan. "I'd begun to lose faith in people before I came here, but everyone in this town has been so wonderful. I'm beginning to think arriving in Mountain Meadow was a miracle not an accident."

* * * *

Jenny was tired when she left the hospital. Between morning rounds and the ones she just finished, it had been a long day. With more retirees in the area, the need was growing for additional doctors and medical facilities to handle their health concerns, but a different patient concerned her now. Jenny told Razawi she would check on Evan as she went home. She wondered what mad impulse had made her volunteer. Evan had been nothing but a thorn in her side. He had dredged up and dissected some of the worst memories of her life, and now she had volunteered to see how he was doing. His house wasn't even on her way. She should have her head examined. On second thought, she wasn't sure she wanted to examine her motives.

Jenny pulled into the drive. Just one light burned in his windows. When she knocked on the door, she got no answer. The door was unlocked. Her hand shook a bit as she pushed it open. Was she really going inside? He would for sure bite her head off if he was here.

"Evan," she called. No answer. "Evan?" This time she called louder, but there was still no answer. Forgetting how he might react to her walking in, Jenny stepped into the foyer and began searching room to room, fear growing that something had happened.

When she didn't find him anywhere downstairs, she dashed upstairs. The bed in his room was rumpled, his clothes from last night lay on the floor, but a quick check in the bathroom told her he was not there. *Calm down.* Tamping down her panic, she ran back downstairs and out onto the porch, shutting the door behind her.

Good. Jake was home. Jenny hurried across the yards and dashed up the front steps to the wide porch. She banged on the door, shifting from foot to foot. As soon as the door opened, Jenny launched in.

"Oh good, Jake. I came by to check on Evan, but..."

"...I wasn't home?" Evan's cool voice rumbled from above her head, completing her sentence.

Jenny stared at him. Afraid what her eyes might reveal, she blanked her expression. "I see you're doing all right, Evan. Dr. Razawi will be glad to hear that. Well," she allowed herself a small, professional smile, "now I see you're doing so well, I'll be on my way."

"Don't you want to come in and say hello to Jake and Holly?" Evan asked. Jenny stopped with her back to him. Tension tightened her shoulders underneath her wool overcoat. "Will you come in if I promise to play nice?"

She was so tired of this, so tired of trying to fight what had never died, at least not on her part.

"I can't. I can handle the occasional glimpses of you, but I can't deal with all this verbal sniping, Evan. That's your forte, not mine," she finished on a husky whisper.

Laura Browning

She heard him stop just behind her. The tension increased until she thought she would scream.

"Jenny…" Evan began. She turned just in time to see Jake step into the doorway with Noelle on his shoulder.

"Hi, Jen. Did you come to check on Evan, or Holly and Noelle?"

Ignoring Evan, she responded, "Evan, but I can see he's all right, so I'll head home."

"No way. Holly would kill me if you didn't come in to say hi. Have dinner with us. We're throwing burgers on the grill."

Jenny smiled in spite of herself. "Jake, it's two weeks till Christmas. People don't grill this time of year."

"I do."

"Besides, it's been a long day. I…I lost a patient today. Heart attack. I'm not the best company. I should go. I'll check in on Holly and Noelle tomorrow."

Evan touched her then. She drew away, but she saw from his narrowed gray eyes he'd felt the tremble in her body. "Stay," he murmured. "You could use some company. If I'm the problem, I'll go home."

Jenny stared at him. Since when had Evan Richardson become a human being?

Jake eyed them. "I'll let you sort this out. Noelle's hungry and Holly wants to nurse. There will be plenty of food for everyone."

Jake disappeared. Evan still had his hand on Jenny's arm. "Why are you doing this?" she whispered.

"What?"

"Why are you being nice?"

He quirked a brow. "You think I can't be?"

"I think you choose not to."

"Holly's former fiancé stopped at Tarpley's. He saw the article and started asking questions," Evan commented. "She could use some company."

"Oh no," Jenny cried. "We have to keep him away. You know she had to put a protective order in place. Someone should stay with her and the baby during the day."

"I am."

She gaped. "You?"

Evan grinned, a mischievous expression she hadn't expected to ever see again, and her heart lurched. "When she saw my bandage, I told her about my terrible concussion and how you sent me home, but I needed someone to check on me, and she invited me to stay with Jake and her for the next two days."

Jenny laughed, amazed she could. "Oh, Evan, that's brilliant. Now she won't feel like she's a prisoner with a watchdog." She reached out to squeeze his arm but pulled her hand back when she felt the warm, hair-covered skin of his forearm. Evan covered her hand with his, holding it in place.

"Stay, Jenny." His voice was urgent. "Don't let me drive you away from your friends."

She blinked and bit her lip. Where was the sarcasm? The taunting? Did she even dare trust this Evan? "Okay."

He took her coat and her bag and hung them on the hooks on the hall tree. Then he let Jenny precede him down the narrow corridor to the kitchen at the rear of the house. They paused, feeling a little like they had stepped into a Norman Rockwell painting. Tyler chewed his pencil as he pondered the textbook in front of him. Holly sat in a chair nearby, nursing the baby, and Jake had just popped a French fry in her mouth before leaning down to kiss her. Anyone looking at them could see they were falling head over heels in love with each other.

"They look so right together," Jenny marveled, "like they're already a family."

"They are," Evan confirmed from behind her. "Even if they don't know it for sure, they already are."

She glanced over her shoulder, and he stared back. A fleeting instant of might-have-beens hung in the air between them. Jenny swallowed.

"Hey, Jenny," Jake called. "Evan convinced you to stay. Great."

Jenny smiled. "Yeah. He was right. I do need to be around people after the day I had today, and you are the people I want to be with." Her voice broke on the last words, her chin trembling. Evan squeezed her shoulder, and Jake gave her a hug, lifting her off her feet.

"Hey." He laughed. "This is a no-cry zone unless you're under seven pounds, and even as tiny as you are, Doc, I don't think you'll qualify."

Jenny had to laugh in return. "Put me down, Jake Allred. Can I help with anything?"

"Tyler's homework," Holly said. "I can handle the math, but he's working on health and science now, and that is not my thing."

Jenny settled in the chair next to Tyler's, seeing he was studying foods and how they converted into energy. She glanced at Holly and Noelle. Peace radiated from the two of them. Love made them and everyone around them glow. It sounded corny, but looking at mother and daughter was like seeing the Christmas season come to life.

Chapter 8

Evan awoke with an image of Jake and Holly permanently imprinted on his brain. He'd gotten up several times during the night. Jake had come in to look in on him during the two times Holly nursed Noelle. Evan awoke on his own the next time. Padding along the hall to the bath, he passed the open door of the nursery and paused. Holly sat in a rocker nursing Noelle by the muted glow of a nursery lamp. Jake was on his knees next to the rocker, one arm curved along the top and the other resting alongside Holly's as she held the baby. Holly had smiled at Jake, and he'd leaned in to kiss her.

Evan had hurried away. When Jake stopped by a short time later, Evan had snapped at him to let him go back to sleep. Now, in the light of morning, he knew why the scene had left him angry. He envied Jake. Evan had wanted with Jenny what Jake had found so easily with Holly. Since the very first time he set eyes on Jennifer Owens, when she was just a leggy teen who hadn't quite grown into her body yet, Evan had wanted her. She was small and feisty and smart. What Jenny Owens lacked in money and family she made up for with attitude and academics.

Evan had wanted her as he'd tugged on her hair and kicked at her desk with his big feet. He had wanted her as they sat through Advanced World History with Mr. Pendergast, who delighted in sharing stories of his days in Vietnam. Evan had wanted her the first time he stole a kiss from her behind the football bleachers when she took a break at halftime with the other cheerleaders, and he fell in love the moment she slapped his face for it.

They had started dating during basketball season, but he'd never tried to do more than hold her hand and kiss her. They kissed a lot, but for two years that was all. The guys teased him, everyone except Jake, and the girls gave Jenny a hard time. By their junior year, they were such an acknowledged couple no one gave them grief, and even though they hadn't gone all the way, they were intimately acquainted with each other's bodies.

Then came Christmas vacation of their senior year. It had been the most beautiful thing. Both virgins, they were nervous and a little uncertain, but so in love with each other it didn't matter. They were careful, using condoms because she was too embarrassed to see the town doctor for birth control pills.

Evan stared at his reflection in the bathroom mirror. They had been so careful and so correct until prom. But someone spiked the punch that night, probably with her daddy's moonshine, and they both got tipsy—and horny. They made love in the car and then again at the hotel room near the interstate. They had stayed there all night, coming again and again. Neither had given a thought to birth control.

Evan looked down now in self-derision. He was half-hard just at the memories.

They had talked about their future together. She would be the town doctor and he was going to right wrongs and put the bad guys in jail as an attorney. Well they'd both achieved their goals; just their future as a couple had vanished.

He showered and padded downstairs in his bare feet, still feeling morose and disinclined to talk. Holly puttered in the kitchen with Noelle on her shoulder. She gave him a quick smile before reaching into the cabinet with her free hand to grab a coffee cup.

"The coffee's still fresh if you'd like some. Black, right?"

"Yeah," he said pleased she remembered. She poured the cup and handed it to him. "Thanks, Holly."

"No problem. How are you feeling?"

"Like a fraud for not going to work."

She grinned. "But you are working. You're my security force, and much better-looking than a pit bull."

Evan chuckled. "I'm glad you can joke about it."

Her green eyes sparked. "I refuse to allow Spence to make me shed one more tear. I refuse to allow him to intimidate me. Just two weeks to Christmas, Evan, and we should be celebrating."

The kitchen timer beeped just then. "Oh. Those are the cinnamon rolls. I made more because Jake and Tyler ate all the ones I baked earlier, and I thought you might like some. Here." She handed him Noelle and Evan froze.

"Just lay her against your shoulder. Put one hand under her little butt and the other behind her head." She smiled at him. "Just like that. You're a natural. I'll get the cinnamon rolls out. Do you want an egg?"

Evan's head spun. He'd been dropped next to a tornado of happiness. "Uh. No egg. The rolls are fine."

A desperate need for oxygen forced him to take a breath, and he was relieved to discover it didn't make the warm little bundle in his arms cry. While Holly bustled around removing the rolls from their pan and placing them on a plate, Evan peeked at Noelle. She had a tiny little bow of a mouth, a button nose, and dark lashes resting against her pink cheeks. She wiggled one tiny hand out of the blanket she was swaddled in, and when he stuck his finger against her miniature palm, her fingers latched onto his with surprising strength. Evan's eyes widened.

"She grabs right onto your heart, too, doesn't she?" Holly whispered next to his ear.

"Yeah." He sounded breathy and a little hoarse, not at all like the cynical, sarcastic commonwealth's attorney known throughout the district as a real hardnose. He flushed, glad no one was around to see.

"Here," Holly said with a smile. "I'll take her so I can put her down for her morning nap. Help yourself. I'll join you in a few minutes."

His hand trembled when he picked up his coffee cup. He rubbed a faint ache in the middle of his chest and reached for a cinnamon roll. Would Holly laugh if he asked to hold Noelle again? There was just something about them. It reminded him a little of Christmas morning when he was young.

* * * *

"Jake?" Ernie stuck his head inside the office door. "Betty Gatewood's here to see you with a couple women from the church."

"Are they here to thank us for finding the nativity toilet paperers?"

Ernie grimaced. "'Fraid not, son. I think this might be more personal business."

Jake groaned as he rose from his chair. He'd been expecting this. In a town as small as Mountain Meadow, word would already have gotten around Holly Morgan was living at his house. He was just surprised it had taken this long. He stepped into the lobby and plastered a smile on his face.

Patience, Allred.

"Good morning, Mrs. Gatewood, ladies," he greeted them. "What can I do for you?"

"Is there some place we could speak in private, Lieutenant Allred?" Betty Gatewood's posture and tone were far from friendly.

Jake kept his smile in place. "Sure. Please come back to my office, ladies. It might be a little cramped, but we'll make do." He held the door and allowed them to precede him before easing past their combined bulk and gesturing them to the chairs. "Please, sit."

All three ladies sat as one just as if they were obeying the direction of the preacher from the pulpit. All three perched on the edge of their chairs, hands gripping their purses as though bent on choking the evil demons from them.

"Lieutenant Allred," Betty Gatewood began.

"Just call me Jake, ma'am. After all, you've known me most of my life," he added with a grin that faded when none of the three women responded.

"We're here to speak about your current living situation…and to find out what you intend to do about it."

Jake decided to be obtuse. No way was he sharing the fact part of Holly's presence was a matter of protection. "Well you know, I bought that big Victorian house over on Maple, right next door to Evan Richardson, and I'm very happy there, so I don't believe I'll be moving anytime soon."

Mrs. Gatewood huffed, "That is not what we're referring to."

"Oh?" He wasn't going to make this any easier for them.

"You have that young woman living with you, the single woman who just had a baby."

As if he couldn't figure that one out. Jake's good humor faded. "You're referring to Holly Morgan and Noelle. I also have Miss Morgan's younger brother, Tyler, living with me. You forgot him."

Her companions shifted, but not Mrs. Gatewood. "You are still young and might not have given much thought to it, but there are certain expectations about the way our top law enforcement officers should behave. Living with a woman of low moral fiber is not acceptable."

Jake leaned forward, resting his elbows on his desk and loosely clasping his hands to keep from flipping all three ladies the bird or punching Betty Gatewood in her sanctimonious face. "Let me clear up a few things for you, Mrs. Gatewood," he began. "First, I am not *living with* Holly Morgan as you mean it. In return for room and board, Holly agreed to cook, clean, and wash laundry for me. Second, I took her, Noelle, and Tyler in because Doc Owens asked me. The old Crawley place was too isolated and unsafe for the baby. Third, Holly's here with her brother to escape an abusive ex-fiancé.

"Accusing her of low morals without knowing the first thing about her says more about you than her. And finally, Mrs. Gatewood," Jake snapped, patience be damned, "were you a man, I would already have punched you in the nose for insulting Holly. As it is, I'll just ask you to leave."

The woman's eyes glowed with spite. "My husband is on the town council, Lieutenant, and I will be sure to pass on to him how you threatened me in front of witnesses."

"You do that, ma'am. Now if y'all will excuse me, I have work to do. You ladies have a Merry Christmas. You remember that holiday don't you, Mrs. Gatewood, when a young woman gave birth to a son out of wedlock?"

All three ladies gasped as if the devil himself had popped up and yelled "boo" before they fled the Mountain Meadow police station faster than Franklin County moonshiners running from the revenuers. Jake pursed his lips.

There was nothing like holier-than-thou hypocrites to push a guy right into a marriage proposal. And damn it, he didn't care if they had known each other for just days, he was asking Holly Morgan to marry him. All he'd needed was someone criticizing her for him to realize he wanted her, her baby, and her brother. Jake's feelings were already way past friendship. He knew it and so did she. They were a family. Jake pushed out of his chair, heading for the front of the station.

"Ernie?"

"Yeah." The older man eyed him.

"I need to run to the bank for a few minutes. Won't take me long."

Ernie tilted his head. "Cashing it in and leaving town?"

"Nope."

"Well if anybody could drive a man to it, Betty Gatewood could."

Jake shrugged on his jacket. "Gonna get my grandma's ring out of the safety deposit box."

Ernie's bushy brows met his receding hairline. "That's a might fast, isn't it? You and Holly haven't even been on a date yet, have you?"

Jake chuckled, knowing he was blushing, but feeling he had to explain. "Nope, but I guess helping a woman bring her baby into the world, you kinda skip a few things."

"I s'pose."

Jake whistled as he shoved his hands in his jacket pockets and headed across the square. No, they hadn't dated in the traditional sense, but they had shared some pretty steamy kisses. Add the intimacy of living under the same roof, and they'd already established a relationship. He just hoped Holly felt the same.

* * * *

Holly was in the basement doing laundry. Just watching her work around the house exhausted Evan. He'd never seen anyone with as much energy—well, maybe Jake—but especially someone who'd just had a baby a few days ago. Wasn't she supposed to need everyone waiting on her? All she'd asked him to do was keep an ear out for Noelle.

"If she wakes, it's because her diaper's wet or she's hungry," Holly explained. "If you'll just change her diaper and bring her down, I'll take care of the hungry part. Okay?"

Evan kept his eyes anywhere but on Holly's chest as he nodded and hoped like hell the baby would stay asleep. Still, he hovered near the bottom of the stairs to make sure he would hear her move.

His phone rang and he checked the caller ID. His office. "Richardson here."

"Oh, Mr. Richardson," Wanda Sue, one of his clerks, gushed. "We all hope you're feeling better, sir."

Evan's mouth twisted. "Right. And I should also believe you just mailed your wish lists to Santa too, I suppose."

"Mr. Richardson."

"Just cut to the chase, Wanda Sue."

"Your daddy called looking for you, said he couldn't reach you at home. We told him you were in court like you said to…"

Evan heard a soft mewl from upstairs, and his eyes widened.

"Whatever… That's fine. I have to go. The baby's crying."

"Baby? What baby?"

Evan started to punch End and stopped. "Say, Wanda Sue…don't you have a couple kids?"

"Yes, sir. One seven and one three."

"Think you could talk me through changing a diaper?" Dead silence met his request. "Well?"

"Of…of course, sir."

"Great. Hang on."

He dashed up the stairs two at a time. Cradling the phone against one shoulder, he picked the now squalling Noelle up, balancing her on his other shoulder. "Okay. There's a table here with diapers, some of those wipe things, some lotion, and some powder. Where do I start?"

"The first thing you do is lay the baby on the changing table and unfasten the dirty diaper."

Evan squeezed the phone between his ear and his shoulder. "Do I hear laughter in the background?"

"No, sir," she assured him in a voice that sounded just a bit choked.

By the time he ended the call, Evan had a lot more respect for Wanda Sue. He couldn't care less what his office thought of him at that moment. Noelle watched him with her big, gorgeous eyes, her little lips pursed, and he was lost. He smiled as he cradled her in the crook of his arm and headed downstairs. He had just reached the last step when he heard the knocker tap a couple of times. This place was busier than his office.

Jake needed to put in a peephole. Evan eased the door open until he saw Jenny's blond hair and then pulled it the rest of the way.

* * * *

Jenny turned, the smile on her face fading into a short gasp at the sight of Evan smiling into the face of a newborn. Her medical bag dropped out of nerveless fingers. For just a moment, their eyes met and held, then she blinked and swallowed. Jenny jerked her gaze away, bending down to grab her bag.

"I…I came to check you and Holly." Her voice was strained.

"Come in," Evan said, looking almost as rattled as she felt. Just then Noelle's alert little face, with her waving arms and kicking legs, crumpled into a howl. "Shh," Evan cooed and began rocking her back and forth. Who was this man—an alien straight from *Men in Black*?

"She might need her diaper changed."

"No," Evan assured her. "Already did that. She must be hungry. I'll take her to Holly. Come on in."

Jenny raised her hand. "Whoa. Back up just a minute. Did I just hear you say you changed her diaper?"

Evan coughed. "Yes. Well I had help."

"Help?"

"Wanda Sue, one of my clerks, talked me through it over the phone."

Jenny's lip twitched. She couldn't help it. She reached for the baby. "I'll take her."

Evan pulled back. "I have her. Holly told me to look after her."

"Well, offer the tip of your pinkie to her to suck on for a minute until she can get the real thing. It might stop her crying." Jenny followed him as he bounced the baby on his arm and led the way down the hall to the basement stairs. "Evan, are you telling me everyone in your office now knows you changed a diaper?"

"Hmm. I suppose."

Jenny examined his broad shoulders and his well-cut dark hair and began to chuckle. As Evan continued down the steps, she had to stop and sit. She was laughing so hard she had to wipe her eyes.

Holly appeared and studied the two of them as she reached for Noelle. "What's up?"

Jenny waved her hands as she continued to laugh. Evan scowled at her and spoke to Holly. "One of my clerks called me and while I was on the phone, Noelle began crying, so Wanda Sue talked me through changing her diaper."

Holly smiled. "Well that was mighty nice of her. You must have some excellent employees. I hope you appreciate them."

Evan's mouth opened and shut like a fish gasping for breath, or as if the idea of appreciating his employees had never occurred to him before. "I do now."

Holly started up the stairs with Noelle. "Well, I'm done here. I'll make Tyler carry everything later."

"I'll do it," Evan offered, which made Jenny laugh harder. Things had gotten a lot merrier since Holly and Noelle arrived.

* * * *

Tyler came home from school Friday with a huge grin. Evan let him in. "Hey, kid, how was school?"

"I aced my spelling test, but I got a B on my math quiz."

"Hmm. I'm not much help with math. You need Holly or Jenny."

Tyler grinned. "One more week and we're out for Christmas break."

Evan stared out the door, noticing for the first time all of the decorations sparkling on houses and lawns up and down the street. There were two weeks until Christmas? He recalled Holly mentioning it, but it hadn't sunk in at the time. "We need decorations and a tree."

Tyler grinned. "You are so right. I was beginning to wonder when anyone around here besides me would notice."

"Notice what?" Holly asked as she walked down the hallway from the kitchen. She was in the middle of cooking Evan's going-away dinner. Jenny had stopped by earlier and told him she'd take the stitches out in a few more days, but didn't see any reason why he couldn't go back home. Holly smiled as she sat nearby cuddling Noelle. Jenny kept coming by on the pretext of seeing the baby, but Holly was positive there was more going on. Something had passed between Evan and Jenny, easing the hostilities. In fact, Jenny had agreed to return for dinner after she finished evening rounds.

Holly touched Noelle's cheek. Yes, everyone deserved a little holiday magic. Noelle opened her eyes and Holly could almost swear the baby winked.

"It's two weeks till Christmas, Holly. We don't have any decorations. Neither does Evan. I'm tight with the two biggest scrooges in town."

Evan laughed. "But we have Christmas decorations. We have Holly and Noelle."

Tyler rolled his eyes and Holly sighed. "Like I haven't heard those jokes my entire life, Evan. Changing diapers has blunted your wit. Where is that rapier-edged tongue I first met?"

Evan placed his hand over his heart. "I have fallen in love with your squirming bundle of blankets, and it's changed my life. I'm a reformed cynic, a recovering curmudgeon, a..."

"Seriously sentimental softy who we all love?" Holly finished.

Evan blinked. "You do?"

Holly smacked him with her towel. "Not like that, silly. You just can't compete with Jake as far as I'm concerned, but you're one of the best friends I've ever had."

"Thanks, Holly. It's mutual." Evan's natural austerity vanished.

"Eww!" Tyler groaned. "This is gettin' all gooey. Is that what adults are like all the time? 'Cause if it is, I do not want to grow up. Oh! I have an idea. Since we're celebrating Evan going home—not that we don't want you here—why don't we go get Christmas decorations and trees? Then we won't look like we belong on another planet."

"How about after dinner?" Holly suggested, a sparkle lighting her green eyes. "All of us. Like a big party."

Evan rolled his eyes. "Please tell me this doesn't mean we'll be descending en masse on Walmart?"

Holly grinned. "Think how it would boost your image." She held up a hand like she was reading from a banner. "Evan Richardson, commonwealth's attorney, relates to the common man."

"And I am accomplishing this by buying Christmas decorations at the local discount giant?"

"Well yes," Holly deadpanned, "but we'll help you and Jake's image by buying trees at different places—one from the Presbyterian church's Boy Scout Troop lot, and one from the Mission Outreach lot the Baptist church is sponsoring."

Evan tilted his head and stared at Holly, "Are you sure you're an accountant? Is there a minor in marketing in there somewhere?"

Holly laughed. "No, but I am catching on to how this small-town thing works."

* * * *

Jenny closed her office door and laid her head against it. She had just explained to an elderly woman that her husband of more than fifty years was unlikely to recover. The stroke he'd suffered had left him in a vegetative state. Jenny had called the woman's son and daughter so they could be with their mother and help her make the necessary decisions about their father. His living will requested nothing be done to prolong his life, so Jenny was sure they would ask that life support be removed.

She hated this part of her job. She'd pursued medicine to save lives, not end them. She clenched her fists and squeezed her eyes shut. Each loss was a reminder of her failure to heal herself. Oh physically, she was fine. Emotionally she'd never been the same after she lost her baby, then lost Evan.

She rubbed her temples with shaking hands.

When her office phone rang, Jenny slipped it from its cradle. "Dr. Owens."

"Jenny, my dear," the voice on the other end was as smooth and cool as a python wrapping around its victim, "you appear to need a reminder about our agreement."

Jenny squeezed her eyes shut and her gut twisted. Hearing his voice was like being sucked back into hell. "Good evening, Senator Richardson."

Several minutes later, Jenny disconnected the phone call and fought the urge to vomit. The urge to get in the shower and wash away the sleaze quickly followed. How could someone like Stoner Richardson be Evan's father?

Stoner had made the warning clear enough. Stay away from his son or he would make sure Evan saw every one of the payments the senator had made to her over the years. Jenny shuddered. When had life become so sordid? When had it changed? But she knew the answer. After all, she'd seen the video.

Stoner possessed a video of her being gang-raped by several members of the high school basketball team, but thanks to clever editing and the drugs her own father had given her, it didn't look like a rape. She appeared to be a willing, if not very active, participant. Worst of all, Jenny still couldn't remember the event, only what she'd been shown.

She sat in the dark for another quarter hour. She had told Holly she'd be there by six-thirty, but it was six-thirty now. Evan would be there, an Evan already changed from just a few days ago. This Evan snuggled babies against his chest and volunteered to change diapers. But she recognized this Evan. She had attended high school with him and fallen in love with him all those years ago.

Her hands clenched into fists.

Jenny wanted that Evan back, but could she risk everything to get him? Could she go through that pain again? Stoner would show him everything and make it look like she was not only a tramp, but a cold, calculating mercenary bitch. At the time, Evan had believed what they'd wanted him to believe. If she risked it all again, would the result be any different?

Jenny shrugged off her white coat and grabbed her wool overcoat and purse. She had returned to Mountain Meadow because it was home, but also to lay ghosts to rest once and for all. Screw Stoner Richardson. She would lay it on the line, and if Evan didn't want her... Well, she'd figure something out.

Chapter 9

"Let's wait a few more minutes," Holly suggested. "Maybe a patient kept her late, and she hasn't been able to call." Evan knew she was trying to put a good light on it, but a bone-deep cynicism, planted twelve years ago, blossomed once more.

"Don't, Evan," Holly murmured. "Don't be so hard on her, so hard on yourself. You have no idea how much you've both changed in just a few days."

Jake stood right behind Holly. Evan saw her reach back to find his hand. He and Jenny weren't the only ones who had changed.

Jake met his eyes. "The hospital has been busy the past few days."

"Yeah."

Evan stared once more out the window just as her car stopped at the curb. *She came.* She *was* just running late. He was embarrassed by the relief flooding through him. He swallowed to ease the tightness in his throat. "Jenny's here," he informed them. "I'll get the door."

Something was wrong. She looked...beaten. He couldn't think of any other way to describe it as she grabbed her bag from the passenger side and trudged along the walk. He flung open the door, wanting to wrap her in his arms, and knowing it was a right he no longer had.

"Jenny?"

When she saw him, her entire demeanor changed. One soft smile and his world shifted. "I'm sorry I'm late."

When she reached the top of the steps, he put his arm around her shoulder. "Tough day?"

"More than you can imagine." She relaxed against him for just a moment, and he closed his eyes as he inhaled her familiar scent. Feeling the years slip away, he leaned back to grin at her. "We have a surprise for after dinner," he told her, "but if you're too tired once you hear what it is, we could volunteer to baby sit and stay behind."

She shrugged as if to say it didn't matter, making Evan wonder if there was more than work bothering her. Her expression was still wary. Jenny was subdued as they all sat to eat, but Holly and Jake's happiness was catching, and she began to relax. As they finished the meal, Tyler told her his fears of being scrooged to death if they didn't rectify the situation and decorate. When Holly explained the public-relations aspect to their proposed shopping trip, Jenny finally smiled.

"I like it, particularly since I heard through the grapevine Jake threatened to punch one of the church ladies in the nose."

"Jake," Holly said. "Can't you go to hell for that?"

"It's far more probable he'd be promoted to archangel, if you ask me," Evan commented.

Jenny squeezed his arm. "I would write him a recommendation letter if he took on the church ladies." She laughed. Her eyes met Evan's for just a moment, and he smiled at her.

While Holly nursed, Evan and Jake cleared the table, and Jenny loaded the dishwasher. Tyler was assigned the job of clearing out the back of Jake's truck so they'd have a place for their purchases.

* * * *

Jake glanced from Evan to Jenny, his hands in his pockets. While he wrapped his right hand around the ring box nestled there, he cleared his throat. "Um. If you'll excuse me for just a minute, I'm going to check on Holly." When they just grinned at him, he beat a hasty retreat and padded up the stairs.

Holly was just switching Noelle to her other breast, so Jake lounged in the doorway.

"I will never tire of watching you with her. You're a wonderful mother."

"You're prejudiced."

Now was his opening. Jake swallowed, crossed the room, and knelt in front of her. His heart beat so hard he was afraid he might choke. He could do this.

"I look at you and I see the mother of my child. That's how I see Noelle. I helped bring her into this world. But I see more…a strong woman who refused to let circumstances beat her. I see a woman who's brought laughter and joy to me and my friends."

He stopped for a moment and swallowed. When his eyes met hers, Holly's lips parted. He wanted to hold onto her and never let her go. He wanted her to stay with him forever.

"A week, Holly," he whispered, "and I feel like we've already experienced a lifetime. I want a lifetime with you."

"Jake?" Holly's voice shook.

He dug in his pocket and brought out the small velvet box. Her eyes widened. Noelle had finished nursing, so Jake took her while Holly readjusted her clothing. He put the baby to his shoulder and burped her before settling her in her crib so he could finish what he'd started. When he turned, Holly still held the closed box in her hand. God, he'd never been this nervous in his entire life.

"Open it," he urged. "It was my grandmother's."

She flicked the lid back to reveal the sparkle of an emerald ring surrounded by small diamond chips. "It's beautiful."

He brushed her cheek with his fingers. "I could give you candlelight and music at some restaurant. We've never even been on a date. But these moments here with you, Noelle, and me will be so fleeting, and they're so precious. I love you, Holly. I want to marry you just as soon as you say you will."

His last words were hoarse, so he cleared his throat, his heart hammering as he waited for her answer. When chagrin flitted over her expression, his breath caught. She was going to say no. And how the hell would he deal with that? He needed to say something. "I know we haven't known each other long, but I don't think that will change a thing."

"Oh, Jake. I love you. I didn't expect it. I didn't want to...but I do. I would marry you tomorrow, but we can't...you know."

He laughed in utter relief. Sex. She was worried about when they could have sex. "How long will it be before we can...?"

"I'll have to ask Jenny."

Jake's breath came out on a small, embarrassed huff. "Wow. That is one disadvantage of small-town life. It's a little awkward to think we have to ask one of my best high school friends when we can make love."

Holly giggled. "Put the ring on my finger. Jenny's a smart woman. She might figure it out if she sees it, so neither one of us will actually have to ask."

Jake, not much on long, personal conversations to begin with, grinned. "What a great idea. That's why I love you."

* * * *

Jenny's gaze zeroed in on the ring as soon as they came downstairs with Noelle. She caught Jake's eye, and he couldn't help the grin on his face, then she spoke to Holly. "The first time you walked into my office Holly, I took one look at you and knew you were perfect for him. And I'm so glad I was right." She kissed Holly on the cheek then hugged him.

Jake set her away from him suspiciously. "So the box of food..."

Jenny blushed. "Was just a way to throw you together." She grinned at Tyler. "Little did I know Tyler had already accomplished that."

The boy grinned and ran forward to hug Jake. "Cool! Does this mean you'll be my big brother?"

Jake returned his hug. God, he already loved this kid like the little brother he would soon be. "Yeah."

Evan stepped forward, kissed Holly's cheek and clapped Jake on the back. "Fast work, bro. Didn't know you had it in you. But you've got yourself one fine woman. You'll have to be sure to tell Sam."

Jake met his friend's gaze and arched one brow. "Am I the only one who'll have to confess something to Sam?" he inquired.

Evan's gaze slid to Jenny. "Maybe not."

Tyler bounced around them. "This calls for a celebration. And this time of year that means *Christmas decorations*...which we don't have. Cut me some slack here. I'm in fifth grade. Andrew Jones's house has *five* lighted reindeer out front, and one even moves its head. I'm losing face."

Jake and everyone else stared for a moment, then burst out laughing. Evan hooked an arm around Tyler's neck. "So you're saying this is a case of needing to keep up with the Joneses. Would that be correct?"

Jenny snickered and Holly giggled. Tyler glared at them, then replied, his expression serious. "Yes, sir."

"Well, by all means, then." Jake grinned. "Let's go shopping."

"Never," Evan drawled, shaking his head as if he were in pain, "did I think I would hear those words come out of your mouth. You are unmanning our entire gender."

"Stuff it, Ev. You'll find out soon enough."

They were still laughing as they piled into Jake's truck. While Holly and Jenny pushed carts, Holly carried Noelle in the sling Jenny had brought her. Lord, Holly was pretty with excitement putting color in her cheeks.

Jake trolled behind Evan and Tyler, who were like kids in a candy store, until Holly tugged on his sleeve.

"Should we be spending this much money?" she whispered, biting her lip and looking at everything in their cart.

Knowing he could, put a smile on his face mainly because he could do something to make her and Tyler happy. "Don't worry about it. I have income other than my salary from the town. We can afford it."

"Besides," Evan, who had caught up with them, added, "this is for two houses. Jake and I are going halves, and in case you hadn't already heard, my family's loaded."

Laura Browning

Holly's eyes rounded and she just laughed as Evan winked at her. With the decorations stashed in the back of the pickup, Jake drove to the Presbyterian Boy Scout Troop's tree lot. The minister happened to be volunteering, and half the church was there as well. He smiled as he peeked in at the sleeping Noelle, but his eyes settled on Evan and Jenny who stood next to each other behind Jake and Holly. Jake sucked in a deep breath of satisfaction. So the minister saw what he had.

"The doctor and the lawyer. It's good to see the two of you. It would be even better to see you in church on Sunday."

Evan flushed. "Point taken, Reverend."

They decided Evan would buy his tree there, and then they moved two blocks to the Baptist church's Mission Outreach lot. Jake helped Holly from the truck, his heart beating just a little faster when her eyes widened at the tree selection. She took such pleasure in everything.

As she cradled Noelle, she tugged Jake's arm. "Doesn't this smell fantastic?"

Pastor Joe approached, looking far more angelic than Jake knew him to be. He arched a brow at Jake before smiling at Holly. "Hi. I'm Pastor Joe. You're Holly, right? And this must be Noelle."

"You know me?" Her eyes widened even more, making Jake chuckle.

Joe grinned back at her, amusement sparkling in his sky-blue eyes. "Let's say I've already heard of you. Jake and you are the talk of the town."

"As I'm all too aware," Jake said with a grimace. He should be used to the gossip by now, but it sure was harder to take when you were the subject of it. "Joe...uh...plays cards with us sometimes. He's new around Mountain Meadow, too."

"Yep. My first church, but things are working out pretty well." He glanced at Tyler. "We're building our youth ministry. I love working with kids."

"Reverend Taylor," a voice Jake couldn't fail to recognize called from across the lot, "we need your help for just a moment to move a tree."

Jake spotted the hostile glare of Betty Gatewood. He smiled, eyes narrowing as he stepped closer to Holly and put his arm around her shoulders. She, bless her heart, tucked a strand of hair behind her ear and, knowingly or not, showed off the ring Jake had so recently put there. Joe's eyes followed the glint.

"Is that an engagement ring, Miss Morgan?" he asked with a tilt of his head as his amused gaze slid once more to Jake. No doubt about it. Joe would be telling Sam before even Evan could get to the phone.

Holly blushed. "Yes. Jake asked me to marry him."

"Well, congratulations. I love weddings, and I love officiating at them even more. Have you set a date? Maybe before the new year?" Joe smirked as he held Jake's gaze.

"No need to rush things," Jake mumbled and narrowed his eyes to glare at Joe.

Joe grinned in return. "I'd love to see you Sunday. If you'll excuse me right now, I better check on my other helpers."

The church ladies' eyes followed them as Holly and Tyler inspected several trees before picking one. Jake leveled a look on the knot of them gathered near the wreaths, but all they did was tighten their circle. Evan bought a pair of wreaths for the double front doors on his house, and then they all piled back into the pickup truck.

As Jake pulled out of the parking lot, Evan turned in the seat and asked Holly. "So was our combination holiday-shopping-and-public-relations excursion successful?"

"Oh I think so." Jake hoped so. And now that he had his ring on Holly's finger, he'd better hear a whole lot less gossip about her.

"How are we going to do this?" Jenny asked as they pulled into Jake's driveway. "It's almost ten now."

"Let's do Jake's house tonight and we can decorate mine tomorrow," Evan suggested. "We can make a party out of it."

"All right!" Tyler cheered. "Now you're getting the idea. It's Christmastime!"

Jake and Evan set the tree in Jake's living room, then satisfied it was straight, they trooped outside to fulfill Tyler's dearest wish by assembling three lighted reindeer for Jake's yard and three for Evan's. Tyler looked so excited, Jake wished he'd thought of decorating sooner.

The kid stood out on the sidewalk in between both houses. "Three, two, one," he called. "Light 'em up!"

Jake and Evan plugged in extension cords and a half dozen glowing reindeer now stood or grazed in the two front yards…and two of them moved. Tyler danced in circles. "Oh! This is so cool, dudes. You got to come see."

Jake joined Evan and Tyler on the sidewalk, and they all gazed in an ecstasy of male bonding over their electrical and mechanical feat.

"He's right," Evan said. "That is cool. My dad never let us put fun stuff like this at Richardson Homestead. Too undignified."

"Hmm," Jake agreed. "We never did either. We lived so far off the road, Dad didn't see the point. Who'd see it? But this is great."

"Yeah," they all said at once and stood for a moment staring at the glittering lighted deer and listening to the faint click and whine of the two moving ones.

"Who wants hot chocolate?" Jake asked.

"Me."

"Me, too."

"Let's go."

* * * *

Holly's eyes clouded just a bit as Jake boosted Tyler up so he could top the tree with a glittering angel. The clock in the hallway struck midnight as they all sat back to look at the tree's bright decorations and sparkling lights.

Holly sighed as she snuggled against Jake's chest. A month ago, she'd known she'd have no gifts for Tyler and feared she wouldn't have a tree. Now everything was different, largely due to the man who had his arm wrapped securely around her. "This is turning into the best Christmas ever."

Jake kissed her forehead. Tyler was curled at the other end of the couch, his eyelids drooping. Holly smothered a yawn.

"It's late," Jenny said. "I should get going."

Evan stood. "I'll walk you out." Holly shifted to show them out, but he held up his hand. "Stay where you are. We'll see ourselves out. You're all invited to my place tomorrow. Two o'clock. We'll decorate then grill steaks."

"Grilling in December." Jenny laughed. "Guys and grills."

When the door shut behind them, Jake searched Holly's gaze before he tilted her chin to kiss her. The shyness was all but gone from his hazel eyes, but oh the heat was there.

Tyler woke enough to look at the two of them, say, "Eww," and dash up the stairs to bed. Holly giggled and Jake chuckled, but his laughter stopped when she wrapped her arm around the back of his neck and pulled him down so she could kiss him again.

"Jenny said since I'm no longer spotting she thought we could be intimate in a couple more weeks."

"Mmm." Jake nuzzled her ear and slid his warm palm along her rib cage under her sweater. Holly loved the feel of his hands, slightly rough but amazingly gentle. She also loved the destination she knew he was heading to. "Did she say anything else?"

Holly kissed him, tugging at his bottom lip with her teeth. "Yes," she whispered against his mouth. "She said to be careful because you were a breast man."

Jake had just begun to rub the heavy globe of Holly's left breast and stopped. "I'll kill her," he growled.

"No." Holly smiled. "I like breast men, but only if they're named Jake."

"Are we allowed to play…?"

Her hand slipped to his belt. "Yes."

Jake groaned against her lips, pulling her with him as he lay back on the couch. His erection pressed into her soft belly. For just a moment, she stiffened.

"Hey." Jake raised her chin. "Everything okay?"

This was Jake, Holly reminded herself. Gentle Jake who would never hurt her. The knowledge gave her confidence. She nodded. As he threaded his fingers into her hair, Holly teased his lips with her tongue. He groaned again and held her still as his tongue plundered her open mouth. She tasted chocolate and inhaled the rich male scent of him, the tang of spice and musk all his own.

Heat pooled between her thighs, setting off a throbbing ache low in her belly, and now she was the one groaning.

Jake tugged at her sweater, pulling it over her head. His hazel eyes burned dark and hot as they raked over her naked breasts. As his gaze touched her, Holly's breath escaped in short, shaky gasps. He raised his head and captured one of her nipples between his lips. His suckling sent a shaft of desire to her very core and made her cry out.

Jake broke contact. "Am I hurting you?"

"Just the opposite." She sucked in a shaky breath.

Her breasts had never been sensitive, but now she was afraid if he touched her again she would go right over the edge.

"Holly?" he murmured.

"Do it again."

He teased her with the tip of his tongue and then took her once more into his mouth. Holly gasped, clutching his dark hair in her fists to hold him against her. Wave after wave of pleasure crested and crashed over her. Holly bit her lip to keep from crying out as she longed to. She sagged against him, burying her face against his neck. Jake stroked her back with his broad palms while her trembling eased and her breathing returned to normal. Only then did she become aware of his erection still pressing against her.

She followed instinct as she slid along the couch, her fingers going to the button on his jeans. She slipped it free and unzipped his fly, gazing at him. "Your turn," she whispered and wrapped her fingers around him.

"Oh yes." He sighed. She held his heated gaze as she took him between her lips. With her mouth and her hands, Holly soon had him gasping out his pleasure.

* * * *

Evan and Jenny reached her BMW. As she started to open the passenger door to put her bag back in, Evan stopped her, his arms trapping her against the car. "Would you like a nightcap? You could tell me about your tough day, and why you were so sad when you first got here. I listen pretty well for a cynical prick."

Jenny met his steady gray gaze. "Evan, I didn't—"

"You did. It's a small town, Jenny. Word gets round. Doesn't matter, though, because it's true. Or was. Come over. Have a brandy with me."

She studied his lean face. All she saw was sincerity, and she remembered her vow earlier to let him know everything so there would be no more lies or secrets between them.

"Okay."

Jenny was leaping off a cliff, but it had to be done. They couldn't remain where they were. Not if they were both going to live and work in Mountain Meadow.

Evan held the door for Jenny. She hadn't noticed the other night when she'd been searching for Evan what a beautiful house he owned. The wide front hall was two stories high with a large chandelier, and an L-shaped staircase. To the right was a formal dining room, and to the left a large living room. They didn't speak. Evan took her coat and bag, then dropped his arm around her shoulders.

"Come on, Doc. I'll give you a brandy and lend an ear."

Doc. Said in a purely conversational tone, yet it made her melt. "Do you know that's the first time you've called me Doc without making it sound like 'bitch'? It's always been either Dr. Owens, or Jenny."

He set two glasses next to each other on a silver tray and unstopped the decanter sitting nearby. He paused before pouring the brandy. "My way of keeping you out, I guess. As long as you weren't Doc Owens, you didn't have any permanence."

"Does that mean you've changed your mind?"

He handed her the glass. "I have. Have you?"

How should she play this? She had no idea because there was still so much *baggage*. Jenny sipped her drink. "I don't know."

He took her fingers and started to lead her toward the couch, but she shook her head. "I need to sit in a chair. There's a lot I need to say, Evan, and I can't be near you to say it. I have to be able to think."

She cringed, realizing just how much she had already admitted to him with that statement.

"Is this about today?" Evan's voice was gentle.

Jenny sighed. "Not really. But I'll start there." She took a sip of her brandy, hoping it might give her courage. While she formulated her thoughts, she stared into the flames from the gas logs he had lit. "I had to tell a woman today her husband of more than fifty years was not going to recover from his stroke. It's left him in a vegetative state. She's so lost, Evan. I called her children so they could help her make the decision to take him off life support."

She glanced at his quiet face, his features outlined by the glow of the fire and continued. "I got into medicine to heal others, because I couldn't heal me. I wanted to make other people's lives whole because mine had become empty and unbearable."

Jenny blinked tears from her eyes, but couldn't quite prevent the slight hitch to her breathing. When Evan started toward her, she waved him away. "No. If you touch me now, I'll never get all of this said. And it's important, Evan. It's important that all the lies, the secrets, and the deceptions come to an end." She closed her eyes for a moment to regain her composure.

"I thought for a long time I was sparing you heartache. I thought if I kept my mouth shut, life would just go on with you hating me as much as I hate myself. But I've seen how nasty and cynical you were with everyone." Jenny stopped and wiped her eyes. "You never laughed. You never smiled. You were just as miserable as me."

She sipped her brandy. "I thought about that earlier tonight because in the past week, you've been so much more like the Evan I fell in love so long ago. The way you've been with Noelle—it opened my eyes. I started thinking about what had happened and what you said the night you took me home."

"Jenny," he interjected, his voice hoarse. "It doesn't matter anymore."

"It does," she countered. "Because until you know everything, I can't go on. We can't go on. While I sat in my office tonight, my phone rang. The caller was someone I've heard from off and on over the years, reminding me of...things. When I ended the call, I was going to go back home and forget I promised Jake and Holly I would be there for dinner because I knew you would be there, too."

Evan's hand shook just the tiniest bit as he sipped his brandy. She let her gaze wander over him until she met his eyes. "But then I decided I would go. You see, over the past three days I've seen you fall in love with a baby. I've seen you go out of your way to help Holly and Tyler...and Jake. You were once again *my* Evan, and I want you back. I told myself I would tell you everything and let you draw your own conclusions." She was so afraid that what she had to tell him would rip them further apart.

"I'm listening."

Jenny swallowed the rest of the amber liquor and set the glass on the small, antique table next to the wing chair where she sat. Hands clasped together in her lap, she stared into the fireplace.

"The night I told you I was pregnant was the most beautiful night of my life." She began. "You were just as happy as me that we had created a life together. I hadn't suspected what the changes in my body meant, so by the time I knew for sure, I was almost three months along. Did you know a fetus at that stage can wiggle its fingers and toes?" A living being that had never really had a chance.

Evan's face went pale and taut. "Do we have to go back that far?"

Sorrow and pain flooded her. "Yes."

"Go on, then."

"After you left, I confronted my father. I told him I was pregnant with your baby. That we loved each other. He was furious. H-he slapped me, told me I was a slut just like my mother, and asked me if I wanted to end up like her. I told him I was going to be a doctor, and you were going to be a lawyer. He just laughed and said I was a *stupid* slut if I thought either one of us would be able to do that and raise a brat at the same time.

"I walked out, telling him I was going to leave. He must have called your father right afterward."

"What the hell does this have to do with my father?" Evan snapped, once again reverting to the cold, cynical man he had become over the years. A man like his father, but Jenny hoped to stop that tonight.

"Please, Evan. Let me tell the whole story, and then you can decide."

He sat back, but tension that was not there a few minutes earlier now tightened his posture. "All right."

Jenny quaked with fear she dared not show. If he wouldn't accept his father's role in this mess, she would lose. *They* would lose. Taking a deep breath, she continued. "The next day, you asked me to meet you at Mercer's. I got ready and told Daddy I was meeting some girlfriends. After his reaction the night before, I was afraid to tell him the truth. He fixed dinner, but I didn't think anything about it. He did on occasion. I didn't want to make him any angrier, so I ate. He'd made fresh tea, and I craved liquids. I swallowed the first glass fast like I often did, and then ate some of my supper."

Jenny stopped, swallowed, and tucked her hair behind her ear. "By the end of the meal, I was dizzy and confused. It scared me because I thought there might be something wrong with the baby. I told Daddy, and he suggested I lie down in my room. I admitted I was supposed to meet you, and he promised to let you know."

"He never called," Evan stated. "I waited at Mercer's for two hours before I drove to your house, afraid something had happened."

Jenny's mouth twisted. "Something did. Only I didn't know it. I was out cold. The next thing I knew, at the time, was waking the next morning. I was in my bed...naked...and starting to cramp. I called Daddy, but he didn't answer. When I dragged myself from bed, I discovered he'd left to run moonshine across the state line." She paused, her eyes locked on the fire as the horror of what happened flooded through her. The pain of that day would never go away. No girl should have to face what she had. "I stumbled into the bathroom because the cramps just got worse. It hurt so much I doubled over. Something was wrong. I put my hand between my legs and when I brought it back there was blood." Jenny stopped, trying to compose herself before she continued. "I needed to call Doc, but another cramp hit. I crouched...and I passed—"

"Jenny. Stop." Evan's voice reverberated with pain.

"It was our baby. A little girl. She was so tiny, but everything was there. Arms, legs, fingers, and toes."

"Stop!"

She ignored him. She had to. If she didn't say this now, she'd never be able to do it again. "I just stared for a minute, and then I got a towel and put her in there. I thought maybe if I could get to the phone, maybe Doc could put her back..." Jenny paused and sighed. "Stupid, but I was just a kid and I was in shock, I think. It didn't matter. Daddy had seen to that. He'd cut the phone line before he left. I went back to the bathroom and held her while I bled. It stopped after a while, so I got dressed." Jenny shivered. "I was weak but afraid to leave her there, so I put her in the wooden chest you'd given me for Christmas. I padded it with material so she'd be nice and warm."

Jenny stopped. She sobbed, and with tears still streaming down her face, continued. "I carried the box and a shovel up the hill to the spot under the tree where you and I used to go to make out. I dug a hole for her and buried her. She would have been a Christmas baby had I carried her to term."

Evan tossed back the rest of his brandy and stood. His movements were jerky and uncoordinated. "Please, Jenny. Stop. It happened a long time ago."

"Don't you see? It's still happening, and you need to know it all. I'm sorry if it's painful for you, but it's not easy for me either."

"No," he choked as he poured them both more brandy, "I can see that."

She took her glass and sipped. She stared into the flames for a while, lost in memories. "I'd cleaned the house by the time Daddy returned. I didn't tell him what happened. I was afraid he'd make me dig my baby up and throw her away." Jenny's jaw clenched. "He fixed the phone line as soon as he got back. After all, he did a lot of business over it. So I tried to call you, but your mom said you'd gone out. I tried to call the next day, but you still weren't there. When I missed graduation, I was surprised you didn't call. By Sunday, I knew something was going on, so I walked through the woods and got old man Crawley to give me a ride to your house."

"And I was washing my car," Evan supplied.

"You looked so strange," Jenny whispered, "as if you hated me."

"I did. I wanted to kill you." His expression now reflected some of the pain he'd felt then, plus a bone-deep remorse.

"I understand now," she murmured, "but I didn't then. I told you I'd lost our baby and all you did was laugh and say, 'Our baby?' in such a cold, hateful voice. Something started to die in me. Then you started in about how it could be yours or half the basketball team's for all you knew, and how I'd probably gotten rid of it."

"You ran away, down the drive," Evan recalled. "I was furious. I went wild. Took off in my car and left town."

Jenny closed her eyes, forcing her breathing to even out. "I didn't have that option, not then. I walked back to town and stopped by Doc's house because I had started bleeding again." She paused when Evan released his breath on a huff. They had made so many mistakes. "He examined me. I told him about the baby, but he said I had bruising and tearing consistent with sexual assault, and he started questioning me." She laughed without humor. "Of course, I couldn't tell him anything because I didn't know what had happened. I'm sure Doc thought I was protecting you, but since I wouldn't say anything, he couldn't do anything. I knew something must have happened the night I was supposed to meet you, but no matter how hard I tried, I couldn't remember. I asked Daddy, but he denied anything happened.

"I admitted I lost the baby and you broke up with me. He hugged me and kissed me and told me how sorry he was." Jenny's voice tightened with the rage she'd suppressed for so long. "He *drugged* me and sicced those boys on me. Then he told me how sorry he was, but now there'd be nothing to stop me from going to Carolina. He'd saved enough to send me there—so he said."

"You don't think it was his money?" Evan frowned.

"I know it wasn't. Now. At the time, I needed to believe, so I never questioned it. He told me everything on his deathbed. Even then, I didn't want to believe, but when I tried to return the next payment deposited into my account, the first phone call came."

"Phone call from whom?" Evan asked. Jenny wasn't sure what she heard in his voice. Doubt? Trepidation? Dawning knowledge?

"Your father."

"Impossible." Evan denied. The way his expression began to close off again made Jenny plow ahead.

"I vowed never to tell you this," she whispered. "There'd been enough pain. We'd lost our child. We lost each other. My relationship with my father was destroyed long before he confessed what he did. There was no point in telling you and destroying your relationship with your father. But it won't go away, Evan. Even after all these years, it keeps coming up."

Evan stared at her, his gray eyes narrowing. "Who called before you left your office?" he demanded, then answered his own question. "My father? What did he say, Jenny? Tell me what he said."

"He told me to stay away from you, not to even think of trying to reestablish our relationship because he had plans for you, political aspirations. And the daughter of a mountain moonshiner didn't fit. Then he reminded me of our agreement."

Evan recoiled. "What agreement? When did you make any agreement with my father?"

Jenny stared into the fireplace. "I agreed to meet him after he called the first time. I was in my last year of medical school, waiting to hear about my residency. It's a very political thing. I'd gotten some excellent recommendations, but I knew all that could go up in smoke. One word from a U.S. Senator, and I could find myself practicing medicine in some obscure Central American village." Jenny swallowed. Surely Evan could understand. After all, his job was an elected position. But then he had never had to live hand-to-mouth as she so often had. His future had come with the backing of a United States senator. How could he understand unless she laid it all out there?

"We met at a bar and grill in Winston-Salem, where I was going to medical school. He had his laptop. I didn't understand why at first. He insisted on getting a booth in the back corner. He made me slide in first, and then he slid in next to me," Jenny shuddered. "I nearly panicked, feeling I was trapped.

"He left the laptop closed to start," she continued. "His hands, so like yours, were folded on top of it. He explained his money had gone into my account each and every month. He'd paid for my education and my living expenses at Carolina, and he was paying them at Wake Forest."

"Why would he do that?" Evan asked in confusion.

"That's what I wanted to know. Your dad told me my father called him all those years ago and told him I was pregnant, and then demanded to know what he intended to do about it. Your dad told him he wanted us split up. So they joined forces. My dad would break us up, and your dad would pay for my education.

"According to Daddy, your father got him the drugs. Daddy claimed once I passed out, the boys were just supposed to strip me and themselves, shoot a video, and allow you to walk in and see us all together."

"Shoot a video?" Evan echoed.

Jenny shuddered. "Yes. Except after you left, so did Daddy, and the boys, who were just supposed to clean up and go home, decided they couldn't pass the opportunity. After all, you'd had exclusive use of me for four years. Not only was I captain of the cheerleading squad, but I was a stuck up little bitch who thought she was better than everyone else."

The old frustration made her grip the arms of the chair as though she could rip them apart. Why couldn't she remember?

"Did they tell you that?" Evan gaped.

"No. Your father did. He said it had been edited from the original video so it would look like I was willing."

"He showed you a video of them gang-raping you?" Evan's question was so appalled, Jenny almost denied it just to save him more pain, but then she remembered she'd promised there would be no more lies.

"He had it on DVD on the laptop." Just saying it out loud made her want to vomit.

Evan's face flushed and his hands clenched.

"He showed me after I told him I wouldn't take his money, and I was going to the police to report all of it. Someone would do something, even if he was a senator. He told me if I ever tried to approach you or anyone with what happened he would be able to show I had taken money from him for eight years, and if he needed to, he would go public with the video of my little sex party."

Jenny downed the rest of the brandy. "So now you know it all." She had bared everything. Like a condemned man, she could now only await her fate. She set her glass on the table, feeling some relief, but also incredible emptiness. Evan showed so little emotion. She wondered if he'd heard her at all. "I put a headstone on our baby's grave. It's not very big, but then neither was she. I named her Hope Richardson. She should have been our Christmas baby."

Jenny smoothed her hand along her sleeve, as if the movement might somehow soothe the turmoil inside her.

Evan stood near the window, looking out at the lighted reindeer in the front yard. The clock over the mantel chimed one. Jenny stared at it. "I should go. It's—it's a lot to think about."

When he didn't turn she swallowed past the lump choking her. Turning on her heel, she grabbed her coat from the hall tree and hurried to the door. She had gambled and lost. The story was far-fetched and based on the word of a dead man. Stoner Richardson would never admit his part, and she couldn't remember any of it. Yet she asked Evan to believe the absolute worst of his own father.

Jenny was empty. She had nothing left. Nothing at all.

Chapter 10

Evan was still trying to process everything when Jenny grabbed her coat. The lack of expression in her eyes bothered him. The front door opened. He had to stop her. He was across the living room and into the front hallway in a few long strides. With one hand on her arm and the other on the door, he prevented her from opening it any farther.

"Don't go," he ground out. "Please, Jenny."

She dropped her bag and he reached for her, pulling her against him.

"How you must hate my family," he stated. "How you must hate me."

"No," she protested, before admitting, "I did for a while. Then when I came home, I realized I wasn't the only one damaged by all this. You hurt, too, but I thought telling you would make it worse."

Her hands crept up until they fisted in the cashmere sweater he wore. Her trembling became shudders and she cried as if her heart would shatter. Evan kicked the door closed and held her, rocking her against him as he had Noelle over the past two days. And it struck him just how traumatic this past week must have been. He remembered her face when she'd walked in and seen him holding Noelle, so at ease with the infant, as if she were his own. They'd had their own baby...or would have.

Evan's eyes closed and his throat tightened. He stroked Jenny's hair and back, and when her crying didn't stop, he carried her into the living room and sat on the couch, her slight weight curled against him.

"It's going to be all right. I promise. Everything will be all right." And then he lost it too and tilted his head back against the back of the couch. Tears leaked from the corners of his eyes, but he continued to soothe her. "Don't, honey. Please, forgive me. Forgive me for seeing what they wanted me to instead of believing the girl I loved."

She touched his cheek. "Don't, Evan. Don't cry."

"I want to see her grave in the morning. Will you take me?" He needed the reality of it.

"Yes."

They stared at each other, their breathing uneven and choked. He inhaled her scent and closed his eyes. Like being fourteen all over again, he experienced the same overwhelming attraction and remembered what heaven was like the first time he'd kissed her.

"I want you, Jenny," Evan said in a shaky voice. "Is that bad...to want you right now?"

"No." He read passion in her golden eyes. It might have been twelve years since he'd last seen it there, but he had no trouble recognizing it. "I can't think of anything except getting you skin to skin." He growled. "I need to feel you. I need to heal you...and me. My feelings never left, they just got twisted. Our parents twisted what was a wonderful, beautiful thing, and I fell for it." The pain poured from him, but Jenny held him. He needed his catharsis as much as she had.

"When you came back, looking so cool and unapproachable, it just reinforced all the lies my father fed me. I attended your party to taunt you. I wanted to make you pay for all the suffering *I* had gone through." He stopped and buried his face against her hair, a shudder of remorse shaking through him "How can you even stand to look at me?"

"I love you," Jenny said. "It never went away for me either. It just... froze...like me. I haven't been with anybody since..."

"Don't," Evan stopped her. "That doesn't count. You weren't a participant, you were a victim, and Jenny...There is no statute of limitations on sexual assault in Virginia if it involves a felony."

She laid a finger across his lips. "Not now. We can talk about it later."

Evan ran his fingers through her short hair. "Come upstairs with me."

She nodded, and he carried her up the wide steps, not setting her down until they were inside the master bedroom. He slid her coat down her arms and kept his eyes on her face as he undressed her. They stopped often to kiss, heat flooding him like he was a kid, but his body no longer belonged to a lanky eighteen-year-old. A thick mat of hair covered his muscled chest and stomach. Hers was no longer the rounded form of a teen. She was fine-boned, sculpted, more slender in her arms and legs, and more voluptuous through her breasts and hips.

He touched her in wonder, rediscovering and arousing new hunger. When they were both naked, he lifted her and wrapped her legs around him. She excited him as no other woman ever had. He held her with his hands splayed on her back as he bent to kiss her throat then her breasts. His erection pressed hard and throbbing against her belly. A flush of desire stained her cheeks and made his own arousal skyrocket.

"I don't want to wait, Evan. I need to feel you inside me."

He lifted her higher. "Then put me there, Jenny," he rasped.

She reached between them, guiding the tip of his cock to where she was already slick and wet. They both groaned as they touched. He pushed inside, completing and healing them, and he wanted it to last forever.

* * * *

Tyler bounded into the kitchen the next morning and plopped himself at the table. Jake paused in playing with Noelle while Holly added the finishing touches to cheese omelets.

"Doc Jenny's car is out front," Tyler informed them, "but I don't see her anywhere."

Jake's gaze collided with Holly's as she carried Tyler's plate to the table. Jake said, "I think she said something about checking back in on Evan this morning."

Tyler shrugged. "Whatever. Seems kind of weird, though, to park in front of our house." He shoved a bite of omelet in his mouth, smiled, and polished everything off in record time. After gulping his glass of orange juice, he announced, "I have to go. I told the Tarpleys I'd be over first thing this morning."

"Don't forget we're supposed to help Evan at two this afternoon," Holly called after him.

They waited just a heartbeat after the door shut behind Tyler before they were both running to the living room window to look out front. Sure enough, Jenny's car sat where she'd parked it last night for dinner. Holly chewed on her lower lip. "I hope everything's okay."

Jake put an arm around her shoulders. "I hope everything's better than okay. The fact her car is still sitting there is a good indication it is." He sighed.

"What's wrong?" Holly asked in sudden concern.

Jake looked woebegone. "I bet he doesn't have to wait two weeks or more to…you know."

Holly sputtered with laughter. "Jacob Allred! You're not supposed to think about your friends doing that."

"All I can think of is doing that, except *I'm* not allowed to with the woman *I* love."

Holly felt a blush heat her cheeks and glanced at the baby resting in her arms. "Noelle's asleep again. We could try some of those creative alternatives like last night."

"I thought you'd never suggest it." Jake's hot gaze dropped to Holly's breasts, and he whispered in her ear. Her eyes widened and she smacked him.

"Jake! That's just wrong." But there was a twinkle in her eye. Oh, yeah, she was on board with a little playtime, and so was he, as his body was making more than obvious.

He followed her upstairs, his eyes admiring her derriere. As soon as she closed the door to the nursery, he arched a brow. "How about a shower?"

Holly frowned in confusion. "All right, but I thought you wanted to…"

Jake grinned. "I do, but we can play in the shower. It's big." His hands were already plucking at the zipper of her robe as he slid it down with a snick that echoed in the silence of the room. "You have far too many clothes on."

He loved the way her lids dropped over her vivid green eyes. His fingers stripped the robe from her and then slid the straps of her gown off her shoulders. When the material caught on her breasts, he leaned forward to tug it away with his teeth.

"Oh…Jake…" she whispered.

With a soft growl he carried her into the bath. While he adjusted the shower with one hand, he caressed her with the other. When the temperature suited him, he stripped off his clothes and stepped with her under the steamy spray. Lord! He was afraid he'd come before they even got started. The steamy heat made her milk let down, a drop of pearly liquid hovering like dew on her nipple. He licked it away with his tongue, smiling as Holly gasped and clasped her fingers in his hair.

Jake cupped her bottom, pulling her hips against him so his cock nestled against her while he bent to cover her mouth in a deep kiss that left them both panting.

"Touch me, Holly," Jake muttered against her lips. "These next weeks can't go by fast enough."

She wrapped her hand around his shaft and stroked while he fondled her breasts and teased her nipples. Her touch made his legs tremble and he leaned against the shower wall, his skin attuned to the glide of her hands, and the pulse of the shower spray. When she knelt in front of him and covered him with her mouth, Jake lost control, his fingers twining in her hair as he climaxed.

He sagged against the shower wall, then felt for her arm. After pulling her to her feet, he hugged her tightly.

"What about you?" he muttered. "This can't be all about me. I don't want it to be."

Holly put his hand on her breast. "Then touch me here."

He smiled. "Gladly."

* * * *

Jenny and Evan made love almost until dawn, their bodies never seeming to get enough of each other. After the first time, when they couldn't think of anything but getting as close as possible, Evan mentioned birth control and the fact he had nothing. Their eyes met in the glow from the reindeer still lit on the front lawn, and what he saw in hers told him it didn't matter.

"I want to give you another baby," Evan whispered at one point during the night. He pictured her growing large with their child, a child he'd move heaven and earth to protect this time.

He watched her, worried it might be too much, too soon. When she smiled, her feelings shone through. "Yes, Evan. This one conceived at Christmastime."

Her smile transformed him, making him feel years younger. He kissed her on the forehead, and they slept. Now a new day had arrived, one he hoped would bring them even closer together.

"Good morning, sleepyhead."

Jenny stretched and sighed with contentment, then groaned. Like him, her muscles must have been protesting at all the ways they'd moved and bent last night. "What time is it?"

"A few minutes before nine. Don't move. I have to get something, but I'll be right back."

He walked naked to the dresser on the other side of the room, grabbed what he was after from the top drawer, and sauntered back.

"You're beautiful." Jenny whispered.

Evan laughed. "I'm glad you think so. Now close your eyes."

Jenny did, a small smile playing around her mouth. He turned her hand up, setting the ring on her palm. She swallowed, and her hand trembled. "Okay. Now you can open up."

She stared into her palm where a simple marquise-cut diamond in a white-gold setting rested, the cool metal already absorbing the warmth of her skin. She said nothing. Tears gathered in her eyes and she blinked. "Evan?" she choked.

This was so much more intense than he'd imagined, but then everything between them had always been intense. "It's the same ring I planned to give you twelve years ago. I kept it. My grandmother gave it to me to give to you. I had it sized. I don't know if it will still fit, or if you even want it. God I'm making a real botch of this." He stared at the case. "Marry me, Jenny. Please. As soon as we can. We've already wasted so much time.

And if this ring brings back too many bad memories, we'll buy a new one for a new start…"

She touched his lips with her finger. "It's perfect." She slid it on and found it still fit. "It does bring back memories, but only good ones, Evan."

He crushed her to him. "I love you so damn much I ache with it. I wish I could melt into you so we would never again be apart."

"That sounds like a serious illness, but fortunately, I know just what to prescribe."

"And what would that be, Doc?"

"A regimen of love, kisses, regular sex, and maybe a few of our own squirming bundles of blankets will do the trick. But I think it fair to warn you there is no cure, so the treatment must continue your whole life."

He lowered his mouth to her. "And beyond," he whispered.

They ate breakfast in bed, licked the crumbs off each other, and made love one more time before they showered together.

"Take me to see Hope," Evan said once they were dressed. He had to face this one part of their past. Jenny had lived it, but he needed to know it in his own way so they could move forward.

"Okay," Jenny agreed. "It's a hike up the hill behind my house, so I'll need to stop and change."

He nodded. "Grab some clothes so you can spend the night here. We'll go to church in the morning."

When they at last climbed the hill, Evan's hand trembled as he knelt, traced his fingers over the engraving, and read the words underneath. "Like our love, born too soon. You will always be our best and brightest Hope."

His voiced cracked. Evan struggled with the emotions buffeting his big frame, but in the end he lost. His broad shoulders shook and he covered his face with his hands. "I'm sorry. I'm so sorry. If I had only believed in you."

Jenny leaned over him and wrapped her arms around his back. "We can't live with what might have been. We have to move forward. We have a chance to start again. We have Hope. We have her inside us."

Evan pulled her onto his lap. Jenny wiped his face and held him until he found the inner core of strength that had helped him get through so many other rough spots. He smiled and blew a breath out between pursed lips. "'Wow!' as Tyler would say. If anyone in my office saw me now, they'd have me committed once they got over the shock."

Jenny smiled. "No. They'll love the new-and-improved Evan just as much as I do."

He touched the tiny headstone again. "Let's get married soon. I want to start a family," he glanced at her with a wry expression, "if we haven't already."

Jenny glanced at her watch. "It's almost noon. You told Jake and Holly to come over at two."

Evan glanced at his own watch. "Shit! I don't have a scrap of food in the house."

"You mean the toaster pastries we had for breakfast won't be enough?"

"Smart ass."

They walked hand in hand down the hill and drove to Tarpley's. As soon as the door jingled and Susie Tarpley saw the two of them hand in hand, she bustled around the counter and gave them both a big hug.

"This is a sight for sore eyes. Oh heavens. Jim," she called to her husband. "Come here. You have to see this."

Evan and Jenny blushed as every eye turned their way. Jim rounded a corner and his lean face broke into a wide smile. "Evan Richardson and Jenny Owens. And is that a ring I see on her finger?"

Susie held Jenny's left hand. "It is." Her knowing gaze lifted to Evan. "Your grandma's, isn't it?"

"Yes, ma'am," Evan answered. "We've taken a few detours, but Jenny's agreed to be my wife."

"That's wonderful, son," Jim Tarpley clapped him on the back. "I'll take that as a sure sign all's gonna be right with the world this Christmas."

"What can we help you with?" Susie asked.

Jenny grimaced. "Everything. I've seen his kitchen. There's no food in it, and we have guests coming over in less than two hours."

Tyler poked his head around the end of the aisle. "I'm one of them, and I'm starving."

Jenny sent Evan to get drinks, and Tyler followed him with a cart. As Evan added two bottles of wine and a twelve pack of beer, the boy commented, "I like ginger ale. Since you and Jenny are engaged now, like Jake and Holly, does that mean Jenny's car was outside our house all ni…"

"So where is the ginger ale?" Evan interrupted as he clapped a hand over Tyler's mouth. He grinned weakly as Pastor Calloway's wife walked past, her lips pursed, but Evan hoped that really was a twinkle in her eye.

* * * *

Jake was installing a peephole in the front door when his cell phone rang. He saw the station's ID.

"Jake here."

"It's Ernie. Look, I know you're off this weekend, but I thought you should be aware we've had some more activity with the nativity."

Jake rolled his eyes at Ernie's attempt at a play on words. His boss should try the stoic route. It worked for Jake. "More toilet paper?"

"No. This time someone stole the baby Jesus and the manger from the Presbyterian church, but that's not all."

Jake sighed. "There's more?"

"Yep. Our thieves also got away with Mary and Joseph from the Baptist church."

"What makes you think we're dealing with the same thieves? Couldn't it be rival church-lady gangs? I heard they've been moving along the interstate."

Ernie was laughing so hard from the other end Jake had to hold the phone away from his ear.

"Oh Lord, Jake. Anyway, the church ladies have formed a posse. A mixed group from both churches is out canvassing the neighborhoods."

Jake slapped the phone back against his ear. "I'm sorry. Did you just say ladies from both churches are *together* canvassing town?"

"Yes."

This was bad. There could be bloodshed. "I'll get my uniform and be right in. I think I still have a couple of flak jackets in my storage building. I'll bring those and the billy clubs too."

"Jake?"

"Don't worry, Ernie. I'll be there to help."

"Jake."

"What?"

"They're at Mercer's drinking tea and munching doughnuts. Together."

"Wow." Jake sagged against the pillar, his mouth hanging open.

"You could call it a Christmas miracle. And I have one more for you."

"What's that?"

"I just watched our commonwealth's attorney and Doc go into Tarpley's together. Holding hands."

Jake grinned. "That one I already knew. They left our place last night at midnight, and Doc's car was still out front this morning."

"So have *you* popped the question?"

Warmth spread through him as he thought of Holly. "Yeah. She said yes."

"Have you set the date?"

"New Year's Eve." Jake told him.

"That's mighty quick."

"Not quick enough."

"Maybe you can do it together. You know, you and Holly, Evan and Doc. A double wedding."

Jake chuckled. Wouldn't that just make Sam Barnes's day? "That's a great idea."

Holly was inside using his computer to work on accounts for her boss while Noelle slept in a basket nearby. Jake paused in the doorway to study her a moment. The faintest crease knitted her brows, and she had a pencil tucked behind one ear.

"Ready to hang out your shingle yet?" he joked.

She grinned. "I think I'd like to hold off until the sign can read 'Holly Allred.'"

He smiled. "Evan and Jenny are official. That's the word from Ernie. He thinks we should do a double wedding."

Holly laughed. Jake was beginning to see the sister Tyler had tried to describe to him. She did have a way of surrounding herself with happiness. He wasn't sure how, but he did know he would do almost anything to keep her just that way.

* * * *

Jenny opened the door to Jake, Holly, Noelle, and Tyler just after two. Evan stood right behind her. Jenny took one look at all their faces and glared with mock ferocity at Tyler. "You told. You promised you wouldn't tell."

"Jake already knew," Tyler protested. "By the time I got home, it was old news. Everyone in town knows. I'm surprised it's not already being broadcast on the local radio station."

Jake coughed. "It is. I heard it, along with our engagement, while I was shaving."

Jenny ran her finger over her smart phone. "It's already on Facebook, too. You can thank Susie Tarpley for that."

For a second, they just stared at each other, and then Holly started laughing. "I love this town. I love everyone and everything in it." When Jake, Jenny, and Evan just stared like she'd lost her mind, she continued. "Don't you see? Everyone *cares*!"

"Cares?" Evan scoffed. "Everyone wants to stick their noses in everyone else's business is more like it."

"No," Holly commented. "In a bigger town, no one knows you so they don't have to care. I had to come here before anyone bothered to lift a finger to help Tyler and me—and we had grown up in Lynchburg."

The discussion continued inside the house with Jenny backing Holly. They continued their debate while they set Evan's tree and trimmed it. Finally Evan said, "Okay. For argument's sake let's say you're right Holly. Everyone in Mountain Meadow does care at some level. If that's true, then explain why someone swiped the baby Jesus from the Presbyterian nativity, and Mary and Joseph from the Baptist manger scene."

"No!" Jenny exclaimed. "That's terrible, Evan. Is it true, Jake, or are you and Evan just pulling our legs?"

"It's true. Ernie told me this morning. He even said the Presbyterian and Baptist church ladies were out together canvassing the town to find them."

"Hah." Holly pounced. "There you are then. That proves I'm right."

"Someone stealing Jesus proves you're right?" Evan asked. "I'm afraid your logic has even me muddled."

"Let me explain."

Jake and Evan crossed their arms across their chests. Even Jenny was doubtful. "It does seem to be a bit of a stretch."

Holly grinned and sat on the floor next to Noelle's infant seat. "The thieves have an ulterior motive. They're building their own nativity which is a combination of the Presbyterian and Baptist nativities."

"So this is like a church merger?" Evan tried to puzzle out the next step.

"Yes." Holly smiled as if Evan were her prize pupil. He checked to see how many beer bottles he had already emptied, concerned he'd consumed more than he thought. "The thefts have brought the two groups of church ladies together, uniting them in a common goal so they can put aside their differences. It's genius."

"It's insane," Jake drawled. "I'm still throwing a couple of flak jackets into the back of the truck to take into work on Monday if the missing manger figures haven't reappeared. I can't see where this truce will last. I've already had Betty Gatewood and her fleet of flowered dresses breathing fire at me."

"Maybe it's a generational thing," Evan surmised, studying Holly as if she were some sort of exhibit. "After all Holly, you're what, twenty-one or twenty-two?"

"Almost twenty-three," she mumbled.

Tyler passed by on his way back to Evan's study where he had discovered a gaming system hooked to a large-screen TV. "Her birthday's Christmas Eve. Mom and Dad named her Holly because her birthday was so close to Christmas. Kind of cool, don't you think?"

Jake, Jenny, and Evan stared at Holly, who blushed in embarrassment. "Thanks, Tyler," she muttered.

"Anyway," Evan went on with an even bigger grin. "We're almost thirty-one. There's eight years, so maybe it's a generation gap that makes her so optimistic."

Holly stared at him. "That's a bunch of bull—"

"Holly!" Jake exclaimed, and even Evan raised his brows, afraid his penchant for profanity had rubbed off on her when he'd never heard her say anything more than hell, and only in context of the actual place.

"…headed pessimism if I ever heard it," she continued with a mischievous grin at Jake. "It's not generational, it's attitudinal. You choose to be pessimistic. I choose to be optimistic and believe in peace on earth, goodwill toward men."

Evan looked skeptical. "I've had a lot to be pessimistic about."

Jenny took his hand. "But we've both learned a lot in the last few days about how important it is to believe. So for the sake of the season, maybe we should try to look at it from Holly's perspective."

Holly just smiled. "You'll see."

Evan fired the grill around six. Impending snow hung in the air again, but it didn't deter either him or Jake. They leaned against the patio's brick wall, sipped beer and waited for the grill to heat.

In the kitchen, Holly nursed Noelle. Jenny set the salad on the table and sat across from them.

"You don't mind if I watch, do you?" she asked Holly.

"Not at all. My breasts seem to have become public property."

"I bet Jake likes that." Jenny chuckled.

"Jenny."

"Well. He was always going on about breasts in high school. I just figured he was fixated."

Holly giggled. "He is."

Jenny's mouth dropped open and she laughed so hard she had to wipe her eyes. Evan walked in to grab the steaks. "What's so funny?"

Holly smiled. "I was just telling her about Jake's fixation on breasts."

Evan blushed and stuttered, backing out of the door with the platter of steaks in his hand. Jenny smiled. "He is," she said, deadpan, and they both smiled at each other. Jenny looked back to where Noelle was suckling her second course, her little hand resting against Holly's breast. "She's nursing well, Holly. Don't forget your one-month checkup. I'll bet Noelle will have gained a lot of weight. She's doing great from what I can see."

"Thanks. Can I ask you something personal?" Holly inquired.

"Okay."

"In the hospital, you saw Noelle's name on the birth certificate and looked like you'd seen a ghost. Why?"

Jenny blinked. "I never talked about it until last night when Evan and I aired it all. I was expecting his child back in high school. A lot of things happened, but to make a long story short, I miscarried near the end of my third month. I held her in my hands." She smiled at Holly through the tears in her eyes. "A perfect little girl. She should have been born at Christmas, and I didn't want her to be forgotten, so I gave her a name— Hope Richardson."

Holly's mouth parted in surprise. "Oh, Jenny. I'm so sorry, and then you saw Noelle's middle name. But Evan never said anything."

"He didn't know. Not until last night. It's a long, ugly story that will probably have to come out, though I wish it didn't."

"Why will it have to come out?" Holly asked. "No never mind. You don't have to tell me."

"I do. You're a friend. So's Jake. It involves a felony sexual assault... on me. There is no statute of limitations, and Evan's an officer of the court. Now he knows about it, he's obligated to pursue it. I guess the only blessing is Jake won't have to investigate it. It happened on my father's farm, where I live now, and that's in the county. Sam's jurisdiction."

Holly held Noelle to her shoulder. Jenny smiled and held her arms out. "May I hold her while you're putting everything to rights?"

"Of course." Holly laughed. "The way she nurses, I might as well walk around topless."

Jenny glanced outside where Evan and Jake were laughing at something one of them had said. "Not a good idea. That would be way too distracting."

"I'm so happy it's working out for you and Evan. Have you set a date?"

"We're thinking New Year's Eve," Jenny said, "and we wanted to know if you and Jake would like to make it a double wedding."

Holly grinned, touched by the way Jenny and Evan had pulled her into their circle. "Jake mentioned that. We could celebrate our anniversaries together... well part of our anniversaries."

Jenny winked. "Evan wants to start a family right away."

"How do you feel about that?"

"I would love nothing better, especially now Evan is an experienced diaper-changer."

They laughed.

Chapter 11

"Begging for forgiveness or launching another assault on community good will?" Evan asked as they left their house at the same time as Jake and Holly. Where everyone was headed was pretty obvious.

Jake and Evan were in suits, Jenny and Holly in dresses. Tyler had his long hair pulled into a neat ponytail and Noelle was a big bundle of blankets in the infant carrier. The baby had already managed to wiggle a little sleeper-covered hand out of her warm wrapping. She waved it around, making Evan smile.

He cocked a brow at his friend as he jingled the keys to Jenny's BMW. "Which church?"

Jake grinned, "Into the lion's den…Baptist."

Evan laughed. "Presbyterian. Shall we compare notes to see if our nativity thieves have generated unity?"

"Good idea. Then we can report back and see if Holly's goodwill meter is spiking."

Holly stuck her nose in the air. "Make fun of me. I'm telling you other forces are at work. Things you non-nativity-season humans just can't understand."

"Come on," Jenny reminded them. "Let's go before we arrive late and ruin the image we want to project as solid citizens instead of lost souls living in sin."

"What's living in sin?" Tyler wanted to know. "Is that what they call the noises I hear at night?"

Evan barked with laughter and both Jake and Holly blushed to the roots of their hair.

* * * *

The members of the Presbyterian church welcomed Evan and Jenny with open arms. Mrs. Tarpley was one of the first to greet them.

"I told you yesterday, but I'll tell you again, it sure is good to see the two of you together."

Evan kissed her cheek. "It's good to be here with the love of my life. Where is the love of your life?"

Mrs. Tarpley smacked his arm with her church bulletin, her eyes twinkling. "You know Jim and I have agreed to disagree. He goes to the Baptist church, and we've still managed to stay married all these years."

Several glances came their way during the service. Evan stretched his arm out along Jenny's shoulders while they listened to the sermon, and she scooted closer to him when they sang so they could share a hymnal. More than a few sighs went up from older women happy to see the two back together again and younger women disappointed to see the county's most eligible bachelor was off the market.

Two blocks down, reactions were mixed, but for the most part Jake and Holly were also warmly welcomed. Betty Gatewood was one notable exception, but then Jake figured having a police lieutenant tell her he would like to punch her in the nose would have a dampening effect.

Pastor Joe welcomed them with enthusiasm, shaking Tyler's hand and letting the boy know they had a church youth Christmas party that evening he was welcome to attend. Tyler's enthusiasm increased when he noticed their neighbor, Alex Scott, in attendance with his parents.

"Could I go with Alex if he's going?" he asked Holly and Jake. Holly nodded and smiled. Jake saw such a difference in Tyler just in the last week.

"You've brought the whole family," Jim Tarpley greeted them with a smile before clapping Tyler on the back. "Mornin', son. You're looking mighty spiffy."

Tyler grinned. "You, too. Where's Mrs. Tarpley?"

Jim chuckled. "You've discovered our secret. Mrs. Tarpley is a Presbyterian," he said the last word in such a stage whisper Holly and Tyler both laughed, drawing several glances. "She enjoys her church and I enjoy mine, and we've managed to get along just fine."

"Hmph!" Jake snorted. "Wish more people took the same attitude."

"Oh, I think we're getting there. Why I saw a group of ladies from both churches sipping tea and munching doughnuts at Mercer's just yesterday," Jim said with a smile. "There's nothing like the Christmas season to bring folks together. That's what I always say."

Holly's smile was huge as she elbowed Jake. "I said the same thing just yesterday, Mr. Tarpley. There should be more people like you."

"The Christmas season or holiday larceny?" Jake arched a brow and Holly just shook her head.

Pastor Joe preached an inspiring sermon on the need to love thy neighbor. From just behind them, Jake heard a woman mumble, "Seems some folks have taken that to heart."

When he glanced over his shoulder, his gaze met a censorious look from one of the women who had come to his office along with Betty Gatewood. Jake smiled, wrapped his arm around Holly's shoulders, and pulled her close against his side. Holly flicked a quizzical look his way, before refocusing on Joe's preaching.

At the end of the service, Holly picked up Noelle. "If you'll excuse me guys, I'm going to take her to the ladies' room so I can change her diaper before we leave."

"We'll wait for you in the vestibule," Jake said, leaning down to pet Noelle's tiny head with its dark curls.

* * * *

Holly smiled at the woman who held the door open for her. As she had hoped, there was a small sitting area providing her with a place to set her belongings so she could change Noelle. She had heard the woman in the pew behind them and her comment. She had also seen the way Betty Gatewood had glared at them Friday evening and again this morning. And, as Holly had already observed, Mrs. Gatewood was in the restroom fluffing her blue-tinted curls and repairing her makeup.

Holly smiled. "I'm sorry to bother you, but would you mind holding Noelle for just a moment while I get everything set to change her diaper." The older woman looked as though she wanted to refuse, but with the baby already halfway in her arms, she had no choice but to grab her. As Holly worked she chatted. "Thank you so much. Everyone has been so kind to my brother and me since we came to Mountain Meadow. Tyler's had a tough time. Our folks were killed in a car accident just a year ago at Thanksgiving."

"How terrible." Mrs. Gatewood responded.

That didn't sound sincere. Holly would have to work a little harder.

"Then when Doc Owens ordered me on bed rest, I was so worried. Mr. Crawford let me work from home, but of course my hours were cut. I hadn't worked there long enough to qualify for leave." She paused, glancing over her shoulder, where the older woman had now shifted Noelle to her shoulder and was bouncing her. The baby cooed in her ear. Holly grabbed a clean diaper.

"Then the Tarpleys were kind enough provide my little brother with groceries in exchange for doing odd jobs for them, and Doc sent Jake out to help. He chopped wood for us." Holly stood and smiled as she held out her arms for her daughter. "I don't know what I would have done without him," she finished, making sure the older woman saw the ring sparkling on her finger. "My phone was out when I went into labor, and he showed up with Tyler and helped deliver Noelle when Doc told him the weather was too bad to move me."

Holly smiled into Mrs. Gatewood's softening expression and added, "You must be very proud to live in a town where people look out for each other and know what it means to 'love thy neighbor.'"

The woman puffed with pride. "Yes. Yes, I am."

Holly beamed at her. "Thanks again for holding Noelle. Family and friends are the most important things we have."

"Yes, they are." Mrs. Gatewood smiled at Noelle's wiggles as Holly unsnapped clothing to get to the little girl's diaper. "You know the church auxiliary runs a children's clothes closet. You should stop by to see if you can find anything for the baby. Most of the baby items for one as tiny as your precious little girl are almost brand new."

Holly laughed. "A wonderful idea, Mrs. Gatewood. Thank you. I will do that."

"Call me Betty. You have a blessed day, dear," the woman said as she left with a smile on her face.

Holly changed Noelle's diaper and smiled at her daughter. "Always remember, my precious little daughter, the message of the season... peace on earth, goodwill toward men, but then you already understand Christmas magic, don't you sweetie? Just like Mama."

She was humming Christmas carols when she met Jake and Tyler. Jake arched one thick brow. "Are you all right? I saw Betty Gatewood come out of there with a smile on her face, and I was afraid she might have spitted, roasted, and eaten you."

"We had a lovely conversation, Jake. She told me about the children's clothes closet the church runs. I said I would stop by some time this week. You know, we should bring my car over."

He was staring at her as if something about her just seemed to puzzle him. "I'll send one of our guys out to get it."

"Jake?" Holly asked as Tyler walked on ahead of them.

"Hmm?"

"I love you."

He put his arm around her shoulder and smiled at her. "I never would have imagined even one week ago how much my life was going to change all because of you and Noelle."

* * * *

"Can you run me by the courthouse on your way to the clinic this morning?" Evan asked Jenny as they curled into each other in the aftermath of making love Monday morning. Evan could hardly believe it. Jenny was here by his side where she belonged. He touched the golden cap of her hair and skimmed his hand from her back to her bottom. Man, he wanted her again.

"Mmm. Not if you keep doing that."

"Why?" he murmured.

"Because we'll never get out of bed, much less to the car."

He chuckled. "You're right. And I need to get into my office. I've been out two days and had to continue the Hairston trial."

"The DWI case involving the family from Hillsville?"

"Yeah. I was hoping to have it wrapped up before Christmas, but now I'm sure it won't be back on the calendar until January."

Evan stood and stretched, and Jenny's gaze roved over him.

"I will never get tired of looking at your body," she told him. "You've got a great ass...no doubt from all those years of basketball...long, long legs and those feet."

He caught her staring. "Feet aren't the thing most women want to stare at," Evan commented and chuckled.

"They're the biggest thing on you," Jenny shot back with an arch of her brow. He huffed and laughed.

"I guess I opened myself up for that one."

Jenny rolled onto her back and put her arms above her head as she stretched. "You did. Mmm. I guess I should get up too."

Evan ogled the firm thrust of her breasts beneath the covers. "We could shower together."

"Not a chance, Richardson." Jenny laughed. "I have patients scheduled first thing this morning."

A few brows raised when Jenny's red BMW halted at the curb in front of the county courthouse. Evan leaned over and kissed her. "I'll see if I can't get one of the county vehicles until I get the insurance settled on my car. Then you can help me car shop. I was thinking maybe an SUV or a minivan. We can fill it with car seats."

He laughed when she blushed, grabbed his briefcase from the backseat, and got out. Before he shut the door, Evan leaned down and smiled at her.

His step had a little extra spring as he took the steps to the front door two at a time.

God, I love her.

It struck him just how much his life had changed in the last few days, and how by chance it had. If he hadn't agreed to help Jake move Holly's belongings, who knew how long he and Jenny would have continued avoiding each other except for the occasional lurch into open hostilities. Holly and Noelle, the spirits of Christmas. Maybe there was something to Holly's belief in peace and good will.

Evan opened the door to the main office and stepped through. Conversations halted, almost as if someone had thrown cold water on the whole group. He looked around at the clerks and his assistants. Did he really have such a dampening effect on their moods? Had he been as cold and sarcastic as Jenny described him?

He smiled at everyone. "Good morning!"

A nervous cough came from the youngest clerk, then Wanda Sue Gardner stood. "Welcome back, Mr. Richardson. I hope you're feeling better."

Evan's fingers touched the bandage still covering the stitches Jenny had put in his head. "I am, though I can't say the same thing for my car."

There was more silence in the office. Were they scared of him? When had he become such a monster? But he knew the answer, and knew things were going to change from now on.

"Is it true?" Wanda Sue continued. "Are you going to marry Doc Owens?"

Serious faces, hardly daring to show curiosity, regarded him. He smiled again and saw them shift nervously at what must be an unaccustomed action on his part. "Yes. It's true. Jenny Owens and I are going to get married." Just admitting it in public filled him with euphoria.

He grinned then and laughed. Another nervous titter slipped from the young clerk and then the whole office was laughing and congratulating him. Evan accepted their handshakes and hugs and the warm sense of belonging missing before. As he closed the door to his office, he decided the change was for the better. He'd do his best to make sure it stayed that way.

Still, some things couldn't be avoided. There was a twelve-year-old crime for which he needed to ensure someone paid. He pulled a pad of paper in front of him and began making notes. He would need his father's bank records, Jenny's bank records, and *her* father's as well. He would need a statement from Doc Baxter and access to Jenny's medical records.

Most of all, he needed the video. And he would have to be careful. Evan now suspected the man he'd spent so many years trying to please was not at all who he thought him to be. The man Jenny described would have no compunction whatsoever destroying evidence if he sensed a threat. Evan would have to be very, very careful.

He drummed his fingers on the desk, realizing he needed to talk to her. She was smart enough to know that now he knew about it, pursuing prosecution was his job. He could not ignore the commission of a felony. This, he thought, was going to get a whole lot uglier before it was over.

Evan grabbed the phone and punched in a number. "Sam, it's Evan. You got a few minutes to talk?"

"Sure, Evan. I've always got time for you. Come on. One of my deputies just got back from Mercer's with fresh doughnuts, and I made coffee. Good stuff, not that swill Jake and Ernie drink at the police station. We can drink to my apparent psychic powers. Just when are you and Jake tying the knot?"

"Bite me. I'll be right down."

Evan walked out of his office whistling "Jingle Bell Rock" under his breath and could have sworn everyone in the outer office caught their breath. He stopped, stared at them all, and snapped, "Oh for heaven's sake! I'm happy okay? I have not acquired some fatal disease."

"Sir?" Bill Fields, his senior assistant ventured.

"What?"

"We're just a little shell-shocked right now."

Evan stared at them all. "Was I that bad?"

Wanda Sue and Bill nodded, and soon everyone else had joined them. He frowned. Damn. He must have become a real son of a bitch without even realizing it. He had become his father. The thought entered his brain unbidden...and very unwelcome. With a flip of his coattail, Evan pulled out his money clip and grabbed a credit card.

"Do we have any cases in court today?" he asked.

"No, sir," Wanda Sue answered.

He handed her the card. "You and Bill, go get Christmas decorations and let's make this place look festive. Get some snacks, too. We'll have a party...on me. Now, I gotta talk to Sam about something. I'll see you later."

Bill looked at everyone with a puzzled expression. "Does anyone else feel like they've just awakened in London on the day after Ebenezer Scrooge was visited by the ghosts?"

After just a short silence, Wanda Sue snickered and soon everyone was laughing again.

Evan rolled his eyes.

"Whatever," he said, and left.

* * * *

Sam Barnes sat back in his plush leather chair. He was about Evan's height, but broader and brawnier, closer to forty than thirty. He'd played football for Tech for a couple of years before an injury sidelined him, and he was already in his second term as county sheriff. He'd been running for reelection when Evan had run for commonwealth's attorney.

He gave Sam a couple of minutes to bask in the glory of being right about him and Jake before he launched into the real reason he'd sought him out.

"That's one hell of a story, Evan," Sam said, rubbing his chin, "but it sounds like you have enough evidence to go after the rapists and your father. The key is that video if Jenny doesn't remember what happened. You need to consider a few things before we go ahead with this, Evan."

"Sam, I don't have a choice. I have to proceed. I'm an officer of the court and I know about it. Besides the fact I would be in violation of the oath I took to uphold my office, it's the right thing to do."

"Even if it puts your father behind bars?"

Hearing it put so bluntly made him want to cringe in denial, but he had a job to do.

Evan clenched his jaw. "Yes. I'll have to recuse myself from the case and request a special prosecutor. Any suggestions? I'd like to make sure it's someone competent who's also not been touched by my father's rather long political reach."

"Let me think about it."

"One other thing, Sam." Evan sighed. "If my father gets wind of this, you can bet your bottom dollar he'll destroy any evidence he can."

"Then we'll have to get all our ducks in a row, quietly and quickly. Let's keep this just between you and me until we ready to make the arrests. When we do, we'll need some additional help. I'll have to bring Ernie and Jake in to assist with any arrests inside the town limits."

"No problem. Listen. My parents are holding their annual holiday party this Saturday. I've been trying to avoid them, but I could go."

"You can't take the evidence, Evan."

"I know," Evan mused, "but I might be able to get him to give it to me."

"How?"

Evan's smile wasn't pleasant. "I would need Jenny's help, but I have the feeling that won't be a problem, not after what he's put her—us—through."

* * * *

Jake took off his ball cap and scratched his head as he stood next to Pastor Joe, staring at the nativity. Someone had swiped Melchior, one of the three Wise Men. Jake had just come from the Presbyterian church where both Balthazar and Gaspar, the other two Wise Men, were also missing. This was just getting stranger and stranger, but there did seem to be a pattern.

"I'm beginning to think Holly's right," Jake admitted.

"In what way?" Pastor Joe asked.

Jake chuckled. "We were talking about it Saturday. Evan and I maintain it's just thieves, but Holly has a different theory."

"What's that?" The young minister dug his hands in the pockets of his down vest as he stared at his denuded nativity.

"You have to understand, Holly has come to believe in the goodness of man since she came here. She thinks the thieves are trying to bring the feuding between the Baptists and the Presbyterians to an end. Somehow, she believes all of this has a larger purpose that will be revealed."

Joe laughed. "Well, we can only hope she's right. But I must tell you, there's been a lot of bad blood between the two congregations over the years. It was one of the first things I heard about when I came to town."

Jake eyed his fellow poker player. He looked more like he'd come straight from the farm than the pulpit, but both worked well for him at the card table. "I take it you don't subscribe to that, though."

Joe tilted his head and smiled. "You were in the congregation Sunday. You heard my sermon."

"Point taken."

"Holly seems to have found another fan," Joe added as he dug his toe at the metal spike that had anchored his missing wise man to the ground.

"Who's that?" Jake studied the blank spot where Melchior had stood between the other two wise men.

"Betty Gatewood."

Jake's head jerked back to Pastor Joe's face. "I'm sorry. Did you just say *Betty Gatewood* was saying nice things about Holly?"

"Indeed. She was the one who discovered the theft this morning. When I mentioned I would contact you, she said she'd spoken with Holly yesterday, and how lucky someone with your volatile temperament was to have found a woman as sweet and kind as Holly Morgan."

Jake blinked. Well it appeared even if she hadn't softened toward him, Betty Gatewood had changed her mind about Holly. He grinned and snapped his cap back on his head.

"Well. That's pleasant news indeed, Joe. I'll have my men keep an eye out for the Three Wise Men, as well as Jesus, Mary, and Joseph. But to be honest, I'm beginning to think we might have to wait a while to see where Bethlehem turns out to be."

The young minister arched a brow. "You thinking they're all going to turn up there in a stable?"

Jake grinned. "Seems likely at this point. You want me to beef up patrols?"

Joe rubbed his cheek. "I suppose. My congregation will expect that, though I must say it would be nice to subscribe to Holly's theory."

Jake laughed. "This time of year is special for her. Noelle's original due date was the twenty-fourth, which happens to be Holly's birthday."

"Holly and Noelle. Christmas angels."

Jake smiled. "That's how I think of them."

Chapter 12

Thursday evening, the Mountain Meadow Town Council was slated to accept Ernie Jones's resignation and appoint a temporary chief until council members could complete official hiring procedures to fill the vacancy. Ernie attended along with Jake, and most of the small police force. Sam had also shown, and despite Jake's protests, Holly was there with Tyler and Noelle.

The council read Ernie's resignation letter and voted to accept it with a note added into the minutes thanking Chief Jones for his years of service. At that point the motion was made and seconded to appoint Lieutenant Jacob Allred as temporary police chief until such time as applicants could be reviewed and a new chief hired. When the mayor asked if there was any discussion on the motion, Betty Gatewood's husband John cleared his throat.

"I'm not sure Lieutenant Allred is the right man for the job. We need someone in the position of chief who is an excellent police officer and can also relate to the public in a positive way." Gatewood paused.

"Are you telling me," Councilman Les Gardner interjected, "you believe the man who delivered Holly Morgan's baby all by himself by candlelight in the middle of an ice storm is not capable of projecting a positive image for the town and the department?"

"He had two flashlights, too!" Tyler jumped up to add before Jake could haul him back into his seat. A nervous chuckle went through the crowd, which Jake now noticed had ballooned to standing room only. He spotted Evan and Jenny in the back and nodded at them.

"He threatened to punch my wife in the nose," Gatewood exploded.

One of the church ladies who had accompanied her whispered into the silence following Gatewood's outburst, "I thought Jake said if she were a *man* he would have punched her in the nose."

"The fact remains," Gardner spoke, "he did not punch Mrs. Gatewood in the nose."

"He should have," someone else in the crowd whispered. "I heard she said unkind things about Jake's Holly."

Every eye glared at Betty Gatewood, who blushed furiously. Jake rested his gaze on the painting of the courthouse hanging over the mayor's head and struggled to keep a straight face. This was turning into a farce. Just when it seemed it could get no worse, the door burst open and the ministers from both the Baptist church and the Presbyterian church entered looking breathless and flushed.

"The thieves have struck again!" Pastor Joe exclaimed.

"They've taken Mary's donkey," the Presbyterian minister informed them.

"And Melchior's camel," Joe added.

The mayor banged his gavel as everyone in the chambers spoke at once. Jake rose to his feet and let out an earsplitting whistle that immediately silenced the room and made Noelle begin to squirm.

"Let's table the matter of our temporary chief until our next meeting on the twenty-ninth," the mayor said. "We can settle it then."

The motion was quickly amended, seconded, and voted on unanimously. Jake leaned down and kissed Holly and Noelle.

"Sorry, honey. I'd better take a look. Evan and Jenny can run you home. Stay at their place until I get there. I don't want you at the house alone at night." Although he was beginning to believe they had nothing to fear from her ex-fiancé, Jake didn't want to take chances. It simply wasn't worth it.

"You have a job to do." Holly smiled and her eyes twinkled. "I wonder where they'll set their ecumenical nativity?"

Jake laughed. "Still stuck on the thieves with a grand-plan theory, huh?"

Holly grinned. "You'll see. You just need to have faith."

Getting everyone in Jenny's BMW was a tight squeeze, especially with the infant carrier. After Evan strapped it in, he unfolded from the car, looked at Jenny archly and said, "Definitely an SUV. One of those big ones with the additional backseat so we won't have to move all the child seats."

Jenny blushed and Holly giggled as she inquired, "How many child seats are you planning on needing?"

Evan grinned at her. "Three or four. We can always do hand-me-downs for the younger ones."

Laura Browning

Jenny made choking noises and Tyler thumped her on the back. "You okay, Doc?"

She nodded, narrowing her eyes on Evan, "Very funny, Evan. It's not nice to antagonize your doctor, especially right before she takes your stitches out."

"Cool," Tyler said. "Can I watch?"

* * * *

Spence Dilby sat in his rental car a few houses down. The cop returned home a few minutes later and headed for the house next to his. With nimble fingers, Spence twisted the cap on the hip flask he carried and swallowed another mouthful of scotch. Good. They were beginning to relax. The first couple of days, they had been cautious and watchful, especially the big cop. Jake somebody. Spence couldn't recall his name offhand, but who cared? He did wonder why they seemed to be on the alert. Then he realized it must be Holly's kid brother. Spence had followed him after school the second day, when he realized the kid didn't come straight home, and discovered he hung out at the hick store on the square. Tyler must've seen him. That was the only reason they would have cause to be so careful.

By now, Spence was getting comfortable with their routine. Every morning, the cop and the tall guy next door ran a pretty predictable route. This morning was the first day a marked car hadn't patrolled the street while they were out. A good sign they were letting their guard drop. If that continued, it might be the best time to snatch the kid. With the older kid working in the afternoons, Holly and the baby would be alone.

He'd already stocked the car with an infant seat, diapers, bottles, and formula. From what he'd seen the couple of times he'd snuck close to the house, Holly was breast-feeding. The whole idea revolted him. After all, who wanted to go to bed with a cow? But it should be easy enough to switch the kid over to a bottle.

Spence sat back. Yeah, this would work out great. He could take the baby. After all, she was a Dilby, and he and Seely would have a family without the inconvenience of pregnancy to interfere with getting sex from Seely whenever he wanted. Her not being able to have kids made her the perfect partner from his point of view. He could screw his eyeballs out whenever he wanted and not have to worry she'd get knocked up.

Just thinking about it made him hard. Spence started the car and drove to the truck stop by the interstate. He'd already found a couple of hookers who worked the parking lot there. They'd blow him for a twenty.

* * * *

Evan's cell phone rang early Friday afternoon while he was handing a list to Wanda Sue of the six men he would have Sam and Jake arrest, along with his father. Jenny might not remember the actual events, but she did remember who she'd seen in the tape, and Evan certainly remembered.

"Run criminal checks on each of these guys, and see if you can start the ball rolling to access bank records for them from about twelve years ago. And, Wanda, it goes without saying. No matter whose names you see there, not a word to anyone." She nodded and Evan punched his phone. "What's wrong, Holly? Everything okay?"

"Yes. I just wanted to invite you and Jenny over to our house for dinner."

"What did Jenny say?"

"She was in with a patient so I haven't been able to reach her."

"I'm sure she'd be delighted," Evan said smoothly. "What time do you want us to come over?"

"Six would be good. I have a roast cooking."

"Mmm. With potatoes and carrots?"

"Of course."

"We'll be there. How's my very best surrogate niece?"

"Growing like a weed, Evan. Thanks for asking."

"Do I get to play with her when we come over?"

"Of course."

"You know, darling, next to Jenny, you are the woman of my dreams."

Holly laughed. "Sorry, big guy. I am very taken with a certain dark-haired cop."

He replaced the handset to find Wanda Sue staring at him. "What?" he barked.

"Are you on happy drugs?"

"Of course not."

Wanda Sue just nodded and went back to work.

* * * *

When they arrived, Jenny carried her medical bag with her. Jake raised his brows when he noticed, and she grinned. "I just figured while I was here, I would perform Holly and Noelle's two-week checkups. It's just a day early, but they both seem to be thriving."

"Does that mean?" Jake hinted hopefully.

Jenny punched him in the arm. "No! You still have to wait, but I should be able to give you a better idea of how long," she added when she saw how forlorn his expression was.

When Evan laughed, Jake glared at him. "Just wait, bro. You won't be laughing nearly as much when it's you who's twiddling your thumbs."

"What's this?" Holly asked as she came in from the kitchen.

"Sex." Jenny said. "Jake's still trying to jump the green light."

Holly's cheeks pinkened. "Is that possible?"

"We can talk about it after dinner. I brought my bag so I could go ahead and check you and Noelle."

"Oh good!" Holly blushed when she met Jake's steady, heated stare.

During dinner, Jake entertained everyone with the activities of the now firmly united Nativity Canvassing Committee, comprised of church ladies from both the Baptist church and the Presbyterian church. They still determinedly marched door to door to inquire if anyone had sighted Mary, Joseph, the baby Jesus, the Three Wise Men, the camel, and the donkey.

Jake shook his head in exasperation. "I still have to clear it with Ernie, but I'm considering adding another officer this weekend so we can keep watch over the shepherd and his sheep."

Holly chuckled. "I thought the shepherds were keeping watch over their flocks by night, not Mountain Meadow's finest."

Jake laughed along with everyone else, but his expression was thoughtful.

While Jake, Evan, and Tyler cleaned the kitchen, Jenny followed Holly and Noelle upstairs. After shutting the door to the master bedroom, Jenny set her bag on the dresser.

"Let's examine you first while Noelle sleeps," Jenny suggested, all business now.

After ascertaining everything was going well with the breast-feeding, Jenny palpated Holly's abdomen. "This is good. You're almost back to normal. Any more bleeding?"

"Just some very isolated spotting, nothing heavy."

Jenny performed a pelvic exam. "Your cervix and perineum look good. You didn't experience any tearing. I have to say, your recovery rate amazes me. The thinking is changing on the issue of when it's okay to begin sexual intercourse, but the consensus is you should wait at least three to six weeks. For some women it takes longer. With what I see and feel, I can't see any reason why you can't go ahead." She paused. "It really depends on how you feel."

"I'd like to. That is we…" She stuttered to a halt and blushed.

Jenny patted her leg. "It's okay. I'll give you the go-ahead, but with a word of caution. Avoid any positions that would give him especially deep penetration. If you feel any discomfort…stop. You might need additional lubrication, so be prepared. Just do me one favor…don't tell Jake until after we leave. I'm afraid he might throw you over his shoulder and carry you right back upstairs while we're still here…just a little too much information for me. After all, he and I did go to high school together."

Holly giggled.

"Seriously," Jenny continued. "There are precautions you need to think about. Despite the myths, you can get pregnant while breast-feeding, and you will ovulate *before* your first period. So use birth control. And remember…take it easy."

Holly smiled. "Jake will be over the moon."

Jenny laughed and hugged her. "I suspect he's not the only one. Now let's take a look at baby girl."

* * * *

Jake caught Holly's gaze when she returned. His eyes narrowed. She glowed. There was no other word to describe it. His glance slid from Jenny back to Holly again and he swallowed. Had she given her the green light? Almost more than he could hope, and he wanted to ask her but knew that would be too rude. His eyes rested on Holly again as they all grilled Tyler about his Christmas list. There was definitely something different in her demeanor. His cock stirred, making him shift a little uncomfortably.

As much as he enjoyed Evan and Jenny, Jake was anxious for them to go home. He watched the clock like a hawk. As soon as it hit ten, he signaled Tyler to get ready for bed. When Jenny grinned at him, Jake flushed and cleared his throat. Her reaction though, just made him more aroused. It had to mean she'd given Holly the all clear. He surreptitiously adjusted himself, wishing for once he'd worn briefs instead of boxers.

"We should be going, Evan," Jenny said with a wink at Jake that just made him flush. "I have to make rounds in the morning and find a dress for your folks' party tomorrow night."

Jake dug his hands in his pockets to hide his arousal as he and Holly followed them into the front hall. Tyler was already in bed, and as soon as the door shut behind Evan and Jenny, Jake pulled Holly into his arms and nuzzled her ear. "Is there something you need to tell me?" he whispered in a voice already husky with passion.

She twined arms around his neck, stared into his eyes and smiled. "Make love to me, Jake."

His body sprang to immediate attention. With a rumbling groan, he swung her into his arms and practically leaped up the stairs to the master bedroom. Once he pushed the door shut with his hip, he let her slide slowly to her feet and down the length of his already aroused body. He groaned again as she rubbed against an erection he was sure was the hardest one of his life.

"I'm sorry, honey, but I don't think I can wait for a whole lot of preliminaries right now," he growled and almost ripped his shirt off over his head.

As they frantically stripped clothes off each other, Holly blurted, "Jenny says we should take it easy."

Jake was panting as he pushed her on the bed. "Easy? Like, slowly to see how you react? Or are there things we're not supposed to do?"

Holly ran her hand over his stomach and his dick twitched in reaction. "No really deep penetration. She said something about that, but why don't I just tell you if something doesn't feel right?"

Jake nuzzled her neck and caressed her breasts with shaking hands. "Mm. Sounds like a plan. How's it going so far?"

"Good," Holly choked. "Really good. I haven't done this since…"

He didn't want to hear about Dilby. Not ever. "It won't hurt this time, honey. But if you feel any discomfort, tell me. I'll stop."

They were both breathing heavily as he scooted between her thighs. When he pushed into her, he sucked in a breath at how snugly she gloved him. Once he had fully sheathed himself, Jake simply waited, nuzzling her with his lips and stroking her with his big hands.

"Okay?" he murmured against her mouth.

"Yes, Jake. Oh yes."

"Not too deep?"

"No. It's good."

Relief poured through him. He ached with wanting her, so he began to move. Holly met him thrust for thrust. His passion intensified at the flush of desire coloring her cheeks and glazing her partially closed eyes. He held her hips between his palms and pressed deeper and faster. As she opened her mouth on a moan that only increased in volume, Jake covered her lips with his, swallowing her cries of passion. He found her watching him with the most amazed smile on her face.

"Oh, honey," he choked. "That's it. Watch me." He held her gaze as long as he could until his climax made him throw his head back. Everything inside him churned together, swirling and focusing on where his body joined hers, then exploding with pleasure and relief. As he collapsed, he rolled to his back, nestling her on top of him. "That was beautiful, awesome! I love you so much."

"I love you," she whispered back and leaned her cheek against his chest. He stroked her back and closed his eyes while their breathing settled and the pounding of their hearts slowed. She was his. Complete and utter contentment flowed through him. Dilby's shadow was gone.

"Uh, Jake?"

"What, sweetheart?"

"Jenny did say one other thing I forgot to mention in the heat of the moment." Holly swallowed. "She said we should use birth control."

Jake's breath caught and then he chuckled softly. "Next time. I'd like nothing better than having my baby growing inside you, but your body could use a little rest."

* * * *

"We'll get through this, darling," Evan assured her as he drove to Richardson Homestead Saturday evening. Evan took his hand off the steering wheel to lace his fingers with Jenny's.

She nodded tensely. The subterfuge of the part she would play this evening wasn't what bothered her. Simply seeing Stoner Richardson again made her cringe. The man was a snake. He gave her chills and made her want to hide. There was something so cold and flat to his eyes as if any human part of him had died years ago.

He had begun to infect Evan with iciness as well, but not anymore. Evan had changed. The cold, sarcastic cynic she'd faced outside old man Crawley's place had disappeared. Evan's gray eyes no longer stared at everyone with chilly remoteness; they glowed with laughter and passion.

"Evan? Are you sure you'll be okay overnight?" Jenny worried. "I don't like leaving you with him."

He glanced at her and smiled. "I'll be fine. No matter what else he may be, he is still my father. But I do want you away from there. I don't trust him with you, and I would prefer you weren't around when Sam arrives in the morning to make the arrest. It won't be pretty."

"I know," Jenny murmured, but she still couldn't shake a vague feeling of unease. It had begun earlier in the day when she and Evan went to her house to choose a dress. The choice was between a strapless red satin and a royal-blue silk sheath that was both classic and sexy. They had settled on the blue. As she'd gathered shoes, stockings, and lingerie, she glanced out the sliding glass doors of her room. Evan sat at the top of the hill, under the tree...right next to the headstone for Hope. Even from where she was, Jenny saw him stare pensively into the distance.

He'd been thinking about the coming evening. She hoped what they were doing was motivated by the desire for justice, not purely for revenge.

She had a hard enough time separating the two in her head, so she could only imagine what it must be like for Evan.

His profile now in the glow of the BMW's dashboard lights was lean and aristocratic, definitely not the boy she fell in love with so long ago, but a man with a goal in mind and a detailed plan on how to get there. No matter what, she would stand by him. She only prayed it wouldn't be to pick up the pieces of someone who'd destroyed his father and his family solely for revenge. In the long run, revenge had a way of destroying the very person trying to exact it.

When they turned into the long drive curving to the big house on the hill, Jenny and Evan both took deep breaths. "Ready?" he asked with an arch to one dark brow.

"As much as I can be."

He touched her hand. "I love you."

Their eyes met for a long moment as she squeezed his fingers. "I love you too, Ev." Her stomach churned with nerves, but she wouldn't be any other place but here by Evan's side.

"Put on your game face."

Stoner and Catherine Richardson's party was designed to make an impression. A sharply dressed young man opened Jenny's door and helped her from the car, another was there to take the keys from Evan.

When they walked inside, Evan appeared cool and distant in his tux, and Jenny made sure everything about her body language radiated anger at him. She wrenched her elbow out of his hand as they stepped over the threshold. Stoner and Catherine were there to greet them. Jenny saw the cold triumph in Stoner's gray eyes, and the distress in Evan's mother's.

Even in her fifties, Catherine Richardson was still a beautiful woman. She was tall and fit, her blond hair expertly styled. She was every inch the perfect wife to one of the most prominent men in the country.

"Mother," Evan greeted her with a kiss on the cheek, "you remember Jenny Owens."

Catherine blinked and quickly recovered her composure. "Of course. How lovely to see you again, my dear. It's Dr. Owens now, isn't it?"

"Yes." Jenny smiled tensely. "It's a pleasure to see you again, Mrs. Richardson." She could say that with honesty because Catherine Richardson had always been kind to her. Jenny hoped she knew nothing of what her husband had done.

"Dad." Evan's tone was aloof. "Sorry we're late. Jenny couldn't seem to tear herself away from her patients."

Stoner hadn't missed the sarcasm in his son's voice, and the gaze he turned on Jenny was coldly victorious. He held out his hand. Jenny hesitated a fraction before taking it. How could he look so much like an older version of Evan, yet be so different?

"Good evening, Senator." Her tone was cold enough to freeze the neat bourbon he held in his left hand. Nothing would have pleased her more.

Evan started to take Jenny's elbow again, but she twisted with a small smile at his mother. "If you don't mind, is there somewhere I could freshen up? Evan barely gave me a chance to get out of my work clothes."

As Catherine pointed her to the downstairs powder room, Stoner clapped a hand on Evan's back. "Good to see you again, son. Come with me. Jenny can catch up with you later. I have someone I'd like you to meet."

Jenny ducked into the bathroom gratefully. That had gone well. Stoner was already taking the bait, but even the success of their ploy couldn't overcome the revulsion she experienced being near him. She took several deep breaths, checked her makeup, and reapplied her lipstick. She couldn't stay away long, but she'd really needed a moment to calm herself. Her heart pounded at the base of her throat.

After smoothing her hands over the tight skirt of her dress, Jenny went in search of Evan. He stood near an older man and woman and their tall, rather horsy looking daughter. Stoner was there as well, watching Evan and the girl. As Evan spotted Jenny, his expression grew colder, and it was obvious to her Stoner couldn't be happier. Jenny would love to spit in his eye, but she had a role to play, and she would give it her all for Evan's sake.

As they'd planned, Jenny and Evan spent the evening sniping at each other. Jenny harped on what a cold fish he was, and Evan made comments about her background and her overzealous fixation on her job. The more they argued, the more pleased Stoner appeared, and the more often he tried to guide Evan to the horse-faced woman Jenny had met earlier. After a couple of hours, Evan pulled her into a corner of the main room.

"How's it going?" he murmured, still glowering in a way that would sizzle most people into ashes.

"About time for me to blow up and leave, I think," Jenny replied, her eyes narrowing as if she wanted to take a swipe at him when what she really wanted to do was wrap her arms around him and deep kiss him so no one could doubt he was hers.

"Wish me luck," he whispered as he once more made a grab at her arm. Jenny grinned evilly at him and winked right before she threw her wine in his face. There was an element of being able to just let loose that she hadn't anticipated.

"Go to hell, Evan!" she snapped loudly enough for most of the room to hear. "This was a mistake. I knew it from the beginning, so just find your own way home. I'm leaving."

He wiped the wine from his face with a pristine white handkerchief and glared at her. "Go ahead. Walk out. It's what you do best."

He had been the one to do that so many years ago, but this? This was Evan rectifying that mistake in such a fashion she would never doubt his love again. He was most likely sacrificing his family ties for her.

Jenny spun on her heel and stormed past the shocked guests and her hosts. Out of the corner of her eye, she saw Stoner stop Catherine as she started toward her. A maid hastily handed Jenny her coat, and as soon as the valet saw her, he scrambled to bring the BMW around. Jenny slipped behind the wheel, spinning gravel behind her as she headed down the drive. Along with the relief of finishing her part in this farce, was the worry of leaving Evan behind.

* * * *

Inside the Richardson house, Catherine handed her son a napkin and relieved him of his soiled handkerchief. "Oh, Evan, I'm so sorry."

He smiled tensely and wiped his face. "You're hardly to blame for Jenny's tantrum."

Stoner stepped up and put his hand beneath his son's elbow. "Why don't you join me in my study, son? It will give you a chance to calm down and clean up, and we can talk for a few minutes."

Evan smiled gratefully. "Thanks, Dad. Good idea." As they walked toward the study, the buzz of the party conversation resumed. Apparently even public marital blowups barely rated a blip for the area's social elite.

Evan was thinking how well things were going when his father shut the door. "I'm surprised at you, Evan."

He dismissed a flash of uneasiness and arched one brow. "How so, sir?"

Stoner's gray eyes, so like Evan's, were icy. "Surprised you would consider bringing trash into our home to begin with, but then now you've seen what comes of carrying on with someone so below you."

Evan's expression grew even chillier. "It's just a difference of opinion, Dad, a spat…nothing more. I think you should know I plan on marrying her."

Stoner stiffened. "Really? I thought when you ran for commonwealth's attorney you had finally decided to pursue your political aspirations."

"What does my relationship with Jenny have to do with that?" Evan snapped.

Stoner laughed contemptuously. "Come now, Evan. You're smarter than that. You know any hint of scandal in your past or your wife's could derail your future like that." He snapped his fingers for emphasis.

And what was the scandal that derailed yours, Dad?

Evan carefully controlled his expression as he stared at his father. This part at least he didn't have to fake. "What exactly are you referring to?"

Stoner laughed. "You think I don't know why you dumped her all those years ago. The girl was a slut. I doubt that's changed."

Evan glared at his father, again an emotion he didn't have to fake. "I caught her with one guy years ago."

Stoner arched his brows. "Really? You think it was just one? Is that what she led you to believe?"

"Careful," Evan snarled. Damn, he needed to get himself under control before he blew this whole thing.

Stoner simply stared at his son, as coolly as he might inspect an antique or painting he was appraising, then unlocked the top drawer in his desk and pulled out a disk. He tossed it to Evan. "Here's a little home movie for the two of you to take a look at. Once you've seen it you might rethink things."

Evan shoved it casually into his pocket, carefully hiding his satisfaction. He'd gotten exactly what he came for. "Whatever. I'll take a look at it later. It appears I'm going to need a place to bed down for the night."

Stoner's mouth twisted. "You can stay in your old room. I don't think your mother's put any guests in there."

Evan nodded. "Excuse me, then. You'll understand if I'm not exactly in the party mood."

Chapter 13

As Jenny and Evan planned, she returned to her own house. Neither of them trusted Stoner, so on the chance he had someone follow her, they'd decided the farce must appear real. Unlocking the door and entering the home she'd built after returning to Mountain Meadow, it suddenly struck her it no longer felt like home. Evan's Victorian on Maple Street was home. Wow, just a few days and her life had already changed so much. She smiled. The changes were all for the better.

After dropping her handbag on the table in the front hall, Jenny kicked off her heels, carrying them as she sprinted upstairs and changed into sweats. She was too keyed up to sleep. A run on the treadmill should help. A couple of miles, followed by a movie might be enough to put her to sleep.

While she ran, Jenny glanced once or twice at the dark landscape beyond the window. Nothing was out there. She tried to laugh it off, but she was uncomfortable and ill at ease. Logic told her to attribute it to the events of the evening and being on her own. How quickly she had become accustomed to Evan's presence, with Jake and Holly just next door. Still the feeling persisted something was not quite right. And Jenny'd learned a long time ago her gut feelings could usually be trusted. She used those instincts on a regular basis in her medical practice.

So she remained alert. That's why she saw her attacker reflected in the television screen and managed to roll to the side just as the blow came down that would have struck her in the back of the head. Instead it barely caught the point of her shoulder. Jenny screamed from pure reaction, though she knew no one would hear, and no one was there to help. Her attacker was on her almost before she could scramble to her feet, grabbing her by the arm. Jenny fought the panic. She couldn't freeze or she was doomed.

Her fate lay in the flatness of his eyes. He wouldn't be content with just scaring her. Her gut told her Stoner was behind this, and she would get more than just a warning. This man would take her out of the picture any way he could.

Powerful hands wrapped around her throat, and Jenny struggled for air against his crushing hold. While she tried to pry his fingers from her neck, she kicked, aiming for his knee. Instead, her blow hit him in the shin, and he growled angrily. She struggled to remember moves from her self-defense class.

"Bitch!" he snarled and punched her in the side of the face with his fist. His other hand still held her windpipe, and Jenny swayed as air and blood flow were cut. He would kill her! In desperation, she jammed the heel of her hand against the bottom of his nose as hard as she could. As he jumped back in pain, Jenny scrabbled for whatever she could get her hands on. Her fingers closed on the geode she'd brought back from a hiking vacation. Swinging as hard as she could, she smashed the rock against her attacker's temple. His hold instantly relaxed and he dropped to the ground.

Jenny stood there for a moment, dazed but finally able to suck in the air she needed. Stars twinkled and fizzled in front of her eyes, but she shook off the faintness. As she stared at the man's fallen form, anger replaced her earlier fear. Her jaw tightened and her fists clenched.

"Son of a bitch!" she snarled. She had to find some way to keep the guy immobilized until she could get Evan, Jake, or someone there. Jenny stumbled for the kitchen, yanked out her utility drawer, and grabbed duct tape. She had no idea how long he would stay unconscious, but she wanted to make darn sure he didn't get away. She was tired of being Stoner Richardson's victim, and she was tired of him screwing up her life. Not this time!

Jenny started with her assailant's hands, binding them as tightly as she could, then moved to his feet and finally his knees. Only when she had him immobilized, did she return to his ski mask. Who was he? Someone she *knew*? Her hand hovered over the blue knit mask. A quivering remnant of the scared girl she once was hesitated, but she sucked in a deep breath. Not anymore. Jenny yanked off the ski mask and gasped. She stumbled backward as memories at last flooded her brain in a kaleidoscope of pain.

* * * *

Evan closed the door and studied his old room. It looked almost the same as it had when he was still coming home for college breaks. High school trophies and some college awards rested on shelves or hung on walls. A shrine, Evan thought, as if his mother were trying to remember when their family had still been together. But that had always been just an image. His sister was the smart one. Erin's latest address was in the Virgin Islands, and she used that as an excuse not to visit.

He stuck his hand in his pocket and extracted the DVD. Evan slid it into the player on the console at the far end of the room and pressed Play. His stomach twisted, and he watched it only long enough to verify it contained what Jenny had told him was there. Then he popped the disc, handling it like something poisonous. Pain and fury tightened his throat. How could her father…and his…have subjected her to that? She'd been a girl, and they'd set her up to be brutalized.

Evan forced himself not to march down the stairs, find his father, and smash his fist into his face. What mattered now was getting the arrests and getting the evidence. Jenny was safe at home by now. Evan took several deep breaths, flipped open his cell phone, and called Sam.

"It's Evan. I've got the disc, and I have the warrants. I'm ready to go any time."

"First thing in the morning, Evan," Sam responded. "I assume you'd like to do it before too many people are moving about. However we do it, the shit's gonna hit the fan."

Evan raked a hand through his dark hair. "I know. If it weren't for my mother, I'd tell you to move right now."

There was a pause on the other end of the line. "You looked at it?"

Evan swallowed. When he spoke his voice was tight, "The son of a bitch had them videotape themselves gang-raping her."

"Calm down, Evan. You gonna be all right overnight?"

Evan sucked in a breath. "Yeah. I'll stay in my room. It's probably best I don't see him until we make the arrest. Is Jake ready to go after the ones in Mountain Meadow?"

"Yeah."

"I can see you arrive from my window. I'll be waiting."

Evan hung up and stripped off his coat, tie, and vest. All he had to do was make it through the night without trying to kill his father.

* * * *

Jenny almost called Evan but stopped. If she told him about this now, he would blow the entire case against his father and the others for what had happened to her twelve years ago. Her face and her throat hurt so much that she struggled to think clearly, but she had to handle this without Evan's help so the plans he already had in progress wouldn't be ruined. She dialed Jake instead, her voice not much more than a whisper.

"Jenny?" He sounded groggy. She was sure she'd awakened him. "What's wrong?"

She outlined what happened and her concern about letting Evan know. "Jake? What do I do?"

There was a long pause on the other end, and she heard the rustling of covers as he shifted. "I'll call Sam. It's his jurisdiction, so he'll have to make the arrest. Given who it is, I need to stay out of it, but I can come over if you need some moral support."

Jake had always been there for her as a friend, but she wouldn't take him away from Holly. The two of them needed time to themselves.

"No. I can wait. I've got him trussed like the pig he is so he's not going anywhere. He's still unconscious right now anyway. If you don't mind, though Jake, can I come over once he's taken away? I can't stay here by myself."

"We'll be waiting, Jenny honey. You always have a place with Holly and me. You know that."

Jenny stared at Mike Saunders after she disconnected. He was a former classmate of Jake, Evan, and Jenny, former member of the basketball team, president of the senior class—and Mountain Meadow's mayor. Though it repulsed her to touch him, she checked his vital signs to make sure he was okay. Swelling marred his temple where she'd hit him, but she hadn't broken the skin. Concussion was almost a certainty. Only because she was a doctor did she force herself to make sure he didn't die.

She dropped into a chair in the corner of the room, gripping her baseball bat firmly in one hand. If he managed to get loose, the next time she hit him he wouldn't get up.

Seeing Mike Saunders's face when she knew her life was in danger, finally accomplished what seeing him every day around town never had. It unlocked memories of that awful night. Jenny swallowed and the pain in her throat reminded her of what had nearly happened again this night.

Mike had never appeared in the videotape...because he'd been the one standing behind the camera, the one egging everyone else on. In some ways, it made him worse than the rest of them put together. The other six had been teenagers overcome by rampaging hormones and a power trip, but Mike maintained enough presence of mind, even as a teenager, to not only videotape the entire episode, but make sure he wasn't seen.

Saunders groaned and tried to roll over. His eyes snapped open. Jenny stood where he could see her. "Why, Mike?" she asked quietly. "That's all I really want to know. Why?"

His gaze held contempt. "Are we talking about tonight or twelve years ago?"

"Both."

His lip curled and he sneered, "Money and power, Doc. Money and power, and that's all I'll say until I talk to my attorney."

Jenny's eyes narrowed. "You don't have an attorney good enough to save you."

As soon as she was convinced he couldn't get loose, Jenny stepped out onto her deck to inhale the cold night air and stare at the tree on the hill. She felt whole. She'd struck two blows for Hope tonight, and, though remembering what had happened brought additional pain, it destroyed the fear and the emptiness that had haunted her.

Sam's cruiser approached the house with the lights on, but no siren. She was grateful. Even though she had no close neighbors, sirens attracted bystanders. They didn't need anyone witnessing this... for her sake and for the sake of Mike's family. Jenny met Sam out front. He touched her arm.

"You okay, Doc?" he rumbled in his deep drawl.

"Mostly," she rasped. "He hit me in the head and tried to choke me, but I'll be okay."

"You want someone to look at your throat?"

"I'll see to it myself. Sam, did Jake tell you who it is?"

"Yes."

"Well, you should know something else as well. When I took his mask off, I started remembering what happened twelve years ago. Mike Saunders is the one who videotaped the other six."

Sam's relaxed posture disappeared. "You're saying he was in on the gang rape?"

Jenny brushed shaky fingers across her face. "He was first. The tape didn't start until after he'd finished."

"That's a lot to absorb, Doc. You want me to call Evan so he can be here with you?"

"No. I'm afraid he'll go ballistic." Jenny frowned into the darkness. "He's only held on by a thread as it is. I don't want to push him. Right now, Evan's been doing a wonderful job of doing what needs to be done and keeping his head about it. I'll tell him tomorrow, after you make the other arrests."

Jenny desperately wanted him there with her, holding her, just holding her, but this was the right thing to do. Her whole body shook. Sam Barnes pulled her against his thick jacket and his broad chest and simply held her for a moment.

"He's a lucky man to have you," Sam reassured her.

* * * *

Jake couldn't settle back down. After a while, he gave up and eased out of bed, careful not to wake Holly. She lay curled on her side, one palm lying curled near her cheek. Her hair spilled around her head in a tangle of curls. Jake's body stirred. He couldn't get enough of her. He resisted the urge to touch her. She needed the rest. She was a bundle of energy when she was awake, but he saw the weariness at night. She slept like the dead, and very often Jake awoke and brought Noelle to her.

After pulling on sweats, Jake padded downstairs to wait for Sam and Jenny. He heated milk for hot chocolate, stirring it before taking the first sip. A soft creak of the floorboard made him look up. Holly leaned against the door frame.

"Why didn't you wake me?" she inquired softly.

"Jenny called. Mike Saunders attacked her after she returned to her house from the party at Evan's parents."

Holly straightened and moved into the room. "Oh no! Is she all right? Is Evan with her?"

Jake shook his head. "She was afraid to call him for fear it would ruin the arrests in the morning."

"We should bring her here, Jake," Holly stated. When she paused with one hand pressed against his chest, he smiled and touched her cheek.

"Sam's doing that. He'll take care of Mike too. I figured I should stay away with Mike being the mayor." He cupped her chin and gazed at her with concern. "You should be sleeping, Holly. You need your rest. I'll wait up."

Holly's mouth tightened. "I'm not fragile, Jake. I won't break."

He sighed, afraid he'd explained himself badly, but wanting her to understand. "I don't think you're fragile, honey, but you do have a lot on your plate."

Her brows drew together. "Nothing I can't handle…" She would have said more, but a quiet knock sounded on the door.

Jenny stood on the threshold with Sam next to her. Jake didn't like how pale she appeared, her golden eyes wide and shocked.

"She's a little hoarse," Sam said in his deep bass. "Saunders choked her. I can't stay. I still have him in the car. Just wanted to drop Doc first."

Holly stepped around Jake and pulled Jenny inside. "Come on. We'll get you fixed and find you a place to rest. You can stay and keep me company when Jake has to leave."

Holly kicked back into high gear, her arm firmly around Jenny's shoulders as she led her down the hallway toward the kitchen. He worried about Holly trying to do too much, but it was who she was. Jake could no more stop her nurturing instinct than he could stop...himself.

"Don't worry about Doc, Sam. We'll take good care of her until Evan can get here. When it comes to mothering, no one beats Holly. Sure looks like Jenny could use some TLC right now."

Sam arched a brow. "Holly's a might young to mother y'all, isn't she?"

Jake grinned. "You'll understand once you know her better."

* * * *

Evan slept very little. He stood at the window of his room as the sun came up. His shirt collar was open and his tie stuffed into his tuxedo jacket. These last few days had shown him he no longer belonged in the house in which he'd spent his childhood. Sam's car turned into the drive with a crime scene unit behind it and an additional marked patrol car following. Evan hoped that would be where his father would ride, so he would be able to catch a ride to Jenny's house with Sam.

He wanted this over with. All he really wanted was to concentrate on Jenny and their future, but they first had to shut the door on the past. As the cars halted out front, he ran his fingers through his hair and absently rubbed a hand over beard stubble before he walked downstairs.

"What's the meaning of this, Sheriff?" Stoner Richardson's tone was arrogant and affronted. He'd known Sam and Sam's father. They were neighbors, if not friends, so addressing him only as sheriff was a deliberate slap in the face.

"We have warrants for your arrest in connection with the felony sexual assault on Jennifer Owens twelve years ago." Sam Barnes's farm might sit right next door to Richardson Homestead, but right now, he was all business.

Evan stepped forward and removed the papers from his coat pocket. "I also have a search warrant, allowing us to look for additional copies of the DVD which you gave to me last night, and any record of payments made to Jennifer Owens's father."

As the deputy cuffed the former Senator, Sam Barnes stepped close to him and said, "Before you say another word, Stoner, I think you should know Mike Saunders was arrested last night for attempted murder at Jenny's house. He's spent the rest of the night singing like a canary.

Deputies and members of Mountain Meadow's police department are in the process of arresting six other people in connection with the original crime."

Sam spoke to his deputy, "Read him his rights and get him out of here before anymore people awaken." His gaze swiveled to Evan. "You want someone to attend to your mother?"

Catherine Richardson stood at the base of the stairs, her face pale and shocked. "Evan?" she choked. "What's going on?"

He took her hands as his father was led from the house. "I'm sorry, Mother. I'll explain everything in a few minutes and help you deal with the guests." He looked impatiently to where Sam directed his detectives toward Stoner Richardson's inner sanctum. "I need to speak to the sheriff quickly, and then I'll be right back."

Sam stood at the threshold of Stoner's study when Evan put a hand on his arm. "What's this about Jenny's house? Is she all right?"

"Sorry to spring it on you, Evan," Sam said. "Jenny's okay. She's at Jake and Holly's. I dropped her off as I took Saunders in. Look, once you get stuff squared with your mother, I'll run you by Jake's. It's probably better if she explains it all."

Evan nodded, concern for Jenny and his mother warring within him. His face was probably as pale and strained as his mother's but for very different reasons. After he took her into her sitting room he shut the door behind him. This wasn't going to be easy.

"Did you know about this, Evan?" his mother asked tightly. Always so in control, but this time cracks were obvious in the quiver of her chin that she couldn't quite hide. Each tremor was like a knife to his heart. He would have spared her this if he could.

"Yes." He met her gaze calmly.

"You came into our home last night knowing this was going to happen this morning?" She shook her head as if she couldn't understand it. "Surely you can't be implicating your father in a rape from twelve years ago? Or any rape. We're talking about a former United States senator."

Evan fisted his hands in his pockets. "I am aware of that, but I have to tell you, if I didn't have very strong evidence, I would never take the step of having my own father arrested."

"You're destroying our family!" she snapped. Her normally composed face was even more tightly drawn with the strain of controlling her emotions. He wanted to deny her words, but he had known going in what the results would be.

Evan sighed. "I don't have a choice. A crime was committed. I've seen evidence of it. It's my duty to see justice is done."

"You would prosecute your own father?" His mother was incredulous.

"No, Mother. I will recuse myself from the case and request a special prosecutor. But I think it fair to warn you I may be called as a witness."

Her composure crumbled. "I don't understand this. You are no son of mine."

Evan's gut twisted. He focused on the one good thing that had come out of this whole mess: the restoration of his relationship with Jenny. "I'm sorry you feel that way. I had hoped you and I would be able to salvage something out of this."

"I notice you don't mention your father."

Evan regarded his mother with a cool, even stare. "Stoner Richardson quit being my father the day his actions killed my unborn daughter." His mother gasped, but Evan refused to acknowledge the shock she'd just received. "Would you like me to help you with your guests?"

She looked at him blankly. "No. You do what you need to, Evan, then leave. I can't talk about this with you."

Evan accepted her condemnation with a nod and left the home he'd grown up in. He waited on the front steps, with the collar of his black wool overcoat raised against the December chill. He was cold, but the cold went far deeper than the freezing air; it went to his heart. He was leaving a chaotic mess behind him, but his focus was already shifting. He was impatient to get to Jenny, worried about what had happened after she left last night. Sam said his father was now also implicated in attempted murder. God! Would it never end? All he wanted was to marry Jenny, settle down, and raise the family they should have started years ago.

Another half hour passed before Sam and the other officers reappeared. They carried with them several file boxes, a handful of DVDs, and his father's computer.

"Hop in, Evan," Sam said quietly, "you look half-frozen."

* * * *

Jake processed three of the six suspects through his office, all of them protesting their innocence. They would go over to the courthouse where the county jail was. Mountain Meadow's police department had only one holding cell, not designed to house anyone for more than an hour or two.

He was empty. He had forced himself to bury his own emotions as he processed the arrests of men with whom he'd grown up. They weren't just suspects. They were former classmates, businessmen, and members of a community harboring a lot more secrets than he'd ever suspected.

The situation with Jenny and Evan, begun so many years earlier, was affecting him in a way he'd never expected. Coming home had seemed like returning to a sanctuary, a place where he could hide from the horrors of his last years in the Middle East. Now he understood, Mountain Meadow had problems as serious as any area. He'd just been lucky so far.

All he wanted was Holly. He wanted to touch her and be warmed by her love and her optimism. At a time when it was almost impossible to believe in the goodness of man, he needed her faith in her adopted town. She made him clean. She made everything clean. And she believed when doubts consumed him.

After making sure they were read their rights, Jake swept his gaze over them. "Gentlemen, I advise you to say nothing else until you've talked to your attorneys."

He spoke to Officer Brandt. "Call over to the jail, see if we can bring them over."

"Jake," Bob Summers called. "Surely you're not going to walk us through the square…"

Jake spun on him but then forced himself to relax. Innocent until proven guilty, that was the law.

"We'll walk you around back."

All three heaved a sigh of relief, but Jake wondered how long that would last once court proceedings actually began.

Once the call was made and the jail said they were ready, Jake helped Brandt walk the suspects over to their new temporary homes. He was silent as they returned to the station. He glanced at the clock. His weekend off, and it had turned into a series of arrests he'd never forget. He needed Holly, needed to feel her innate goodness.

"I'm headed home, Brandt. Call me if there's any problem and you can't reach Ernie."

He had just turned into the driveway when his cell phone rang.

"Jake! It's Evan. How's Jenny?"

"I'm just getting back. When I left this morning, she was more pissed than scared, but that could be a front. She needs you. Are you about wrapped?"

"Sam's giving me a lift there now."

"See you in a few minutes then. Jenny will be relieved. I'm not sure she slept all night."

Jake saw the relief on her face when he walked inside and told her he'd just gotten off the phone with Evan. He said gently, "Jen, he's going to be livid when he sees what Saunders did to your face and throat."

"I know," she rasped. "If you don't mind, I'm going to wait on the front porch for him."

"Go. I need a cup of decent coffee. When y'all are ready, come in, we'll eat a big breakfast."

* * * *

Jenny watched him go inside. She leaned against the porch railing waiting. She was exhausted and at the end of her rope. She had managed to hold it together all night, but she ached for Evan and the warm comfort of his arms. When Sam's car stopped in front of the house, she was already halfway down the walk before he could get out. Evan shook Sam's hand before getting out of the car. As soon as he did, he opened his arms to Jenny.

They held each other silently for a heartbeat, and then he eased her away. His eyes darkened as he took in the bruise high on her cheekbone and the bruising along the slender column of her throat. "Ah, Jenny!" His voice was hoarse. "What happened? Why didn't you call me?"

So much aching regret lay in his voice that tears started to her eyes, but now wasn't the time. She made her voice as normal as she could.

"He must have followed me. I started to call you, but I was afraid you'd be so angry it would mess up this morning's arrests."

He gathered her close and simply held her. She leaned into him, feeling the tension recede. With their bodies touching, they drew strength from each other, as they always had. They stayed that way until Holly called to them.

"Come inside before you freeze! I've got coffee, homemade cinnamon rolls, eggs, and bacon."

Evan tucked Jenny's hair behind her ears. "That sounds so good. You haven't lived until you've eaten some of those rolls."

Jenny smiled through her tears. "Breakfast in a tux?"

Evan looked at himself wryly. "It would have been a little difficult to make people believe we'd had a fight if I brought a change of clothing."

Jenny touched his lean cheek. "Was it bad?"

"You're worried about me?" Incredulity flooded his expression. "Mike Saunders tried to kill you last night, and you're worried *I* had a tough morning?"

He wrapped her in his arms and held her against him so he could plunder her mouth. Jenny, mindless of anything else and needing him desperately, wrapped her arms around his neck and held on for dear life.

"Hey!" Jake yelled from the front porch. "Come inside before the neighbors call to complain. Besides, Holly won't let me eat until y'all are here."

* * * *

Jenny and Evan decided attending church would show a united front. The situation would get worse before it got better. At the Baptist church, Jake deftly fielded several questions by letting everyone know the investigation was really in the hands of the sheriff's department and the commonwealth's attorney. Jake had simply assisted.

As Sam said, the shit was really going to hit the fan, and it had already started by the time they went to church. None of the men arrested had been members at either the Baptist church or the Presbyterian church, but it seemed almost the entire congregation knew several men were behind bars, including former Senator Stoner Richardson and Mountain Meadow's current mayor, Mike Saunders.

Not until afternoon did Evan and Jenny finally have a chance to talk. He handed her a glass of wine and sat next to her on the couch. His long, sensitive fingers gently brushed her throat.

"Tell me about it, Jenny."

"I went to my house as we discussed, but I was feeling restless, so I changed clothes and ran a couple of miles on the treadmill. It didn't help. I just had a gut feeling something wasn't right. I sat in the den to watch a movie when I saw his reflection on the screen. I managed to dodge the first blow, but before I could get away he grabbed me and started choking me."

Evan put his arm around her shoulders. "Did you know it was Mike?"

Jenny shook her head. "He wore a stocking cap. I started to freeze, but then…well, I just got mad, you know? I thought no way was I going to be a victim again. I tried kicking him in the knee, but I missed and hit his shins. Well that just made him angry, and he hit me in the cheekbone."

"How did you get loose?"

"I jammed the heel of my hand into his nose. He let go long enough I was able to grab hold of the big geode on my table and hit him alongside the head with it."

Evan smiled at her as he stroked her cheek. "I wish I could have seen that. It helps me, helps the anger I'm feeling to know he probably looks a whole lot worse than you do."

Jenny grinned. "Oh, he does. I bloodied his nose and his head."

Evan leaned over and kissed her, then met her golden eyes insistently. "There's more, though, isn't there?"

Jenny wrapped her arms around her bent knees. "When I pulled the cap off his face, it all came back Evan."

"What do you mean it all came back?"

Jenny swallowed. "He was there, twelve years ago. And I remembered all of it."

Evan was nonplussed. "Mike? The night you were gang-raped? I never saw him, and he's not in the video…" He stopped. "Son of a bitch. He was the one shooting it, wasn't he?"

"Yes. But he participated, too, Evan. He was the first."

God, he wanted to kill him. Evan pulled her onto his lap and cuddled her against him. His hands stroked the back of her head and rubbed her shoulders and back. "Everything feels so tarnished. Here we are at what should be one of the most joyous times of the year and we're dealing with this." He paused. "Did you tell Sam?"

"Yes. He's getting additional warrants so he can go through Mike's house. He's hoping he might have been arrogant enough to hang onto the original videotape." Jenny nestled her cheek against Evan's broad chest. "What about you? Are you okay?"

His hands tightened on her for an instant. "My mother didn't take it well. She told me to do what I had to do and get out."

"Oh, Evan." Jenny stroked his cheek. As much as he tried to hide it, she saw the hurt and disillusionment in his face. "How much of the legal proceedings will take place before Christmas?"

"Not much. With the holidays, it's likely only the arraignments and referral of the case to a grand jury will happen. But the press will have a field day with it. And I don't just mean locally, honey. Dad's name alone will probably draw national attention. Are you ready?"

"With you next to me, I can do anything."

He kissed her again, his mouth hard and passionate. They were both desperate for reassurance, for validation what they were doing was the right thing for everyone. Their kisses and caresses grew more heated, until Evan carried her up the stairs to the big master bedroom. Afternoon faded to evening as they touched and kissed and finally came together, arousing and then soothing each other's emotions until they fell asleep, emotionally and physically spent, in each other's arms.

Chapter 14

"Oh for heaven's sake!" Jake exclaimed, smacking the palm of his hand against his forehead when he saw the two ministers walk into the station the following morning. "It's my fault. The shepherds and their sheep are gone, right? And I promised to put on extra patrols to watch over them at night."

"It's okay, son," Reverend Calloway said. "We understand you can't be everywhere at once. And you did have a few other pressing matters to attend to."

"I feel rotten about this. Let's take a look. Maybe they will have left some clue." After grabbing his cap, Jake glanced at Ernie. "I'll be back in a little while."

"Don't forget," Ernie said. "We've got the arraignments this afternoon for our three prisoners. And it might be a bit of a zoo around the courthouse right now. I believe the mayor and the senator are due in court at nine."

Sure enough, when Jake emerged from the police station, there were news vans from several agencies, and a satellite truck with a network logo on the side. Great! Just what they needed the week before Christmas.

* * * *

Evan dreaded facing the media feeding frenzy as he headed downstairs to the courtroom from his office. He'd been surprised and a little overcome when he'd walked into the office, and his staff had greeted him with hugs and hands on the shoulders, asking if he and Jenny were all right and whether there was anything anyone could do for them. Evan looked at Bill, his assistant with the most experience.

"I need you to represent the office in court today. I'll be there, but I want to be as hands off as possible until we can get a special prosecutor in here to handle the case. Let's push for a change of venue as well. There are too many locals involved for us to ever impanel an impartial jury."

"Hell," Bill had said, "Two of the suspects *served* on the last grand jury panel."

And that was perhaps one of the most telling comments about the case. None of the suspects was scum of the earth. They were excellent students and athletes in high school. Many had gone on to college and successful careers with families of their own. But crime knew no class boundaries in this case. Had Jenny's father still been living, they would be prosecuting everyone from a moonshiner to a former United States senator.

The two men walked into the courtroom and were barely able to keep from stopping in surprise at the crowd gathered. Knowing the case would generate interest and seeing it were two different things. Evan saw Amanda Brown from the local paper rubbing shoulders with a reporter he recognized from Washington, DC. Bill took the lead chair and Evan sat next to him. The suspects paraded in and sat on a bench along the wall. Evan felt his father's glare, but refused to look at or even acknowledge the older man. Far too much had happened. He was no longer a young boy looking for approval, or even the teen who'd hoped to follow in his father's footsteps. Evan realized now he'd started backing away from his father years ago, and not just because of Jenny. Evan sensed a core in Stoner Richardson as cold as his name. He couldn't remember a time when his father had been anything other than harsh and remote. Evan could be harsh as well, but his single-mindedness was reserved for the pursuit of what was right, not what benefited himself.

The clock outside struck nine and the bailiff called the court to order.

* * * *

Evan's phone rang not more than an hour after he finished in court. He punched it, "Evan here."

"It's Holly. Are you okay?"

Evan smiled. "Sure, darlin'. Thanks for asking. How's my favorite baby girl?"

"Sleeping, eating, and pooping. Oh, and I think I caught a smile from her today, but it might have just been gas. Would you like to bring Jenny over tonight and you can both stare at her for a while to see if she'll do it again?"

Evan laughed, and everyone in his office relaxed. "Would this involve dinner, too?"

"Of course. I figured we could throw steaks on the grill because I know how much you and Jake like to freeze your bottoms off while you do the guy thing on the back porch, but I've also made this really great homemade pound cake, and…"

"What time?" Evan interrupted. If her pound cake was anywhere close to her homemade cinnamon rolls, he might just ask Jake and Holly to let Jenny and him move in.

Holly giggled. "Shy, aren't you? That's what I love about you, Evan. The usual time, six. You want me to call Jenny or will you."

"I'll call her. I need to let her know what went on in court today."

Despite everything hanging over them, Evan and Jenny were both smiling within a few minutes of arriving at Jake's house. Being around Holly and Jake made others happy because they were so obviously in love.

Evan was overjoyed his friend had finally found someone who could match his loving, giving nature. Jake had always been the one in school who'd been everybody's buddy—male and female alike. Guys knew they could rely on him, and girls discovered he provided a very sturdy shoulder to cry on, but there had never really seemed to be anyone serious until Holly.

And wasn't it just like Jake to jump unhesitatingly into an instant family? He'd not only acquired a little brother who was more like a son, but also a brand-new baby girl. And anyone watching him with Noelle and Holly knew he would do anything to make sure they were happy and secure.

* * * *

Jenny wished she could be as upbeat as Holly about everything, but life had taught her painful lessons. She still watched her back, wondering when fate would deal one or all of them another crippling blow. For a while, Jenny thought the court case would be that blow, but since Evan had recused himself, most of their responsibility would rest in testifying. Jenny knew that wouldn't be easy, but they would have each other to rely on.

So what made her so uneasy? She tried to shake the feeling, but it had served her well in the past. She just couldn't fathom what threat might be out there.

As they sipped coffee and cut into Holly's luscious pound cake following dinner, Jenny jumped wholeheartedly into the wedding plans Jake and Evan were hashing out. She asked Holly, "Are you really going to let them plan the entire wedding?"

Holly laughed merrily. "If it makes them happy, I'd even let them pick out my dress. It's not the details; it's the people. New Year's Eve, I will marry the man I love with my whole heart, and next to me will be my very best friends who will also marry. We will share our love and our lives. What more could I possibly want?"

There was a moment of stunned silence. They all sat motionless and stared at her. Evan was the first to move. He knelt next to her. Framing her face in his big hands, he gently kissed her forehead. Holly blushed and Jenny saw just the faintest shimmer of tears in Evan's eyes. "You have taken one of the toughest days of my life and put it into perspective for me. All I have to do is hear you, and it restores my faith in the goodness of man. Are you sure you're human?"

She touched his hand with hers. "All too human, Evan, because it hurts to see my friends in pain. If I've made you happier, then I've justified my reason for being."

He smiled at her, then Jake. "If I haven't already told you, I'm really glad the two of you found each other."

Jenny leaned around Evan and touched Holly's cheek. "And we're both honored we'll be sharing your wedding day with you."

"Oh gross!" Tyler said into the emotionally charged moment. "Now all of you have that gooey look Evan gets when he looks at Jenny and Noelle. I'm going to bed."

* * * *

Spence watched Holly most of Tuesday. For a short time, he even peered inside the windows and caught her nursing Noelle. It disgusted him. He had the car stocked with what he needed—diapers, bottles, formula. Spence even had an infant car seat properly installed in the backseat. Now all he needed was the opportunity, and this morning he finally heard what it would be. As the boy left to go to that tourist trap country store where he worked, he heard Holly tell him she was going out later. She needed to run errands at the Walmart.

You couldn't ask for a better opportunity. The place would be packed these last few days before Christmas. If he could just get close enough, find something to distract her, then he could grab Noelle. Spence took a sip from his hip flask. This would work. And once he had her, he'd take the baby back to Seely.

He'd taken precautions to cover his tracks. Spence told his family he and Seely were skiing at a different place. Hell, he'd even made the reservations under a different name where they really were. That way, his family would truly believe they were telling the truth if they had to give the police any information. He'd purchased a car last week, and would return the rental he was now driving east of here where he'd stashed the other vehicle. Then he'd drive back to the ski resort.

Seely would have the kid to take care of, and once the heat died down, they'd go back home. It was a great plan. Spence had absolutely no worries. Everything would be perfect.

* * * *

Holly watched Tyler walk down the street that morning while she hummed Christmas carols to Noelle. The baby was more active now, staying awake for longer periods, and Holly was pleased to see the little girl had a very sunny personality. Holly knew she was right. Noelle had smiled. It hadn't just been gas.

"It's you and me, baby girl, the Christmas elves. I think your good cheer power might be just a bit more than mine. What do you think?"

Noelle blinked and her little mouth curved. Holly kissed the baby on each cheek, inhaling her sweet fragrance. She would never get enough of it.

After closing the door and locking it, Holly took the infant back upstairs and laid her in her crib so she could get ready to go. She had a million things to do to get ready for the upcoming holiday weekend. There was food and presents to buy. She would stop by the jeweler's first. She had found an old pocket watch of Jake's that no longer worked. He admitted it had belonged to his grandfather, and he'd always treasured it; he just never took the time to have it fixed, so Holly had seen to that for his Christmas gift. Tyler was a different matter, and after talking with Jake, they had decided he deserved the video gaming system he'd been so keen on. That was the main reason she was headed to the discount store with Jake's debit card in hand, and she figured she could purchase most of her groceries there as well.

More than an hour later she loaded Noelle in the infant carrier in the backseat of the car and drove down the highway. Shopping options were minimal, so folks tended to hit the huge store for socializing and shopping. Today the shopping was paramount and getting harried as people rushed to buy last-minute gifts and necessities.

With the jostling crowds, Holly decided to leave Noelle in her carrier and put it in the basket. She was afraid to use the sling in case anyone bumped into her. She pushed the cart to the Christmas wrapping section first to get paper, boxes, bags, and bows. Noelle slept peacefully despite the crush of people. Once she was done there, Holly maneuvered to the back of the store where the electronics were located.

What a crush! Wall-to-wall people made it difficult to get through with the cart. As she waited for an opening, a woman just in front of her bumped a display of DVDs, knocking them all to the floor. The woman was so embarrassed, and Holly felt sorry for her.

"Here, I'll help."

She looked up, her face red with mortification and exasperation. "Oh thank you. I came on my lunch hour to finish shopping for my little girl, and I just didn't think it would be this crowded at this time of day."

Holly smiled reassuringly as she collected the DVDs. "It does get a little hectic. We forget why we celebrate this time of year. Your daughter must be very special for you to brave these crowds."

The woman beamed, her face relaxing and a smile actually appearing as she picked up the last of the DVDs. "Oh she is. Heather's nine."

Holly stood and smiled at her. "Well you and Heather have a wonderful Christmas."

"You too, and thank you."

Holly grabbed her shopping cart. The infant carrier and blankets were still there, but not exactly as she'd left them. Coldness trickled through her. She touched the blanket with cold, stiff fingers. Gone. Noelle was gone!

"My baby." It came out the first time as just a whisper of sound. The disbelief still outweighed the horror. "My baby!" This time her voice was stronger. "*Someone's taken my baby!*" Holly shouted.

The store clerk behind the register pushed his way through the crowd. "Ma'am?"

Holly gasped for breath. "Noelle! My daughter! Someone's taken her!"

Why didn't they understand?

"Could she have wandered away?"

Holly blinked at the clerk. "Wandered away? She's only three weeks old."

The clerk pulled a walkie-talkie from his belt. "I need a Code Adam issued on a newborn infant girl. She was taken from electronics in the last five to ten minutes." He looked at Holly. "What was she wearing?"

She took a deep breath, trying to calm herself, but inside creeping coldness and almost certain knowledge settled. Spence had gotten her. "She had on a pink snowsuit and…and underneath a Christmas sleeper that was green with red trim. Please! You have to find her."

She swallowed jerkily, thinking her heart might beat right out of her chest. The clerk patted her back as he relayed the information, and two burly security guards hurried their way, but Holly saw all of it through a fog. The only thing she could really hear anymore was the frantic beating of her own heart and her shallow, uneven breathing. Somewhere deep in her consciousness she acknowledged the bitter irony of the Christmas carols playing over the speakers in the stereo section.

* * * *

Spence had tucked the baby inside his leather bomber jacket and walked out the doors of the huge store right before he heard the Code Adam go out over the loudspeaker. After walking casually through the parking lot, he unlocked the rental car, bent inside the vehicle, and slipped the baby from inside his jacket and into the infant car seat. Somehow, amazingly, the girl still slept. It had all gone even easier than he suspected thanks to that stupid woman knocking over the DVD display, and of course Holly just had to help. She had always been a little too good to be true. Well, that's what being nice got you—the purple shaft with the barb-wire cluster.

Spence looked at the sleeping baby, feeling only curious detachment, not any real tie to her at all. Hard to imagine one night of really bad sex had resulted in the kid strapped in the car seat.

He hoped she wouldn't make noise. He didn't like crying babies. Plus, Spence still had a bit of a hangover. He'd never spent much time around kids and didn't really want to have much to do with her. The kid was for Seely and their parents. He hoped Seely knew something about babies. Spence pulled out of the parking lot just as the sheriff's cars slid to a stop in front of the store with their lights flashing.

* * * *

Jake had just left Mercer's where he'd met Evan for lunch when his phone rang.

"Lieutenant Allred?" the unidentified caller asked.

"Yes. Can I help you?"

"This is Joshua Patterson, manager of the Walmart. I have your fiancée with me, Holly Morgan. She needs to speak with you."

Jake's senses went on high alert. He heard Holly's ragged breathing through the phone. "Holly? Honey? What is it?"

"Noelle. He's taken her!"

Jake stumbled and had to lean against the corner of Mercer's building. Evan stopped too and put a hand beneath his elbow. "Jesus!" Jake breathed. "Are you sure?"

Holly cried softly. He heard her even through the phone, and it broke his heart. "Who else could it be?" There was a long pause. "Jake, I need you." Four little words that ripped him right in two.

"I'll be right there."

He jammed his phone in his pocket and began swearing a blue streak, his voice cracking with pain. "The son of a bitch has taken Noelle. We let our guards drop, and he's fucking taken her!"

Evan held Jake's shoulders and shook him slightly. "Jake! Hold it together. You still got lights on your truck?" At Jake's nod, Evan hurried him across the square. "Get in. I'll drive. You radio the chief, let him know what's happening."

Two sheriff's cars, with lights still flashing, idled in front of the store. As soon as Jake and Evan arrived, a deputy was there to escort them to the business office where Holly was seated. She was in a daze, her face pale and her eyes unfocused.

"Lieutenant?" The deputy standing near her said, "We haven't been able to get anything out of her."

Jake squatted in front of her and Evan sat next to her. While Evan stroked her hair from her face, Jake rubbed her icy hands.

"Holly, honey," he rasped. "I'm here. Can you hear me, sweetheart?"

"Jake?" she whispered, but she didn't seem focused on what was happening, and her skin felt so cold.

"I think you'd better get hold of Doc, Ev." To the deputy, he ordered, "Bring me a couple blankets. She's having a stress reaction." He'd seen it so many times in the military, but seeing it in Holly was a thousand times worse.

"Jake?"

"What, hon?"

"It's time to nurse. Noelle will be hungry. Do you think he'll feed her?"

"I'm sure he will, but we'll find her so you won't have to worry." While Evan wrapped the blankets around her shoulders, Jake stood and spoke to the deputies. "Sam deputized me, so there's no problem working this together. I can give you a name of a prime suspect, but we'll need to see security tapes. If you can pull them, I'll get her to ID the person. In the meantime, begin looking for Spencer Dilby as a person of interest in this. Family's from Richmond; he may also have ties to Lynchburg."

Jake knelt in front of Holly. "We're going to get the security tapes for that part of the store. I'll need you to look at them Holly. You'll need to look so you can tell for sure if it's Spence. Can you do that for me?"

She nodded, burying her face in Evan's shoulder. He cradled her head against his wool coat. "I'll stay with her while you get things set. The faster the better, as you and I both know."

Jake hated to leave her. He desperately wanted to be the one holding her and comforting her, but his first priority had to be getting a BOLO out for

Spence. He'd never met the man, but he was filled with an overwhelming urge to smash his fist in his face.

* * * *

Spence drove east first until he reached the small community where he'd stowed the SUV he'd purchased. He had almost finished transferring everything from the rental car to the SUV when the baby began to wiggle and shift. She waved her fists and her face reddened. Now what the hell was this? He had stuff to do. Didn't she know any better? Noelle added a loud, indignant cry.

Spence's eyes opened wide as he stared at the squalling baby. Damn! That was the most earsplitting sound he'd ever heard. No wonder so many parents seemed like they couldn't hear their kids. They weren't tuning them out as he'd always thought; they were deaf from the god-awful noise.

After stumbling through the mysteries of how all the clothing went together on the tiny, wiggling body, Spence discovered the dirty diaper. Nose wrinkled in distaste, he changed the baby and got all her clothing back on, but still she cried and seemed even more pissed than before. He poured formula in one of the bottles and shook it before offering it to her. She rooted at it, touched it with her small mouth, then turned her face away, screaming all the harder.

"Well *shit*." He glared at the baby and muttered, "You'll sure as hell eat once you get hungry enough."

He slammed the rear door, slid into the driver's seat of the SUV, and blasted the radio to drown out the baby's squalling as he headed back to the mountains along a different route. He had mapped out a way along back roads. While shorter in mileage, the twisting and turning of the narrow highways made it infinitely more time-consuming.

The baby fell asleep eventually and Spence smiled. Fatherhood wasn't so tough after all. He pulled his flask out and took a swig. Just a few sips would help calm his nerves.

* * * *

Within an hour of the Code Adam, Jake seated Holly in front of a security monitor. As they scanned the tapes, Evan stepped through the door with a state trooper. Introductions were quickly handled and the trooper stepped over next to Jake. They watched as Holly bent to help the woman who'd bumped the DVDs. In the bottom left corner of the screen a man stepped forward amid the chaos. Everyone else's eyes were focused on the scattered DVDs as the man removed Noelle from the infant carrier. For just an instant, his face was visible.

"There. Freeze it." Jake told the computer tech.

Holly gasped. "It's him, Jake. It's Spence." She started to shake.

Jake put his arms around her, feeling her lean into him. Focusing must be so hard for her. Between Evan and the other lawmen there, terms flew around the room she would be unfamiliar with. They had already put out an Amber Alert, and were in the process of issuing an All Points Bulletin for Spencer Dilby. As long as he stayed in Virginia they would be working under state kidnapping laws, but they had put the feds on alert just in case Dilby headed south into North Carolina. The family had a house on the coast, so law enforcement agencies there were also put on alert. Officers contacted the Dilby family in Richmond.

Jake bent his head to her. "Honey, I need to ask you about the woman you helped."

"Woman?" She still appeared dazed.

"The woman who knocked over the DVDs. You helped her pick them up."

Holly smiled. "Yes. Rebecca Austin. She has a daughter, too."

Jake stroked her cheek. Only Holly could have gotten all that information from just a chance encounter. "Honey, do you have any reason to think she might have done that on purpose? That she might have helped Spence?"

Holly's eyes widened with horror. "Oh no! She was so embarrassed at what had happened. No."

"Okay," he soothed. "That's all I needed to know. Look, I'd like you to go with Evan. He'll take you home. I'll bring your car later."

"Wh-where are you going?" Tears welled. "I need you." It tore him apart, but he had to help. He cupped her cheeks in his hands, and leaned his forehead against hers.

"To the sheriff's office, honey. I wish I could be two places at once, but I can't. I'm gonna find her and bring her home."

He doubted seriously if Dilby had any clue how to care for a baby.

"I know you will, Jake. I'm being selfish. You'll find her. I know you will." Holly made an effort to pull herself together, her jaw clenching.

"Not selfish. I love you. I promise I'll find her." Jake walked with her and Evan out to the truck. After Jake tucked her in the passenger seat, he stared hard at Evan who had just vaulted into the driver's seat. "You'll stay with her?"

Evan raised a brow. "Of course. Jenny's going to meet us at your place."

Jake watched them leave, fury and desperation swirling inside him. He knew, without a doubt, if he could get his hands on Dilby at that moment...he'd kill him.

Chapter 15

Jake rubbed the heels of his hands against his gritty eyes and rolled his aching shoulders. Nearly midnight, and so far the only thing they'd hit were dead ends. By continuing to look through the store's surveillance tapes, they had tracked Dilby leaving the store and located him getting into a car in the parking lot. He had beaten the store lockdown by mere seconds. So they were still looking for the car, a rental. The state folks contacted Dilby's parents and were told he and his fiancée had headed to a resort in Northern Virginia, and indeed there was a reservation there under their name, paid for in advance, that Spence checked into on Sunday, but when the state guys got there, no one had even stayed in the room.

A check of other resorts hadn't revealed any reservations in Spence's name. They were trying to get a recent photo from the family right now, but they weren't being very cooperative.

"Jake," Sam said firmly, "go home. Holly needs you there as much as you're needed here. And you look like shit."

Jake stared at his friend. "I promised her I'd bring Noelle home, and all I'm doing is sitting here. I feel like my hands are tied, damn it."

"We will bring her home, Jake," Sam reassured him. "It just looks like it's going to take some time. Go home. Be there for Holly. You know the ropes, and you know as we get leads it's easier and faster to have local guys follow up."

He pulled in the driveway a quarter hour later. Only the lights in the living room were on. When he opened the door, Jenny greeted him. His eyes went beyond her into the living room, where he saw Evan still in his dress shirt and suit slacks, but there was no sign of Holly.

"Where is she?" Jake asked hoarsely.

"I sedated her, Jake," Jenny said. "She went from being almost in a stupor to being manic. I gave her something so she could settle down. She's upstairs sleeping right now. I take it you haven't found Noelle yet."

How he wished he could give any answer other than the only one he had.

"No." Jake took off his cap and his leather jacket. As he hung the coat on the hall tree, everything crashed in on him. He braced one hand against the wall. He was going to lose it. He raised his hand to cover his eyes. "What if he's not taking care of her? She's like my own, Jen." He cringed as a short sob escaped. "I delivered her, for God's sake, held her while she took her first breath. I feel like I'm being ripped into pieces."

"Sh." Jenny soothed him. Her arms wrapped around him from behind and she hugged him fiercely. "Come back to the kitchen, Jake. Have you had anything to eat?"

He shook his head as tears continued to roll down his cheeks. Then Evan was there with him, putting his arm around his shoulders and guiding him back to a chair at the big kitchen table. Jenny heated leftovers, poured him tea, and they both sat and kept him company while he tried to eat.

Between bites, Jake told him the leads they had pursued so far, and the dead ends they'd hit. "Evan, even though Dilby is Noelle's biological father, we can make the kidnapping charges stick can't we?"

"Most likely. There will be a lot of factors in our favor. He's not listed as the father on the birth certificate first and foremost, so legally he'll have to prove paternity. From what I understand from Holly, he initially denied being the father. Most importantly, though, he's endangering the life of a child so young by removing her from the care of her natural mother. Yeah. We can make it stick. There are other avenues as well, but we can pursue those only if we have to."

Jake nodded. He went back to eating, his movements methodical. Years in the army taught him to feed the furnace even when battered psychologically. When he finished, he took a deep breath, blew it out. "I'm ready to see Holly. Anything I should know?"

Jenny nodded. "One of the orderlies at the hospital brought a breast pump. Holly needs to keep pumping milk along the same schedule Noelle was nursing. You'll need to pour the milk out while she's sedated and for twenty-four hours after she's not. I saved the milk from the first two pumping sessions before I sedated her. It's in the fridge in bottles, but we'll get to that if we need it as soon as we have Noelle back. For right now, you concentrate on her."

"I need to work on the investigation," Jake said running his fingers through his hair for about the millionth time. He had promised Holly. He couldn't disappoint her.

"Call me or Evan," Jenny said. "We'll stay with her and Tyler. She needs another adult to lean on now. But, Jake, she needs you most. She's not nearly as self-sufficient as she seems, and I think we all tend to forget because she's always so upbeat."

Jenny was right. Everyone took Holly's upbeat outlook for granted, and he had been no exception. Well, that would change.

She was curled up on the bed they now shared. Jake kicked off his boots, but stretched out next to her still fully clothed. She immediately curled into him and he wrapped his arms around her. Heaven help him. She and Tyler and Noelle were his life. His throat ached.

"I love you," he whispered to her in the dark and silent room.

* * * *

Holly sat in Jake's office working on the computer. While the police concentrated on Spence, she learned what she could about Celia Segal. She had to do something. She didn't believe Spence would deliberately hurt her baby, but he knew nothing about children, and she'd already seen from the way he dealt with Tyler he was not a patient man. So she pinned her hopes and prayers on Spence's current fiancée.

Her research turned up extensive coverage of Seely's accident. Even focused on clues that could lead her to Noelle's location, Holly's sympathy stirred. She suspected a lot of the accident details had been kept from the press. No one was immune from tragedy, and even coming from a fancy background didn't make one bit of difference. As she continued to scan any news she could find about Celia Segal, one thing became abundantly clear. Seely wasn't just an avid skier, she was fanatical. Holly knew the police were checking other resorts once the first one turned out to be a red herring…

The phone rang and Holly snatched it. "Hello?"

"It's me, honey." Jake's voice sounded a little less tired than it had. "We've located Spence's rental car. It's about an hour east of here. I'm getting ready to…"

"I want to go with you."

"Holly…"

"Jake…I need to," she told him, letting her intensity show. This was not an option. "I can't stand just sitting here any longer."

She let the silence hang. When she heard his sigh on the other end, Holly closed her eyes in relief.

"All right. I'll have Evan pick Tyler up from the store on his way home. I'll be there in ten minutes. Be ready."

He pulled into the driveway exactly ten minutes later, not in his truck, but in a marked cruiser. It drove home to Holly this was business. She closed her eyes and leaned against the wall in the big front hall, trying to calm her breathing and slow her heartbeat.

"Holly?" Jake stepped through the door and grasped her shoulders as he pulled her toward him. "What is it, honey?"

She leaned her head against his broad chest. "It just suddenly hit me. Seeing you in uniform, in the cruiser. It's not some joke. Spence is in big trouble, isn't he?"

"Yes, honey. He is. And all the Dilby fortune in the world won't buy his way out of this. All we have to do is find him."

An hour later, Holly stood dispiritedly next to the cruiser as she stared at the nondescript rental sedan. Spence had left behind a dirty diaper and some fingerprints, but that was it. She clenched her fists in her jacket pockets and walked to the other side of the parking lot where he'd left the car.

She heard Jake's soft footsteps behind her, but didn't turn from where she studied the tangle of underbrush encroaching along the pavement's edge. "I've been trying so hard to stay upbeat, to believe Noelle will be okay. I mean, Spence is her biological father, right? But, Jake, I'm so angry. So *damn* angry! How could he take my baby? She's not some toy or pet to be passed from owner to owner." She clung to the arms he wrapped around her. "He stole our child!" Her words crackled in the cold air.

"We'll find her, Holly. Hang onto your belief." He held her away for a moment so they could get face to face. "I need your optimism, honey. You're what keeps me going. Don't lose faith now."

The truth of what he said shone in his eyes. Although they reflected the same pain she felt, she also saw conviction. If her belief fueled his, then she would stay positive. It was nearly Christmas after all, a time for miracles.

* * * *

Holly sat in Noelle's nursery. She was pumping milk, the whirr of the machine reminding her vaguely of a dairy she'd visited on an elementary school field trip. It felt a little macabre to pump while sitting in the rocker where she normally nursed Noelle, but only there could she relax enough for her milk to let down.

Christmas Eve. Her birthday. Through the doorway, she saw Jake sprawled on the bed, exhausted but still not sleeping well. His nightmares had returned full force, and he would awake with a hoarse shout, then

Laura Browning

struggle to get back to sleep. He looked far worse than she did, and Holly's heart filled with tenderness. He was working himself to the bone on the investigation, and then trying to be there for her as well. As strung out as she was, she could only imagine the fine edge Jake teetered on.

After Spence's rental car had revealed nothing helpful, Jake went to check several other leads closer in. But they were all dead ends. They had talked on the way back from looking at the car and decided to stay close to home for Christmas Eve and Christmas Day. Then Monday, they'd check out some of the ski resorts closer to Mountain Meadow.

She finished pumping and took the milk downstairs to the fridge. She could keep this milk. Jenny had told her to wait twenty-four hours after the last of the drugs.

After pumping, Holly slipped into bed and cradled Jake's head against her. He stirred and she stroked his hair. She loved him so much. Circles lay beneath his eyes, and strain lined his face even as he slept. In some ways, she thought, Noelle was more his than Spence's. Jake had helped her into the world, held her while she took her first breath, and cleaned her. He'd cut her umbilical cord, loved her, and cared for her every day.

Holly did what she did every time she thought of Spence and the anger threatened to overwhelm her. She prayed. She prayed for him to take care of her little girl and bring her back. She prayed some Christmas angel would find Noelle and bring her home. She prayed she could let go of the anger that made her want to stomp Spence into the dirt if she ever saw him again. Holly bit her lip. Better not to go there. She was afraid to give vent to her anger, afraid it would overwhelm her. Like a tidal wave, it would destroy everything in its path, even those she loved.

Christmas was surely a time for miracles. Holly believed that stubbornly and wholeheartedly. Over the last day, that optimistic outlook with which she viewed her world had returned. Jenny and Evan noted it with wonder. Jake, she knew, watched it with the need for reassurance, but also with worry.

The longer Noelle was gone, the less the chances were they would find her. Those were the statistics, but Holly wasn't a statistics person. Her life was built on belief in the goodness of man, and this was surely the biggest test yet of that belief. If Spence wouldn't do the right thing, then maybe Seely would. Nothing she'd read led her to believe Seely was bad, or anything like Spence at all.

Holly touched Jake's cheek, and he opened his eyes wearily. "It's Christmas Eve, Jake, and I know she'll be home with us soon. Today or tomorrow. Noelle will come home."

* * * *

Holly's green eyes glowed with optimism. Jake's closed to hide the defeat he felt. He swallowed with a pain verging on anger. How could she remain so positive? "Oh, Holly, baby, I don't want to see you disappointed…" He had borne a lot of things while he was in the army, but the idea she might not get the answer to her prayers nearly knocked his breath from his body.

She smiled. "I won't be. You'll see. You said you needed my optimism. Well, I'm telling you right here, right now, Jake. Something wonderful will happen. Just believe."

He stared at her. How could she be so sure? So upbeat and peaceful? In some ways it made it worse for him because the pressure to make her hopes reality was so heavy he was afraid he might crack. She touched his face and smiled. "I love you. I will love you forever. No matter what."

He wanted to be able to take some of her serenity inside him. She had taken his loneliness away. She, Noelle, and Tyler. But what had he given her? He was a man of action, yet his hands were tied bringing Noelle back to them. Sam tried to reassure him that where he was needed most was right where he was, but it ate at Jake. He wanted to find Dilby and pound him until he couldn't get up. But they had no leads. In this one area at least, Dilby had covered his tracks.

Jake clutched Holly.

"I'm so sorry," he whispered, his voice breaking. "I've tried and tried, but I can't find her. It's like they've disappeared off the face of the earth. You've given me so much, and I can't help you now when you need it the most."

Holly framed his face between her palms. "Oh, Jake. Never think that. We help each other. We will always help each other. Please. Have faith. If you can do nothing else, have faith. If you can't do that, then hold onto me. I have enough faith for both of us. Maybe it's not your time to do; it's simply your time to be. Be with me. Monday we'll hit the road. But I don't think we'll have to."

Could it be that simple?

They kissed. It began as healing and ended in passion. He groaned as Holly touched him and caressed him, and he gave back to her. He stroked, listening to her sighs of pleasure, and then his lips followed a path across her breasts to the rounded curve of her belly until he lifted her hips and opened her to his most intimate kiss. As she cried out, he rose above her and sheathed himself, moving in a rhythm that brought peace and passion.

As they climaxed, they clung. He gave Holly his touch, his strength, and drew the same from her.

They held each other for a long time, whispering until he fell back asleep, and at last experienced some of her peace, faith, and hope.

* * * *

Ernie Jones looked at Jake as the younger man sat in the chair across from him. "Jake, go home. Be with Holly. Dilby is going to lie low. You and I both know it."

Jake rubbed his hand across his eyes. In addition to working on leads during the day, he had been on the Internet at night sending e-mail and faxing both Noelle's and Dilby's pictures to every law enforcement agency he could think of. Ernie was right, though, and Jake knew it. He stared at the Internet page in front of him. They could try this last ski resort Monday. After coming up empty at every other place, he'd started looking at the resorts they might have visited when Tyler had seen them. Maybe Spence had returned to the same place.

"I so wanted to be able to bring her home for Christmas, and even worse, Ernie, today's Holly's birthday."

When his voice cracked at the end of the sentence, Jake looked away in embarrassment. He had always presented a stoic front to everyone, but the truth was he was as close to the edge as he had ever been, even more so than from the aftereffects of combat.

"Son, there's no shame in showing your emotions for those you love."

Jake crossed to the window. "I've tried to be strong, but I'm beginning to lose hope. Yet every time I look at Holly she tells me to have faith." He studied his mentor. "How can she still trust? How can she still believe?"

Ernie put a hand on Jake's shoulder and squeezed. "Go home, Jake. Take Tyler and Holly and go to church tonight. You may find that faith you're seeking."

Jake nodded, but in his heart he didn't know what good that was going to do.

* * * *

Tyler expressed the same doubts to her just a short time later. "How can I celebrate Christmas when God let Spence take Noelle? I've prayed and prayed, Holly, but God's not listening."

"He listens, Ty," she told him softly. "Sometimes we just have to be patient and wait for the answer." Holly stroked his hair and glanced at the tree in the corner of the room. Her chin trembled, but she wouldn't let Tyler see, nor would she let Jake see. They were as torn up over Noelle as she was, but if she let them see how close she was to breaking, none of them could handle this.

Tyler was smart. It hadn't taken him long to realize Holly had been shopping for him when Spence snatched Noelle. He carried an inner guilt she couldn't erase. And Jake? He'd been working like a dog, trying to be strong for them, and it tore him up inside. She wasn't in much better shape. She sought refuge in routine, but in those moments when she had nothing to occupy her mind, hopelessness took root.

They needed church tonight, needed to watch the children's pageant, to sing songs of joy and hope, Holly's favorite part of the Christmas season. She needed Jake at her side. Tyler would be in the pageant as one of the three wise men, so Holly had invited Evan and Jenny to go with them. She wanted loved ones around her, and if they couldn't have Noelle tonight, they could remember her and pray for her safe return.

Chapter 16

"Come on, Holly. Pastor Joe would understand if I don't want to be Melchior."

Evan lounged in the doorway to the living room watching as Holly put the finishing touches on Tyler's outfit.

Holly gave Tyler *the look* and he rolled his eyes. "You made a commitment," she reminded him. "They're expecting you. What would the manger scene be with two wise men instead of three?"

"A lot like the one outside the church?" Evan suggested. "Which also happens to be missing Mary, Joseph, the camel, the shepherd, and all the sheep. Or was that the Presbyterian church?"

"No," Jake said wearily. "The Presbyterian church is missing Jesus, Balthazar, Gaspar, the donkey, the shepherd, and all his flock. I think. I'm so tired I can't remember anymore."

"Are we ready?" Evan asked. "I'll drive. We can all pile into the Tahoe." He'd offered to drive for the last two days ever since he and Jenny bought his new replacement vehicle. He figured it offered plenty of room for car seats, and Jenny said it offered plenty of protection in case Evan missed any more curves.

They had to be there a half hour before the service was scheduled to start so the youth director could get everyone in their places for the manger scene in front of the altar. Evan's eyes widened as one of the angels burst into tears when the littlest shepherd knocked her sparkly gold halo off with his crook.

Jenny leaned over and pulled Evan down to whisper in his ear. "Would now be a bad time to tell you I'm late?"

Evan smiled vaguely, "Late? We got here in plenty of time."

"No, Evan," she said patiently. "I'm *late*."

His eyes widened as he stared at the angel now being soothed by Mary, a high school student, while Joseph, another high school student, instructed the shepherd to say sorry. Evan smiled in dawning comprehension at Jenny. "How late?"

"Just two days, but Evan, I'm *never* late."

He grinned, feeling brighter and warmer than the star on top of the stable.

Once everyone was in place, the lights dimmed in the sanctuary. All the parents found seats and the rest of the congregation was allowed in.

Holly sat with Jake on her right and Jenny and Evan to her left. Jake put his arm around her shoulders, perhaps afraid the story of the Savior's birth might bring too many reminders.

Jenny found Holly's hand and laced her fingers through it. Evan knew she desperately wanted to share her news with her friend, but she was no doubt afraid it would remind Holly of Noelle.

Evan sat a little stiffly to Jenny's left, his thoughts swirling from the disintegration of his own family, to tiny Hope on the hill behind Jenny's house, to Noelle, and finally to the spark of life even now growing inside Jenny.

Life, he thought, was a series of beginnings and endings more than a circle. Connections and disconnections created a constant struggle to find harmony in so many areas. He now had new hope, and he even began to understand how Holly could sit there near the front of the church looking with such radiance at the cross.

Without conscious thought, he laid his hand protectively across Jenny's stomach. When she stiffened, he removed his hand and looked at Holly. Shining green eyes met his. Her gaze fell to Jenny's stomach and then back, and she smiled at them. She knew, and it was all right.

Pastor Joe stepped into the pulpit.

"Good evening, everyone. Peace and goodwill to all of you on this, the eve of our Savior's birth."

After an opening message from Pastor Joe, the children's choir sang "Away in a Manger" and then Les Gardner's son stood and went to the pulpit, his red head barely visible over the top of it. A small hand appeared and tilted the microphone. There was a rumble of laughter through the congregation.

* * * *

Holly glanced at Jake and smiled as she leaned into his shoulder. His arm tightened around her shoulders, and he stared at her in wonder. She no longer saw the doubt and despair that had filled him. Instead, his steady hazel gaze reflected the same hope to which she had been clinging. He smiled for what seemed like the first time in days, and warmth suffused Holly's heart. It would be okay. She knew it.

"And it came to pass in those days, that a decree went out from Caesar Augustus that all the world should be taxed." The young man began the familiar story in a very serious voice. "And all went to be taxed, every one into his own city."

The little boy continued the story to the part where the angels appeared to the shepherds. Rather than sharing tidings of great joy, the littlest angel seemed to be glaring at the smallest shepherd.

"And the angel said to them, Fear not, for behold, I bring you good tidings of great joy…" The angel stuck her tongue out at the shepherd and he changed his grip on his crook so it looked more like he held a light saber. "For unto us is born this day in the city of David a Savior which is Christ the Lord."

There was a faint stirring at the back of the church, but the little boy continued resolutely, "And this shall be a sign to you; you shall find the babe wrapped in swaddling clothes, lying in a manger."

Suddenly from the back of the church, someone spoke, "Glory be. We've been invaded by the Presbyterians."

And sure enough, as they all gawked, there stood the Presbyterian minister and behind him what appeared to be his entire congregation, but Holly's eyes were drawn immediately to the blond woman and the brown-haired man standing right behind the minister. She had no idea who the man might be, but Holly knew from her research, the woman was Celia Segal. Slowly, Holly stood. When she swayed, Jake jumped to his feet, too. Then Evan and Jenny stood. From the edge of the manger scene, Tyler set down his frankincense and left.

The brown-haired man searched the congregation as he stepped forward with the blonde and the blanket-wrapped bundle in her arms. As the bundle began to move and squirm and squall, the man spoke. "I'm looking for Holly Morgan?"

Holly pressed her hand over her heart, sure it was going to beat right out of her chest.

"*Noelle,*" she whispered, and then she and Jake rushed down the aisle as the combined membership of the Baptist and Presbyterian churches looked on at the unfolding of their very own Mountain Meadow version of the Christmas Story.

Seely held the baby out. As opposed to the Internet pictures that had shown an immaculately groomed woman in stylish clothes, this Celia

Segal was sans makeup and looking like she had borrowed clothes from the guy she was with.

"Holly?" Seely's voice shook. "I'm so sorry. Spence took your baby and…and he wouldn't let either of us go."

Holly knew that look of fear. She'd felt it, too.

She took Noelle into her arms and laughed. The baby instantly quit crying and smiled. All of the pain and fear of the last few days disappeared. It was gone, as though she had snapped her fingers, and God had granted her dearest wish.

Jake was there with his arms around them both. Tyler shoved back his cardboard crown. "Is she okay?"

Jenny hurried up the aisle. "Buck Harris? What are you doing here with Noelle?"

The brown-haired man laughed. "It's a long story." And he put his arms around the blonde's shoulders.

Holly rocked her baby and whispered to Pastor Joe, "Could we finish the service? Do we have room for all the Presbyterians?"

Pastor Joe smiled, his blue eyes twinkling. "We'll make room."

Holly raised her head just in time to see Evan look beyond the group gathered around Noelle, as though he was searching for someone. His gaze stopped on an older woman with silver-blond hair that glinted in the subdued light. Some wordless communication seemed to pass between them. Realization dawned on Holly. It had to be Evan's mother.

Evan tugged at Jenny who caught the direction of his gaze. She smiled at Catherine Richardson and pulled Evan forward. It seemed it was a night for mothers to reunite with their children.

Holly cradled Noelle while she sat next to Jake, finally feeling like the Christmas angels he called them. No longer on their own, they had family, friends, and a cocoon of love surrounding them. Seely and the guy named Buck slipped in next to Jake. Jenny and Evan made room for Catherine Richardson, and the healing began. Around the altar, Tyler and the rest of the children enacted their parts in the birth of the baby Jesus, while to the side the two real shepherds—Joe and the reverend—watched over their combined flocks.

Everything was finally right.

* * * *

Holly unwrapped her infant daughter and touched every part of her as soon as they returned home. She had prayed for a Christmas miracle and gotten exactly that. While Jake called Sam and relayed what had happened, Holly sat in the living room with Noelle and their guests.

She looked at Celia and said, "I can never thank you enough. You know, when Spence first tried to convince me to give her up while I was still pregnant, I wanted to hate you, to hate the woman who wanted to take my baby."

"It was never that way," she said. "But I was so jealous of you. You were able to have a child, while I can't. But what Spence couldn't seem to understand was Noelle belongs with you...no one else."

Jenny sat next to Evan on the couch, studying Buck who stood quietly near the fireplace.

"I guess I should explain. Buck and I go way back. In fact, we were in medical school together. While I opted for being a family practitioner, Buck decided on an OB/GYN practice. I have to know, Buck. How on earth did you end up involved in this?"

He grinned. "I followed the most daring skier I have ever seen down the slopes behind my house. Do you know that's how Celia got away from Spence? She tucked the baby inside her jacket, rode the lift up the mountain, skied to the woods, and waited for Spence to go by before she came to my house."

Holly looked at them all. "I want to hear the whole story if you'll excuse me for nursing in front of everyone?"

Evan chuckled. "Holly, the only male in here who hasn't already seen your bare breast is an OB/GYN, and he's probably seen more bare breasts than Jake and I have in our whole lives combined."

Buck winked as he tilted his glass of brandy at Evan, but his eyes watched Celia carefully as Holly put her daughter to her breast. Noelle latched on greedily, her little hands kneading and patting. A certain wistfulness colored Celia's expression, but she seemed all right.

"Celia," Buck said, "why don't you start."

"Spence had set up a ski week for us," Seely began. "I love skiing, and I thought we might finally be making progress in our relationship. Shortly after we got to the lodge, though, he disappeared, saying he had some business he needed to finish. I went skiing without him. That's how I met Buck. We talked some over hot chocolate, so I knew where he lived.

"Well, when Spence returned, he wasn't alone. He had Noelle with him."

"Why didn't you notify anyone?" Evan asked suspiciously.

Seely shook her head. "I couldn't. I think Spence must have realized almost immediately that I wasn't on board with what he'd done." She stopped and looked at Holly. "I want you to know, I did my best to take care of her. I'm not very experienced with babies—"

"She's fine, Seely," Holly reassured her. "You did a fantastic job."

Seely smiled in gratitude. "Thanks. Spence took my phone and my keys, and disabled the room phone. Noelle and I were basically prisoners."

"So how did you get out?" Jake asked.

"Spence has a drinking problem. I started hiding things in my backpack every time I had an opportunity."

"Couldn't you simply have ripped the door open and screamed for help?" Evan inquired, an edge to his voice.

"Evan," Jenny said. "I'm sure she has a reason."

"I was afraid to," Seely admitted. "He's the baby's biological father. I'm unable to have children. It just seemed like it would be so easy for him to lie and blame the entire thing on me. I figured if I could get Noelle out with me, then we could find Buck and get help from him. I had already told him I was planning to end things with Spence because he really was getting more and more out of control."

"So how did you finally do it?" Jenny asked. "I did hear Buck say you skied—with Noelle?"

Seely shrugged. "I'm good. Spence isn't. Buck's condo was close to one of the runs. I waited until Spence was asleep before I grabbed Noelle and my backpack and took off. I zipped her inside my jacket, got my skis, and headed to the lift. It was tricky, but I was as careful as I could be. Spence came after me, but I was way ahead of him on the lift, and I guess he was too paranoid or fuzzy from the booze to simply say something to the lift operator. Anyway, I got off at the midpoint, finally believing I might just be able to succeed when I skied away from the lift and no one stopped me.

"About halfway down the slope, I popped my skis and hid them at the edge of the berm, then waited for Spence to go by before I ran to Buck's condo."

"I wasn't there," he added in a voice filled with warmth as he looked at Seely. "Had it not been for an emergency delivery, I would already have been on the road to my parents' home. Lucky for Celia, I came back to pick up my duffel. I'd given her a spare key in case she needed to get away from Spence. I just hadn't envisioned exactly how and why she might need it."

"Buck figured out pretty quickly who Noelle was, said he knew Dr. Owens, so we tried calling her. When all we got was the answering service, we decided to drive here. The town was locked up tight, though. That's when Buck spotted the lights and cars at the Presbyterian church.

Laura Browning

We figured it was a small enough town someone there would know how to find Holly."

Buck finished by telling them how the Presbyterian minister suggested they all walk to the Baptist church to witness the very special Christmas gift they had brought. Jake's phone rang. He looked at the caller ID and swiped his finger over the touch pad.

"Hey, Sam…what's up?" The whole room grew silent as Jake listened. When they saw the small smile playing around his mobile mouth and the twinkle in his dark hazel eyes, the tension eased. After he said good-bye, Jake began laughing. By the time he stopped, tears rolled down his cheeks. To Seely's surprise, he came over to her, pulled her to her feet, and gave her a big hug before kissing her on each cheek.

"Wh—what's that for?"

They all stared at Jake. "Sam called the state guys right after I talked to him. When they went to the ski resort looking for Dilby, they were told he was at the hospital."

"The hospital!" Seely gasped. "What happened?"

"Apparently after he passed you, he rounded the next bend, missed the curve, fell, and slammed into a tree. The ski patrol found him lying there with a compound fracture of the left femur, still drunk as a skunk, and madder than hell at someone he kept calling 'Seely.' Would that by any chance be you, Celia?"

Seely smiled, her gaze going to Buck. "It used to be, but lately the name Celia is really beginning to grow on me."

"At any rate," Jake continued. "He's under police guard at the hospital now where he's been read his rights until they can get him in to book him."

After staying for sandwiches, cookies, and coffee, Celia and Buck excused themselves. "I'm sure we'll all see each other again," Buck said, "but I think it's time Celia and I left you alone. You need time to talk and get reacquainted with your daughter, and I think Celia and I need some time to talk too." He handed Jake a card. "Give this to the sheriff. It's my contact information. Celia will be staying with me for a while."

Holly smiled when she saw the look the young doctor gave the statuesque blonde. It held an unmistakable promise, or as Tyler would say, Buck Harris was getting the gooey look. For that matter, so was Celia.

Evan and Jenny were next, their eyes on each other as they said they too had something to discuss. Evan looked at Holly and Jake, his gray eyes no longer icy but as warm as molten silver. The cynic was gone, or at least buried for a time, beneath the golden glow of the woman staring at him. The woman who had loved him for more than half her life.

"We'll catch you all tomorrow afternoon. Why don't you come on over for an early supper?" Evan stopped, his eyes twinkling. "We can throw some burgers on the grill."

Jake chuckled. "Sounds great. I'll bring the beer."

When just the four of them remained, Tyler crossed the room to where Jake was and wrapped his arms around his waist. "I'm glad I found you for Holly. We needed you. I'm glad you're going to be my brother."

Jake's eyes met Holly's for an instant over Tyler's head. As he hugged the boy back, Holly watched his adam's apple bob as though he needed to swallow a lump in his throat.

"Go to bed, sport," he muttered gruffly. Tyler hugged Holly, kissed Noelle, and took off upstairs. Jake extended his hand to Holly. "Let's put our daughter back in her crib where she belongs."

He glowed with love. Holly knew no other way to describe it. His features appeared softened in the rosy glow of the nursery lamp. Never would she have thought when he arrived on her porch, cap in hand, that in less than a month they would be standing together like this. She touched his sleeve, loving the way his hazel eyes warmed as he stared at her, the way a dimple creased one cheek as he smiled, and how dainty he made her feel when he bent and scooped her in his arms.

"Are you taking me to bed, Jake Allred?"

The dimple deepened. "Indeed I am Holly Morgan."

As he slowly undressed her, pausing to kiss and caress each part as he bared it, the clock in the downstairs hallway struck midnight. His lips found her mouth, teasing and tasting while the chimes continued. When it stopped, he rested his forehead against hers.

"Merry Christmas. You are the best present I have ever been blessed with, and I can't wait to marry you next week."

Her heart pounded, not only with anticipation of their marriage, but with the excitement of what would happen in the next few minutes.

Holly feathered his cheek with her fingertips. "Show me, Jake."

Epilogue

The town of Mountain Meadow talked about the Christmas Holly Morgan came to town for years to come, but perhaps the highlight of the whole tale occurred Christmas Day. Everyone who found a flyer tucked in their door arrived at the courthouse square at noon. There, in the middle of the square was a very special Nativity scene made up of a combination of figures from both the Presbyterian church and the Baptist church. In front, a sign read, "Merry Christmas to our own Christmas angels—Holly and Noelle—from a town that now understands the meaning of peace and unity."

Pastor Joe stepped from behind the Baptist shepherd along with one of his flock…Jim Tarpley. And from behind the Presbyterian shepherd, the very Reverend Thomas Calloway stepped along with one of his flock… Chief Ernie Jones. Ernie lumbered forward.

"Jake, we're your thieves. It started out as a way to bring the two churches together, but it got so much bigger with everything else that happened. We'd just all like to tell you and Holly how overjoyed we are to have you here. You've brought about a lot of Christmas miracles."

"You were right," Jake and Evan said in unison to Holly. It was an ecumenical Nativity with only the purest of motives.

She cradled Noelle and smiled at them. "I love Christmas and I love this town, but most of all, I love you Jake Allred."

And the whole town clapped…even Betty Gatewood.

Meet the Author

After a long career in journalism, I changed gears and began teaching English. The change in pace allowed me to ramp up my own love of writing fiction. After a push from my hubby, my hobby morphed into a book contract. When I'm not teaching or writing, you can find me on our farm or in the woods with camera in hand.
I would love to hear from you. Visit my contact page to send comments. You can also keep up with me through my blog: Wake Me Up If I Fell Asleep At The Computer, where you'll sometimes get in on contests or additional excerpts, interviews and free reads!

You'll also find me on Facebook at Laura Browning Author.

Turn the page for a special excerpt of Laura Browning's

Bittersweet

Can love survive a night he can't remember but one she'll never forget?

Anna Barlow is giving herself a fresh start, leaving everything about her old life behind. With a new name, a new career and a new look, everything about her has changed since the night her daughter Becca was conceived. Anna finds out just how different she looks when an emergency farm call brings her face to face with her baby's father…and he has no idea who she is.

Chris Stevenson is on hiatus from the world of competitive show-jumping. He's returned to the family farm to get his life back in order. Nothing's been right for the past year… not since the night that has remained a blank in his memory. When he meets the area's newest veterinarian, Chris feels two things—instant lust and that he's met her somewhere before.

As they struggle to reconcile the night he can't remember, both Chris and Anna must learn to trust each other and the idea of what family really means.

On sale now!

Chapter 1

The cellphone on Anna's hip buzzed. She had turned off the ring in the hope that Becca, nestled in her carseat in the backseat of the pickup, would stay asleep at least for a short while. Days and nights of colic had drained them both. The programmable swing at home wasn't a luxury but a necessity. Miles of uninterrupted driving making farm calls also seemed to soothe her daughter. Saturday night dinnertime had already come and gone, both hers and Becca's, and Anna felt the pressure to nurse. She had been about to pull over to feed her when the phone had vibrated against her hip. Not now. Just this once.

"Dr. Barlow," she murmured into the phone as she slowed the truck and pulled to one side of the secondary road. The clinic answering service secretary was on the line with an emergency farm call. Anna jotted the address and the directions the operator gave her. Still somewhat new to the area, she was learning her way around, so directions were a must. Getting lost on her way to an emergency was not an option. And at this hour on a Saturday evening, no one called a veterinarian for anything routine, but the nature of the emergency wasn't what made this call different. The owner's name made her stomach jump with nerves.

"Please let Mr. Stevenson know I'll be there in five minutes." Anna hung up, checked there was no traffic and pulled onto the road. She found the first available driveway to turn around and head back the way she had come. She glanced at the address again. Main barn, Fincastle Farm. Of course she had heard of it. Who hadn't? The farm had been the signature of the Stevenson family for several generations.

She had held hope that Fincastle would never appear on her client list. Naive of her to think she wouldn't see him. Some sort of veterinary call had been bound to happen sooner or later. Later would have been much better. Never even more so. Maybe she'd luck out and the Mr. Stevenson in this instance would be father rather than son.

Anna swallowed as she turned down the long driveway bordered on each side by tall, white-paneled fences. In the paddocks left and right, high-dollar horses grazed in the glow of the spring moon. Ahead lay a long, pristine white barn. A darker color trimmed the doors and windows. It would be green, she recalled. Forest green, like the curtains around the Fincastle tack stalls at shows. Light blazed from one barn, which must be her destination. Most barns would already be settled for the night.

Okay. She was headed into the lion's den. Chris Stevenson, the man she so did not want to meet. Anna hoped he wouldn't be there. Sure, she'd known the possibility of meeting existed when she took the job in Redfield. Let him not be there. Not tonight, when she was tired and needed to nurse Becca to the point that her breasts ached. The show season had started, after all, so he should already be on the road at some of the smaller warm-up shows.

She took a deep breath and let it out. It didn't matter. She could do this.

After she parked in front of the barn, Anna shoved two more nursing pads inside her bra and muttered a quick prayer she and Becca could wait a while longer. One glance over her shoulder showed her infant daughter still slumbered in the carseat. She rolled down the windows before she got out and checked on the baby one more time. A gentle tug brought Becca's blanket back to where it belonged. After releasing a soft sigh, Anna straightened away from the truck. She pulled the zipper higher on her cotton coveralls and threw her stethoscope around her neck.

"Dr. Barlow?" someone inquired in a deep, masculine voice.

For an instant, she swayed. That voice. So much for being on the show circuit. Anna stepped around the back of the pickup into the view of the man who had emerged from the lighted doorway of the barn. Even as one part of her brain told her it was him, she shook her head in denial. Not with his reputation, and not on a Saturday night. There must be some horse show groupie somewhere who was willing to jump his bones, and that would take precedence over actual work.

"You're not Dr. Barlow? Where is he?" the silhouetted figure asked. Anna could not see his face, or much else, since the light behind him cast his front in shadow. As much as she might have tried, she would never forget his voice. She didn't need to see his face to know the speaker was Chris Stevenson.

Now, though, irritation kicked in. Where was he? She sighed. In this day and age, women veterinarians were more the norm than the exception. Of course, her height, or lack thereof, also played a role. She had encountered similar questions before, so she shouldn't have been surprised when it came from a man like Stevenson.

"Sorry, my mind was on something else. I am Dr. Barlow. I understand you have a horse in need of stitches." Anna's jaw hardened as she sensed his reluctance as well as his outright hostility. "If it will make you feel better, I would be happy to show you my credentials, Mr...." That was a nice touch. She'd make him think she had no idea who he was.

"Stevenson. Chris Stevenson."

"The man himself." As soon as Anna voiced it, she wanted to kick herself. She hadn't meant to say that aloud. He had half-turned, and in the glow from the barn, she saw his frown at her tone, but she was not going to back down now. Stevenson was nothing to her. Not anymore. Not ever. Once he'd been her hero, the object of teenage fantasies. But that was in the past. There was an injured animal to treat, she had a hungry daughter to feed and a painful need to feed her that only increased as time passed. She'd do her job, get the hell out of there and be done with it.

"May I take a look at the injury, or would you like me to call the answering service to see if someone else is available to take the call?" At the moment, she couldn't care less that Fincastle was one of the clinic's biggest clients. She was tired and wanted to go home, so if he wanted a different vet, that was fine with her.

She braced herself as they walked into the light of the barn. As the fluorescent lights illuminated his lean features and fair hair, she realized he looked different. He was harder, but also healthier. The dissoluteness that had begun to leave its mark last summer was gone.

"You'll do," he grunted in response. "Follow me."

Anna cocked one eyebrow at Stevenson's retreating back. At least he was polite enough not to sigh as he said it. Still, what an arrogant jerk! Thank God she need have nothing to do with him outside of professional calls, and thank God he appeared to draw a total blank when he looked at her.

She supposed she should be used to people questioning her abilities because of her petite size. She had received odd looks through veterinary school, and even had to answer some pretty pointed questions when she talked to people about joining their large animal practices. Just over five feet tall, she was slender to boot, and at the time, she had been very pregnant. At least the vets at Redfield were able to overlook her appearance in favor of the credentials she'd set in front of them.

Her biggest relief was Chris seemed not to recognize her. She shouldn't be surprised. She knew she looked a lot different than when he'd seen her, but part of her hardened with hurt and anger. What was she hoping, that he would remember the night they met? He would fall at her feet like the prince with Cinderella? There was no reason for it to stand out in his memory, not like it forever would in hers. He spent plenty of nights bedding besotted bimbos. She'd been another in a long line.

Stevenson stopped so abruptly in front of the stall midway down the aisle that Anna almost walked into his backside. Quivering at the rear of the stall was one of the biggest Thoroughbreds she had ever seen. The horse snorted and rolled his eyes. On his right hip, she saw a jagged tear about eight inches long, a messy wound that would require careful stitching.

Stevenson turned to look at her, his eyes challenging. "Still ready to take this on?" he asked with a sardonic twist to his lips.

Anna gazed at him without batting an eyelash. "I'll get my supplies. Would you prefer to bring him in the aisle or would you like me to do that when I return, since he seems a bit rattled?" Her tone dripped ice.

Stevenson looked her up and down. "I'll bring him. He's a stud, and I give you fair warning, he's always had more than his share of attitude."

Anna bit back the retort on the tip of her tongue about him having something in common with the horse besides their hind ends and nodded before spinning on her heel. She had dealt with bigger horses' asses than this one, and she wasn't referring to the horse.

She sighed with relief when she reached her truck and saw Becca still slept. "Bless you, sweetheart," Anna whispered to the baby.

She checked to make sure her daughter was still dry and stroked a finger over her soft cheek. With one last sigh, Anna opened the tailgate. She always kept a plastic caddy ready to grab, which she stocked with the supplies most often needed. After picking it up, along with a few other items she'd need, she hurried along the aisle. Chris was snapping crossties on the stallion as she approached. The big horse stomped his front foot before kicking out with his right rear leg as if trying to dislodge whatever it was causing him pain. Anna set her supplies several feet away and slipped the syringe of sedative inside the front pocket of her coveralls.

As she approached the horse, she murmured to him, watching his ears flick backward and forward as she continued talking.

"You can release him, Mr. Stevenson," Anna directed in the same even tone she used with the horse. Once he turned the halter loose, the horse quit stomping and stretched his nose toward her.

Anna stopped in front of him. Her face was scarcely higher than the horse's flared nostrils. He puffed at her and she blew back. The horse's head relaxed and both ears came forward.

"That's it, big man. Why be scared of something as tiny as me?"

Anna touched him on the cheek before stepping to his side and stroking his neck. Before either the horse or the man was aware of it, she slipped the hypodermic with the sedative into the horse's vein and delivered the drug. She continued to talk to the stallion as the horse's eyes drooped.

Anna bent to look at Chris from under the tall Thoroughbred's neck. "Do you have a step stool close by, Mr. Stevenson? If not, I can get the one I carry in the truck."

Stevenson's pale gray eyes had lost their sardonic expression, but not the hostility.

"Sure," he responded in a clipped voice. He stepped away, returning in a couple of minutes with a lightweight mounting block. "Will this work?"

Anna smiled. "Perfect. Thank you."

She sensed Chris's critical gaze on her but dismissed it. He'd have to deal with his own hang-ups without her help. Right now she had a job to do. Anna worked with careful efficiency, first cleaning the wound before checking for any underlying tissue damage. She was relieved to see it was only a tear to the hide and did not involve any muscle.

"How did he do this?" She lifted a brow in inquiry. Even standing on the second step of the mounting block, she stood barely above eye level.

"A fool of a groom who was careless with the gate when he tried to bring him in tonight. Bart caught himself on the latch coming in."

"That explains the tearing more than cutting," Anna mused as she returned to her work. She used small, neat stitches, tying off the sutures as she finished each one. As she was knotting the last one, she heard Becca wail. Oh no! Just what she needed. She hoped she might be able to get away from the farm without Stevenson realizing there was a baby in the truck. A baby she preferred he didn't see.

His head jerked toward the barn doorway. "What the hell?"

Anna felt the tingling in her breasts that signaled her milk letting down and knew she was leaking. Becca's cry was like an instant trigger to nurse, and she was already long overdue. She hunched her shoulders and jumped off the mounting block. There was no way around it. At least he hadn't recognized her, and at the moment, that was a plus she would accept with gratitude.

"My daughter. Your stallion should start to wake in the next fifteen minutes," she explained even as she packed. "He should be fine to go in his stall. I'll check on him in the morning."

Anna shoved everything into the caddy and the buckets she had brought with her and turned to escape. The leaks from her breasts grew heavier as her daughter continued to cry. Her entire focus was on getting away and finding a place to nurse. She was not sure how long the nursing pads would hold.

"Whoa!" Stevenson commanded. Anna stopped, her mouth tightening. "I want you here until this horse recovers from the sedative."

Anna frowned then looked along the aisle to the truck parked on the edge of the light spilling from the end of the barn, and the increasing volume of the hungry wails emanating from it.

Stevenson ran a hand through his sandy hair in obvious frustration. "This is my best stud. I want you here in case there's a problem. Can't you call your husband or boyfriend or someone to take her?"

Anna's eyes narrowed. "No, I can't. She's not a puppy, Mr. Stevenson and she's hungry now." No way was she going to let him know there was no husband, not even a boyfriend.

He expelled his breath. "Go get her and bring her in."

Nowhere had she heard a please, but what had she expected? Anna shifted. Now was not the time to worry about manners. "Fine," she mumbled.

As distasteful as she found him and as tempting as it might be, Anna knew she couldn't afford to anger one of her clinic's biggest clients. The job was too new, she needed it too much, and if she alienated someone like Stevenson, it would leave the vets who owned the clinic little choice but to get rid of her. She might be excused for taking a tone with him after he questioned her identity and credentials, but ignoring his wishes about this was different.

She hurried from the barn. As soon as she picked up her daughter, the baby reached for her, making smacking noises with her lips. Anna laughed and felt everything inside her melt. As she cradled the baby in one arm, she used her other hand to unzip the coverall. She bared her swollen breast and leaned against the pickup with a sigh of relief as Becca latched on and suckled. Her tiny fingers pushed against Anna's breast.

"Is everything okay?"

She almost jumped out of her skin as she heard Chris's impatient voice. She threw the blanket dangling from her hand over her half-bared front.

"She was hungry," she replied in a somewhat shaky voice as she angled herself away from the man coming around the side of the truck.

"You can give her a bottle inside where it's light," Stevenson added as if he were granting her a huge favor.

"I'm nursing her, Mr. Stevenson. She won't take a bottle."

"Oh."

Anna almost laughed as she saw him halt. He was tall enough his face was in the light showing from the barn over the top of the pickup. For the first time since she arrived at Fincastle, Chris appeared at a loss for words, and she felt a small spurt of cynical amusement. Of course he would be unprepared to deal with the normal result of the sex act. The only thing he was interested in was the performance, not any repercussions.

He cleared his throat and coughed, his gaze skittering away from her. He shifted his weight from one booted foot to the other, and if the light were better, Anna would have sworn a blush stained his tan cheeks.

"You may still come inside if you'd prefer. Sit in my office, and I'll keep an eye on Bart."

Anna darted another quick look at the man. Perhaps he was human. As soon as the thought popped into her head, she shook herself. No, not bloody likely. "Thank you."

Stevenson looked anywhere but at her as he led the way to his office. It was spacious and furnished for comfort rather than style, with a large antique desk and a couple easy chairs in addition to the leather chair behind the desk.

"Make yourself comfortable," he murmured with an automatic kind of politeness she was sure had been drummed into him, but the words cut off on a choked cough as Anna sat. The receiving blanket slipped, giving him a clear view of the baby nursing at her breast. She pulled the blanket back in place. Anna had long ago lost any embarrassment about feeding her child, and though she didn't push her breast-feeding on people, she wasn't going to apologize for it.

The door shut with a hasty click. Anna leaned back in the chair and sighed with relief. The pressure eased, at least on one side. Now Stevenson had disappeared, she removed the blanket, burped the baby and switched her to the other breast to get some relief there too. If there was one thing she had learned, her daughter had no problems nursing. The baby was strong and efficient. She had finished burping her again and put her own clothing to rights when he knocked on the door.

"Are you... Is the baby through...uh, nursing? Bart's waking, and none too happy."

The impatience was back in his voice, and it hit her the wrong way. Anna stood. The weariness of the long day was catching up with her, and she lost patience as well. As much as she wished to keep him at a distance, sometimes options ran out. "I can't juggle him and my daughter. If you'll hold Becca for a minute, I'll get him settled and in his stall."

Chris looked almost as if she had instructed--"here, take this large, poisonous snake and give it mouth to mouth." To give him credit, he recovered in an instant and held out his arms, uncertainty plain on his face. Anna hesitated a moment before she put the baby on his shoulder, her gut clenching as she gazed at his sun-bronzed forearms and work-toughened hands that rose to cradle the infant. He hadn't recognized her, so it should be safe to let him hold the baby this once. Beyond that, though, she didn't want him near her daughter. She settled Becca's bottom on his muscular forearm and placed his other hand at the back of the baby's head.

"There you go." She left him standing in the middle of the office, a nervous, almost frightened look on his face. Serves you right, Anna thought with a small spark of vindictive satisfaction as she walked away. The only thing that would make it better would be for Becca to either spit up or poop, both things she excelled at doing. Imagining such a scenario made Anna smile.

The horse's ears swiveled forward when he saw her. He quit stomping once again and this time blew at her enough to make a small nicker. Anna's smile widened. She loved horses—always had, and somehow they knew it. Without hesitation, she walked to the muscular animal, stroked his head before clipping on a lead shank, and unhooked the cross ties. To make sure he was steady on his feet and the stitches weren't pulling, she walked him the length of the aisle a couple times before leading him to his own stall. The horse followed her and munched the hay in the feeder as soon as she escorted him inside the stall. After unclipping the lead and looping it in her hand, she shut the door and watched him for a couple more minutes. Finally glancing at her wristwatch, she hurried up the aisle to the office.

Chris stood rooted where she'd left him, as if he were afraid any movement might startle the tiny person in his arms. Curiosity had replaced his earlier frightened expression. Becca had her face turned toward him and watched him from her big, blue-gray eyes. Anna swallowed. The baby had a reputation for not liking strangers, so her daughter's quiet observation of the man made Anna uneasy in a way she did not want to examine. Part of her had hoped Becca would scream bloody murder the moment he touched her, and at least her daughter could have covered him in spit up. Traitor.

"Thank you," she said, reaching for her. "I can take her now."

"I've never held a baby before." Stevenson's deep voice was rough, and he sounded a little embarrassed. He handed her the infant.

His awe made Anna drop her hostility. For just a moment, she felt like she glimpsed the man behind the public persona--and he appealed to her. When she smiled, she saw Stevenson's eyes widen, then narrow with speculation. Her smile turned to a chuckle. "I know."

His gaze swiveled from her to the baby and back. "That obvious?"

Anna pursed her lips. "Yes, but at least you were brave enough to take her." She laughed again before quieting at the curious look he gave her.

Time to go. Right now. Curiosity was not good. The last thing she wanted to do was make Chris curious about her in any way. They had nothing in common, nor should they. She would not take such a risk.

She kept her tone cool. "I'll stop by in the morning to check on your stallion. Good night, Mr. Stevenson."

"Good night, Dr. Barlow."

He turned back to the barn, and she gathered Becca and the rest of her things and headed toward the truck. That was it. He hadn't recognized her. She was relieved. Of course she was relieved. It was the best thing. Her lip trembled and she clamped on it with her teeth until it hurt. He was a despicable human being, which she knew better than most people ever would. The farther she and Becca stayed away from him the better.